THE MELEKE STONE

OLGA SWAN

ISBN: 9798522802349 (paperback)

At early morn' I had a dream
that man would cease his futile scheme
Blazing battles, suicide missions
Murder, hatred, crazed seditions
Plumb the depths, re-appraise
Be none so blind, none so fazed
Halt the fight, tribe v tribe
Suffused with hate and diatribe
But see with eyes afresh from birth
We're all one tribe – that of Earth

Olga Swan

CHAPTER ONE

Meleke is densely-bedded limestone. It is white, rough crystalline, found in the hills of Judea and Samaria. For over three thousand years, meleke has been used in Jerusalem's traditional buildings, it being a material especially prized by King Herod. Today, some people refer to meleke as Jerusalem Stone. However, the latter can refer to a number of different types of stone found and used in Jerusalem. The following story refers only to the lithologic, ancient limestone in its purest, original form: the meleke stone.

St. Antonin Noble Val,
Tarn et Garonne,
S.W. France

June 2019

S AMI SAT ON the old wooden bench of the market town, smoking nervously. Every so often he would shift a little and look behind him, staring into the running stream down below. There was something about the moving water that reminded him of his own life. Boulders, slippery obstructions everywhere, but life still carried on regardless.

Sami understood the reasons why his father had moved the family to St. Antonin. Menes had talked constantly about it while he and his four brothers were growing up in the *banlieues* of Toulouse before they moved to a small village just outside this market town, a little to the north. It was a place where the whole family could play a part in making enough money to live. But what Sami had never known was what life was like in the teeming streets of Cairo, where both his parents came from, and why they had made the difficult journey in the first place to live in France. Sami knew that his parents both spoke French, albeit with an accent, it being the second language after Arabic in Egypt at the time they lived there. All around him were many other North African families who had also made the same perilous journey, but Sami didn't know what could possibly have uprooted both Menes and Layla to a world they knew nothing about. Several times he'd asked his father but Menes had remained tight-lipped.

"The past is gone, Sami, best forgotten. You're young with your whole life ahead of you."

So Sami had grown up largely ignorant of his father's past. But, what Menes could never have imagined nor dreamt of, was that his eldest son was fermenting plans which would ultimately destroy him.

On the evening before market days, Sami's mother, Layla, would be busy in the kitchen, preparing and cooking her favourite foods. She felt proud of her cooking skills and the culinary secrets she had learned from her own mother back in Egypt. Her most prized possession was her heavy, orange earthenware tagine, into which she poured all her love and expertise. Sometimes she would cook chicken, other times fish, but always she would add a blend of special spices to bring the Mediterranean flavours to life.

Whilst she was doing this, Sami's father, Menes, would be filling hessian sacks of couscous, various grains, spices, black olives and dried fruits which he and his five sons would lift into the back of the van ready to be transported to St. Antonin early the next morning. Stepping into the kitchen, the boys would take from their mother a stack of sealed, plastic containers of the cooled meals she had made the night before. Menes had learned that it was important to arrive in the town very early, often just after dawn, to give them enough time to park the van, unload their goods and set up their stall before customers started to arrive.

That morning, Sami had been lying in bed, waiting for his father's call.

"Sami, hurry up. We don't want to be late. Where are you? Why aren't you up yet?"

So, with a grunt, Sami had hauled himself out of bed, grumbling as usual as his feet hit the cold, red tiles of their small house in a medieval village fifteen minutes away from St. Antonin. Their house was big enough to house the family well enough. It had a long winding, stony driveway leading haphazardly to their front door, situated at right-angles to the road. This was quite common in this part of the world, builders often using the sun's position to orient in which direction the main rooms should face. The many ancient trees in the surrounding grounds proved particularly useful on cold winter evenings, when the boys would be sent out to saw more wood to add to the huge log pile out back. Their mother was also glad of the outside summer kitchen where she would store her cooked foods to cool for the following day.

Sami knew he was a disappointment to his father, but his inner feelings were too strong for him to ignore. Whilst his four brothers willingly ran around, eager to help their father, Sami found it harder and harder to continue. Ever since childhood, he had felt immense resentment building up ready to explode. Sometimes it felt like a well bubbling up inside him, ready to burst. These days he hated everything and everybody. The French, the Jews, the authorities. They all colluded inside his head. Why should they have everything, whilst he had nothing?

My family deserve better than this, he whispered to the four walls. Why, his father's very name Menes meant endurance. His parents had worked hard all their lives and for what? This hand to mouth existence wasn't worth it. Watching TV, he would sit there inwardly seething as he saw the rich and famous lining up in Cannes to receive awards they'd done very little to deserve.

From time to time, the French news channels would show frequent race riots. *What was the point in encouraging my father to come to France,* he would inwardly shout at the French government, *when all it's done is make everyone unhappy!*

He had grown up with stories from his father of what had happened in their early days in France, enticed by rumours that the French would provide them with money and housing. However, Menes soon found that in practice the French treated him like a lowly servant, paying him very low wages compared with his French-born colleagues. Over a few decades, millions of refugees had crossed over to Europe from north Africa, instantly creating a 'them and us' culture. The story Menes had been given back then was the French government had come under increasing pressure from businesses to provide more cheap labour, especially since 1945. But, right from the start, the mixing of cultures had not been a happy one. To the French government, Sami's family had come from a country which was deemed part of France. However, the relationship became one which was racist and colonial, leading to inevitable violence between the different factions. *Les gilets jaunes* were everywhere, the ubiquitous yellow emergency vests which all motorists were required to keep in their vehicles, gaining an easily-acquired second use as a symbol of gallic protest. Never since the days of la révolution had French citizens felt such anger.

But, what his father never seemed to mention was what happened when he was an Egyptian army soldier in the Six Day War. Like so many other soldiers involved in the terrors of war, many suffered from post-traumatic stress disorder. In Menes' case, it had caused him to clam up, forbidding anyone in the family to mention it.

But alone amongst his brothers, Sami felt depressed and alienated. He didn't feel that the French treated him properly. Everywhere he looked, he could feel their eyes on him, disapproving for no apparent reason. Despite the President always going on about how France was leading the world in being a secular state, banning all outward signs of religious adherence whilst encouraging private worship at home, in practice Sami wasn't fooled. He saw it everyday on the streets. Racism burned from the eyes of every French passerby, something which was imbued in all of them from their fathers and their fathers before them.

Well, thought Sami, *I for one have had enough of it. I need to make a stand for justice. This is supposed to be the land of Liberté, Equalité and Fraternité. Time I showed everybody that it's not working. Yes, time for me to prove my own, personal résistance.*

Now taking a break from serving customers at the stall, Sami sat nervously awaiting the arrival of his friend Seth, whose father worked in a small local shop repairing bicycles. Sami had deliberately chosen this bench to wait, as it was well away from his father's stall, round the corner from all the trader vans parked in *Avenue du Paul Benet.* Hungrily he eyed the boulangerie on the corner of La Bésserel opposite him. What he wouldn't give for a bite of a fresh, crusty croissant or a demi-Parisien loaf with a ripe Roquefort cheese. But, as usual, his pockets were empty. In any case, the last thing he wanted now was for his father to see him, apparently skiving and not doing his bit to help the family. Only last night, he had overheard his parents talking about him.

"I don't know what's wrong with the boy," Menes had said, grumbling in his usual fashion. To him, it was traditional for sons to work willingly for the good of the family unit. He just couldn't understand his son's belligerence when confronted, and his lack of family feeling. He'd done everything possible to bring the boy up as well as he could, given the difficulties of living in modern day France, so why was the boy so ungrateful? If Sami had grown up in Egypt as he had, he'd certainly appreciate how much better things were today!

Sami could still hear his mother's voice, crying in that particular way of hers "Oh, give Sami another chance. He's still so young. Just give him another chance."

That was all Sami could hear, as his parents went into their bedroom, separate from the one Sami shared with his four brothers. As his parents closed their bedroom door, their voices were too muffled for Sami to hear, but he knew only too well what the outcome would be. His mother always won in the end.

Back in the present, Sami's eyes stared vacantly into the distance, oblivious to the noise from the tourists and traders in the distance Vans full of fruit, vegetables, clothes, bags and jewellery were parked as far as the eye could see, with empty wheeled clothes racks waiting at the kerbside to be loaded.

At last Seth approached, like Sami smoking nervously as he ran towards his friend. "Sorry I'm late. I had to do a job for my father….," his voice trailing off as he scanned the area. "So, what's this big idea you've got?" addressing Sami directly.

"Come," said Sami, pulling his friend across the road, racing through *La Bésserel,* the square opposite, past the playground and the ancient horse trough on the right before expertly snaking his way through the familiar zig-zag lanes which encompassed the back alleyways. He knew from long experience that this was the best route to avoid detection. The last thing he needed right now was to be confronted by his irate father. Ducking and diving around the cobbled chicanes, avoiding the central gullies which centuries ago had swept waste waters towards the nearby river, eventually they emerged into a square the other end of the market area. Sami breathed a sigh of relief. This should be far away from his father's vengeful eyes.

Sami's eyes glazed, confronting the throngs of tourists everywhere. Even though he was born here, he still couldn't get used to all the English voices as they hustled to take a look through the window of the local estate agency, situated on the narrow cobbled lane leading from the café. Clearly, it was every Englishman's dream to own a holiday home there.

Automatically, his eyes flicked around to make sure there was no-one around he knew. Opposite was the ancient *Place de la Halle*, which from medieval times had housed the weekly market. Today, to add to the clamour, it was filled with annoying school children running and shouting through the pillars and oriels.

His glance took on the scene further down the hill. Lining the market street were the many-storeyed ancient houses, each one a photographer's dream, their many windows edged with the colourful cornflower-blue *volets* of the region. With disgust, Sami noticed that hordes of tourists still massed in front of the many galleries, spellbound by the *pot pourri* of artists' easels. Everywhere were examples of vivid impressionist landscapes, with their bright splotches and melange of shades, flowers and cornfields. Cleverly, the traders knew just what the customers would be looking for.

Seth, in particular, paused a moment to see which painting was on display that day. He had always wanted to be an artist, the painting in the shop window reminding him of a famous Pissarro. "Look," he said, pulling on Sami's reluctant sleeve. "Can you see how the artist is showing us what a Sunday afternoon used to look like? I love all those vines and the realistic-looking crépi walls, ready to fall down any minute. To me," eyes glazing in admiration, "I think the artist is trying to show us how the future might look. I must remember how he's used the oils to reflect how the summer's light can easily disappear, leaving behind only darkness."

Sami looked at his friend in disgust. "What are you talking about? You sound like a bloody tourist!"

Scraping back two chairs from the corner café, and relatively hidden by the branches of a tree, Sami ordered two cups of strong black coffee. Nearby, a local brass band was serenading an admiring American family as they sighed over just how quaint this town was. Further along, a man with a talking bird in a cage was entertaining a group of children, whilst various art galleries displayed vibrant impressionist paintings in their windows, all at fantastic prices.

Ignoring it all, Sami leaned his elbows on the small round table as he explained to his friend what he had in mind. "Look, how often do you see your friend Ali? You know, the one who lives in Toulouse?"

Seth thought for a moment. "Well, I should see him next week. I've got to go down there on an errand for my father and it should be easy enough to find him at his market stall. Why?"

Looking all around to make sure there was no-one near enough to overhear, Sami got to the point. "I've decided to go ahead with the plan we discussed the other day. You remember we were thinking about the best place to carry it out?"

Seth nodded a trifle nervously.

"Well it suddenly came to me. Didn't you say that Ali lived in an apartment near the Esquirol metro? Well, I found out that his apartment sits right above a synagogue. Yes," seeing Seth's sceptical face. "No-one knows it's there, so it's ideal for my purpose."

"Well, I don't know," replied Seth. "I'm not sure I want to be involved in this. It's too dangerous."

"Look," replied Sami. "I understand. Really I do. We're good people. Our families are good people. But when does this world every recognise that? What do we ever have to show for it, working day in, day out, trying to eat? When are we supposed to live and enjoy life like so many others seem to do?" looking at the American family laughing and joking as they sang along to the umpah strains of the brass band.

"I know what you mean, brother," said Seth unhappily. "But what can I do?" All I know how to do is fix bicycles. Hardly a skill that you're going to need."

"Ah," replied Sami. "That's where you're wrong, my friend. It's exactly what I need," going on to explain what he had in mind, as Seth's eyes widened.

Two weeks later, they arranged with Seth's friend in Toulouse, to make sure his bicycle was positioned in its usual place in the foyer of the *rez de chausée* ground floor of his apartment building. They made a point of emphasising that, on no account should his family be at home on the Saturday morning they indicated. Sami thought it better to leave Ali in the dark as much as possible as to their true motives. As few people who knew, the better. If all worked well, they should all be out of the way when the mayhem started.

So, under cover of darkness on a Friday night, well after the evening service had concluded and the congregants had gone home, Sami and Seth were let into the apartment building by Ali and set to work on his bicycle. Pulling the rucksack from his back onto the floor, Seth carefully laid a number of items on the floor. With a nudge from Sami, Seth loosened the wingnut holding the stem of the saddle onto the bike frame. Then he pulled off the cracked leather saddle from the bike and proceeded to carefully push a fuse into the tube and then pack the hollow bike frame with the explosive mixture they'd prepared in secret in the shed at the back of Sami's house. Then they tamped the mixture down, before replacing the saddle, making sure that the fuse was hidden underneath the saddle but connected to a trip switch and small nine volt battery. Many of the materials Seth had managed to get from the storeroom at the rear of his father's *velo* shop. The plan was that their friend Ali would nip downstairs soon after the first congregants arrived on the Saturday morning, put downward pressure on the saddle before rapidly escaping out of the back door.

If all went well, a few seconds after Ali hotfooted it out of the building, the activated switch would send a current to the wire and ignite the explosive.

CHAPTER TWO

T HE EXPLOSION TOOK everyone by surprise.

Moshe was running late. Everything these days took so long. First, he couldn't find his *talith* prayer shawl, and his son Simon still hadn't arrived. Fretting, Moshe looked at his watch once again. If they didn't leave now, they were never going to get to the synagogue in time for the *Shabbat* service.

Simon was a dutiful son. Moshe knew that. But he was somewhat lackadaisical in his manner and attitude. Simon's whole ethos in life was peace and love. But, of course, being newly married, his son could be forgiven for not putting his father first any more. However, that morning Moshe didn't need slowness; he needed his son to hurry up if ever they were to get to the morning service in time. Walking over to the kitchen window overlooking the front driveway, Moshe again spoke out loud "Come on Simon. Where are you?"

Moshe's house was a traditional, stone-built French house

in a neighbourhood on the fringes of Toulouse. The property stood well away from the other neighbours in the road. And that's how Moshe liked it. He had very few visitors but when someone did have the temerity to see how the old man was, they needed to firstly negotiate the gated entrance, painted in the standard blue colour of the region, and drive up the long shingly path to park near the double garage sited at the front of the house.

Moshe stumbled over to the wall cupboard where he kept his motley collection of coffee cups and poured a strong cup of his favourite blend. He'd just swallowed the last dregs when the familiar sound of Simon's old *Berlingo* van could be heard screeching to a halt down below. Scrabbling in a drawer, a glory hole of everything in his life dating back years, he finally found a paper bag that would do. Quickly, he popped two pastries into it before crossing to the salon, opposite. Being continually obsessive about everything in the house, Moshe checked that the flames from last night's log fire were well and truly out and damped down before finally hurrying out of the front door. Patting his pockets, Moshe at last found his door keys and made sure the door was locked securely. Whilst Simon sat patiently in the car waiting for his father to go through his usual routine, Moshe decided he first needed to go back and check whether he'd locked the door.

Reassured, Moshe at last waved to his son before stumbling down the red brick terrace steps, holding on firmly to the metal hand rail lest he slip, and into the car. With a quick prayer to *HaShem,* giving thanks that Simon had at last passed his driving test, Moshe squeezed into the passenger seat of his *Berlingo*.

Hurriedly clicking their seat belts, Simon performed his usual hairbreadth three-point turn in the narrow driveway, missing the stone wall by just inches, before zooming through the town towards the autoroute access road.

Halfway along the A68 autoroute towards their destination, Moshe suddenly remembered. Turning to his son "Did you remember the sweets?" Not for nothing was the old man affectionately called *Monsieur Bonbon* by the children in the synagogue, but it was no use at all if he'd forgotten to bring his usual brand of boiled, striped sweet.

"Don't worry, Papa. I have them," replied Simon, patting his bulky jacket pocket,. "Don't you remember? There were a lot left over last time, so I said I'd keep them in the meantime." His father grunted before relaxing his head against the back of the seat.

But, still fretting about the time, Moshe asked Simon "What time is it?"

"Only a few more minutes to the *Balma-Gramont* exit, Papa, where we can park at the shopping centre and catch the metro to *Esquirol*, just like we always do. What does it matter anyway? We don't need to be there right at the start of the service. Don't think they'll be searching for a *minyan* this morning, somehow. It is *Shabbat* after all."

His father grunted, acknowledging that his son was right. On mid-week mornings, it was often the case that the Rabbi needed to call on his list of stalwart male volunteers to make up the necessary quorum of ten men to allow the service to start.

Now stumbling across the paved frontage of shops that made up the *Balma-Gramont* shopping centre, avoiding the usual beggars at the top of the metro steps, they rushed down to the ticket machines. Moshe was always relieved to have Simon with him at such occasions as he couldn't abide this world of incomprehensible instructions and unfathomable machines. With a blur of fingers, Simon extracted their return tickets and helped his father down another set of narrow steps to the station they needed. In front of the waiting passengers was a glass screen running the width of the platform, intersected at various points by doors, which were currently sealed firmly shut.

Moshe knew why. Years ago, when he'd first arrived in Toulouse, there'd been a spate of terrible accidents, when people had fallen in front of an approaching train. So this new idea of a protective screen was a good one. But, there was something Moshe didn't understand. Turning to Simon "How does the métro driver stop the train so that the train's doors are exactly opposite the screen's doors?"

Simon laughed. "Oh Papa, it's all electronically-controlled these days. Nothing to do with a driver."

Moshe shook his head. Whatever was the world coming to?

In no time at all, the roar of the approaching train assaulted their ears. And; sure enough, as soon as the train was stationary, magically the screen doors opened and they stepped inside. At last, the warning sirens abated, the doors closed and they were on their way. Pushing past pole-clinging youngsters, Simon pulled down two side-facing seats and helped his father sit down. Soon they were speeding sickeningly above and under the tunnel towards *Esquirol*, the station after *Capitole*. In ten minutes, after the nauseous, lurching journey, the train would deposit them a hundred metres walking distance from their destination.

For Moshe, it didn't matter how many times he made the journey, he was always surprised and shocked by his fellow passengers. It may only have been a short trip, but to him it revealed everything that was wrong about the world. These days, youngsters never seemed to give up their seats for older people, they always had mysterious headphones clamped to their ears and wore ripped clothes that he would have thrown out long ago.

He sighed and closed his eyes for a moment as the train swayed and whistled to a stop at *Roseriae* station. He'd come a long way in his life, ever thankful that he'd been spared but for what reason? Why him and not someone else in his family, all of whom had perished in those dark days of Nazism and terror? Maybe *HaShem* had a plan for him. All he knew was that he was now old and still no wiser as to what he alone could do to stop such a massacre to his people ever happening again.

Moshe was nudged out of his reverie by Simon pulling his sleeve. "Wake up Papa. We've just passed *Capitole* so ours is the next stop.

Blinking foolishly, Moshe pushed his wire-framed spectacles further up his nose and accepted his son's arm as he struggled to a standing position, clinging onto the vertical pole as the train sashayed to a halt. Carefully stepping down to the platform, they walked the few steps to the moving walkway and up into the fresh air again. Moshe knew, of course, that if he were strictly orthodox, he should have bought a house within walking distance of the synagogue, but needs must. After the trials and tribulations of his terrible childhood in Poland, he was simply glad to still be alive.

It was as they were walking past the *tabac* and the phone shop towards the corner of the main road, opposite all those touristy cafés with their awnings and outdoor sitting areas, that they stopped in surprise. It was just as they were ready to turn left into the pedestrian section, when they saw the barriers. Police vans and *pompiers* fire engines were lined up across the road and security officials wearing yellow vests were stopping everyone from entering the area. They could hear the steady crackle of conversations coming from digital devices pinned to their uniforms, and every man was armed. In the air there was a definite smell of wood burning, something which always made Moshe freeze in his tracks.

"What's happened?" Simon asked a young woman standing in a nearby shop doorway. She was busy rolling a thin cigarette between her nervous fingers and looked up suspiciously at Simon. From the looks of her, Simon thought, it had probably been some time since she'd eaten anything decent, her shrunken cheeks and grey complexion speaking volumes about her lifestyle.

"Don't know exactly," she muttered, looking all along the road in case anyone could hear her. "Like everyone else here, I heard the bang. Real loud it was. I felt this shop door shake behind me, even though it's nowhere near where it must have come from." A thick plume of pungent smoke emanated from her nostrils, as she continued with a sigh.

Simon nodded to her as they stared at the totally unexpected scene in front of them.

Moshe had already started to move backwards involuntarily, only too aware of his past. Memories of his time in the camp flooded into his brain. Although he was born in Poland, it wouldn't have mattered if he was French. As Jews, all their fates were the same. For French Jews in 1942 it had been that traitor Pétain who had sold them down the river by negotiating with that madman Hitler. It had been only a short time after Pétain had signed that infamous document on board a train to nowhere, that his evil colleague Pierre Laval was arranging mass deportations eastwards of French Jews to concentration camps.

For Moshe, with a similar history, he was only too aware of how lucky he'd been in getting out of that camp alive. If it hadn't been for his life-long friend Hanna and that brave Englishman called Gabriel, he would have been murdered by the Nazis. The gratitude he owed them knew no bounds. It was beyond words. If only the rest of his family had been as lucky back then. Unlike him, they'd all been murdered by the Nazis in appalling circumstances. Moshe knew that, despite the problems of living in modern day France as a Polish holocaust survivor, he was a very lucky man.

Now looking sideways at his son in considerable consternation, he saw that Simon looked pale. Glancing at his father, they knew all too well which building had been targeted. "Come on Papa. Nothing we can do here. Let's go home," shepherding his shocked father to the métro station, retracing their steps back to their car at *Balma-Gramont*. They wouldn't be attending the *Shabbat* service that day or anytime soon by the look of it.

Now safely back home again, Moshe watched the news reports and the excited faces of the witnesses to the tragedy.

He was sunk in gloom. "Why do people so love all the gory details?" he muttered to Simon. "The news is supposed to be a factual service to tell the public what's happening, but so often it merely acts as a medium to feed people the…what did we used to call it?….oh yes, *schadenfreude*… they seem to love!"

He wished his friend Menes was there so that they could discuss all that was wrong with the world. He thought back to when they'd first met. *Must have been soon after I arrived in France,* he thought. *Yes, I remember now. I got lost trying to find the market in Toulouse, and this man suddenly appeared at my elbow*. Moshe smiled at the memory. Straight away, the two men had felt they were kindred spirits. They were about the same age, had that look in their eyes of having lived a bit, but above all Menes had a kind heart. Moshe realised that when the stranger took his arm and said he was going that way himself, so why didn't he walk along with him? Since that day, they seemed to bump into each other often. At first Moshe had thought that Menes was Jewish, with his olive skin and deep-set eyes, but Menes told him he was actually from Egypt.

"Is that a problem?" asked Menes.

Moshe had reflected a while before saying to his new friend. "You know, Menes, I have a philosophy in life. After everything I suffered during the war, I've come to realise something. It doesn't matter what you wear on your head, or what food you eat. The most important thing of all is what's in your heart and in your soul. Nothing else matters."

After hearing this, Menes clapped Moshe on the back. "I think we are going to be friends for a long time."

And so it proved.

But now, after the morning's tragedy, Moshe was again in sombre mood. Banging his fist on the table in frustration, Moshe knew something had to be done, but what?

The solution was to come to him in a remarkable way but with tragic consequences.

CHAPTER THREE

Toulouse
July 2019
Early Saturday morning

H ANNA SISKOWSKI WAS up early that morning. On her kitchen table she lined up all the food she'd bought the day before, checking she hadn't forgotten anything, before packing everything into two carrier bags. Checking her watch, she thought she'd better hurry. She wanted to have time to stow all the refreshments in the *shul* fridge before the others arrived. Then she'd be able to relax and enjoy the service.

As she finally approached the synagogue, she saw them. It always gave her a jolt, reminding her of what had happened to her and Moshe so long ago. The intention of the soldiers this morning, though, was clear. This was no ordinary shopping street. It housed a place which must be protected at all costs.

Ever since the terrorist shootings in Toulouse, the local French military were taking no chances. Every Saturday, two soldiers stationed themselves in front of the heavy, studded oak doors, pistols resting threateningly in black leather holsters at their hip. American-style camouflage uniforms and heavy brown boots always looked incongruous in the Midi-Pyrénées summer sunshine, but families with small children in buggies chattered and pushed by without a care on the pedestrian street. To further convince the onlooker that this was a simple shopping area, planners had installed stone islands all along the thoroughfare so that weary shoppers could sit awhile to catch their breath.

Seemingly a normal Saturday shopping day in the heart of Toulouse.

Hanna paused for a moment a few metres before the door to put her bags down and wipe the sweat out of her eyes. With a grimace, her hand went to the small of her back. She was getting old and her body was letting her know big time. Abstractedly pushing a stray tendril of grey, wiry hair under the brim of her straw hat, she bent painfully to pick up her bags and smiled as she approached the soldiers.

Bonjour messieurs, she said, offering up her bags for their inspection.

Whilst one solder studied her without expression, the other quickly rummaged inside the flimsy plastic bags before giving her the all-clear. They creaked open the heavy doors, allowing Hanna to sidle through with her bags. Adjusting her eyes to the sudden gloom of the interior, she trudged past the metal post boxes on the right-hand wall, nearly tripping over a bicycle one of the upstairs' tenants had left haphazardly parked along the *rez-de-chaussée* wall, before struggling up the two, short wooden flights to the room on the first floor.

"*Shabbat Shalom, Hanna,*"smiled a woman wearing a fashionable *sheitel* wig. Although it had long been the norm for Jewish orthodox married women to cover their hair, this was France so no-one said a wig couldn't be as *chic* as possible. "Have you brought Leah with you today?"

Hanna reciprocated the greeting before replying that unfortunately Leah wasn't feeling well and had decided not to go to *shul* that day.

The Rabbi's wife smiled. If there was one thing she understood more than anything else, it was morning sickness. Hadn't she suffered time and time again before giving birth to her beloved six children?

Leah was Hanna's favourite person in the whole world, a lovely girl who had married the son of Moshe, the old man who shared so much of her terrible childhood during the war. Hanna smiled when she recalled Simon and Leah's wedding last year. She had felt so proud to see such a lovely couple under the *Chupah* wedding canopy. Having lost all her family in the holocaust, Hanna looked on them as *mishpocha*. Family in all but name. And now that Leah was pregnant with their first child, Hanna couldn't help but dote on her like a mother hen. Nothing must happen to this new unborn child. It was imperative.

Walking into the kitchen area, Hanna now deposited her bags of kosher milk, fish balls, cake, orange juice and other kibbles in the kitchen. Relaxing her arms at last, she looked forward to the *kiddush* refreshments after the service, when she could chat to the other women and send the children to the other side of the *mechitsa* barrier, which separated the men from the women. The children always gladly rushed off, laden with plates of food and glasses of wine for the men. Of course, this being *Shabbat,* the main liquor for the men sitting around the far table after the service, would be a large bottle of the finest Scotch whisky. It was the Rabbi's way of wetting the men's throats so that they could fully discuss rabbinical lore.

But for Hanna, making her habitual way to the room which served as the *shul*, she nodded at the Rabbi before sitting in a wooden pew on the right-hand side of the central *mechitsa*. Feeling her age, she was glad of the red cushions supporting her back. Increasingly these days, the walk to *shul* took a heavy toll on her but it was something she'd always done.

Hanna lived in a small apartment on a narrow road running parallel to the *Jardin des Plantes*, a lovely park. Although she had hardly room to swing the proverbial cat within her cramped living space, in the end she had agreed with the landlord to pay the rent on her apartment mainly because of its proximity to the park. Whenever her spirits were jaded, which was often these days, she only had to step out of her apartment, down the outside steps, and across the building's forecourt to transport herself to another world. There was something about walking across the Japanese-style bridge just inside the park gates and breathing in the heavenly flowers below to immediately make herself feel better.

Her apartment was also conveniently near the *Esquirol* metro station, which whisked her wherever she wanted to go. The mechanical, female voice intoning the various stations *en route* always made her smile, interjecting formal French with the local *Occitane* dialect. Sometimes Hanna would spend the day in the town centre, hopping off at *Place Capitole* and enjoying all that the *pink* city had to offer. There was always something to do there cheaply if you knew where to find the bargains. Many a time in the summer, she would wander down to the grassy area fronting the quay, watching the chattering tourists board a boat and chug off along the Garonne river before returning sometime later, laughing and joking.

But each *Shabbat,* the Sabbath day, without fail she would unhook an iron key from a peg in the hallway and walk over to an oak cabinet in the corner of her salon. The squeak of the heavy metal key in the rusty lock seemed to act in synchrony with the creak of her arthritic bones as she grasped a small round object from the murky interior of the cabinet and held it at arm's length to catch the full glow of the sunlight streaming in through the salon *porte-fênetre* patio doors. Quickly kissing the stone's smooth exterior, she popped it as usual in her bag.

Now pausing for a moment to take a breather and reflect on her life, such as it was, she shifted her position a little, better to ease her aching muscles as she let the Rabbi's soothing voice waft over her as she struggled to follow the service in the blue *Siddur* prayer book she'd pulled off the shelf to the right of the ladies' section. At such times, her fingers would absently stroke her small, round stone. It was such a little thing really, but she gained much comfort from its smooth surface. It had reached her via a circuitous route, as her mother Adela had died at Auschwitz. As part of her effects, carefully secreted in their old Polish home, was a handwritten note addressed to her: "Daughter, this is a piece of the actual *meleke* stone taken from the wall built by King Herod in Jerusalem. It has magical properties for our people. That's what I was told and I firmly believe it. Never lose sight of this stone. Above all, don't lose it and, when the time comes, pass the stone on to another female. Don't fail me."

These words had long been imbued in Hanna's conscience, but to whom should she give the stone? She was single and had no near female relatives. So, for now, she preserved the precious stone and kept it with her at all times. There was but one person she had mentioned the stone to, her old friend Moshe, the fellow survivor who attended the same *shul* as her.

A small noise behind her caused her to turn her head. She found herself staring through the glass kitchen partition behind her at the muzzle of a rifle trained on the sparse congregation. It was shocking but a sobering reminder of the times she lived in.

Sometimes in life, sudden and unexpected events have a habit of surprising and confounding the unwary. This was what Hanna had always believed, struggling through life with little money and no apparent prospects of marriage, but what happened next she couldn't possibly have conceived.

Suddenly, without warning, a blinding flash jagged through the room like a thunderbolt. The last thing Hanna saw was a sudden flash of red on the window before falling to the hard wooden floor. Unconsciously, her stiff fingers still clutched her precious stone. Moments later an unearthly rumbling noise shook the tiny, ancient tenement which housed the synagogue.

Up above, the second, third and fourth floor apartments also felt the impact. Later, passers by would say it looked like the whole building was being crushed in a pair of huge pincers. Strangely, they also reported a phenomenon. It looked as if the window on the first floor of the building was momentarily illuminated by an ethereal light coming from within. But for Hanna and the few other early-morning congregants who had gathered on the first floor for their usual *Shabbat* service, each was simultaneously knocked senseless to the floor with the terrible force of the explosion.

Outside, orange flames surged up the front of the building, scorching the rough red bricks to cinders. In the blink of an eye, and that's all the time it took, the heat became intense.

After pulling his unconscious colleague away from the danger zone, the second soldier shakily reached for his intercom and called the emergency services. He had no idea what had happened to their colleague upstairs in the kitchen area. Groggily, he put his hand to his forehead. It came away bloody, but it looked as if it was only superficial. He was lucky, having moved over to his police vehicle just moments before, away from the epicentre of whatever had caused the explosion. But where were the congregants within and the apartment residents above? In a panic, he stepped over where the entrance used to be and found himself yelling to everyone to make their way downstairs, but only silence and a pall of black smoke met his horrified gaze.

Although it shouldn't take long for the *pompiers* firemen and other emergency services to arrive, he knew there were things he could do in the meantime. First, he erected makeshift barriers in a wide area to both sides of the building, whilst sidestepping around the sudden mass of rubble piled up all around him. Bits of masonry were raining down on his head, loose splinters of wood and glass lying fragmented at his feet. Hundreds of tons of rubble had descended to the wooden rafters. At first there had been an eerie silence, but now it sounded as if all hell had been let loose. He could hear shouts in the distance, and now terrible screams and moans coming from the impenetrable wall ahead of him.

He looked around, at last relying on his famed lateral thinking in any situation. Instead of trying to go back upstairs to where he had last seen that old woman, he looked the other way and saw a security door, still intact, leading on to the back entrance. He rushed over and tried the complicated horizontal bar. It wouldn't give. He bent down and grabbed a large piece of masonry. It felt sharp and gritty in his feverish hands. He took a few steps back and hurled it at the glass door. It splintered. Frantically, he pulled away at the splintered glass, not caring about the bloody damage he was doing to his hands, until there was enough room for him to climb through. He lifted his leg and carefully eased himself sideways over the dangerous shards until, at last, he was fully over onto the central courtyard at the back. He ran out and looked up at the upper floors in a vain attempt to see if anyone was at a window, calling for help.

No-one.

Out front, crowds of people had begun to gather, staring morbidly at the scene of the disaster, before moving back to let the *pompiers* through. A distant siren announced the arrival of a fleet of ambulances and police vehicles.

Chapter Four

H ANNA OPENED HER eyes, momentarily confused and not knowing what had happened. She remembered showing her bags to the soldiers, but nothing after that. She scrabbled at the falling masonry, desperate in her attempts to try and go back to the safety of her own apartment, but she just couldn't move. What on earth was she going to do? Her head was dizzy and concussed. She must have been knocked out by a blow on the head, she thought, gingerly fingering a lump on her scalp. She wondered how long she had been unconscious, but looking around her in the gloom, she thought probably not long. Several people lay unconscious. By the side of their outstretched hands lay the shredded remnants of their prayer books, lying open just as they had landed.

She recognised the Rabbi's wife, lying not far from her. *Yes, it must be her*, she thought. She remembered the thick stockings she'd been wearing, always wrinkled at the knee. And the long sleeves of her *Shabbat* white blouse, the *Torah* decreeing that a woman's arms must be covered. Unconsciously, Hanna tugged at the sleeves of her own black jumper, which had ridden up with the force of whatever it was that had knocked her to the floor.

Turning her head painfully upwards again, Hanna's eyes looked up at where the ceiling should be, but all that remained was a wedge of concrete above her head. For a moment, she couldn't make out what was hanging down in front of her but realisation slowly dawned. It was the cord of the brass chandelier, the many lights of which in normal times always managed to cheer her as it cast a warm, rosy glow over the congregation. But now?

No lights.

No warmth.

Just darkness and a deathly pall everywhere.

"But it's *Shabbat*," she cried out. "Why would anyone do this to us on such a holy day? We are all good people and give to charity. I'd help anyone in need. Anyone." But, silence told its own tale. No-one was listening.

Slowly, her eyes closed. As the darkness closed in, she thought she heard the voice of her own mother. "*Mamo*, is that you?" using the childish, Polish word from so long ago. A bright light was blinking in the distance as she tried to stretch out her arms towards the mother she'd last seen so long ago. Oh, how she longed for her warm embrace!

Hanna's life had been so hard. She'd been so young to have had her family snatched away from her in Poland. She kept saying to herself: *what did I do so wrong to earn such punishment*, as salty tears ran rivulets down her bloody cheeks.

Strangely, from far, far away, her mother's voice resonated deep within her brain. "Have courage and be strong," her voice eerily turning to Yiddish. *Vos a Kind zol nit der'Raiden, vet di Muter im farshtain."*

Now Hanna truly realised it was her mother speaking. *Who but Mamo would say that 'whatever a child babbles, its mother will understand!'*

Despite everything, she would be reunited with her beloved mother very soon. Was it seventy years since she'd last hugged her close, or eighty? *N'importe quoi.* Whatever language she spoke these days, Polish, Yiddish or French, the meaning was clear.

Nothing mattered but love.

Only love.

She smiled and closed her eyes, waiting for that glorious moment of reunion.

A loud voice woke her up. "What?" That certainly wasn't her mother, but a deep voice calling down to her from above.

"Can you hear me?"

Slowly Hanna opened her eyes. As she tried to move, she grunted in pain.

But that was all the fireman needed. Down below, miraculously, someone was still alive. "I'm coming to get you. Don't worry. We'll soon have you out of there," breaking open some loose timbers and easing himself gingerly to the floor below.

In no time, a team of *pompiers* firemen, dressed in orange suits with *gilets jaunes,* had lifted down a stretcher. Whilst one man was leaning over her and checking her vital signs, another told her he was about to give her painkillers.

Somehow, the expert team managed to manoeuvre the stretcher, with Hanna now comatose on board, down to the ground floor, where others helped to push it up and onto the waiting ambulance. Leaping on board, two paramedics quickly fixed a drip onto her arm as the vehicle sped off towards the nearest hospital, blue lights flashing, sirens sounding.

In its wake, Hanna's once familiar route across the park towards the pedestrian shopping area, was now blackened. Charred wreckage littered the area, with smoke rising and emergency services still at the scene.

A local news reporter, positioned as near as he could to the site of the incident, was standing in front of a camera: "I am reporting to you live from the scene of the explosion, a synagogue in the middle of prayers on their sabbath day."

The camera panned out to show the rest of the street.

"As you can see," continued the reporter, "in normal times we know this spot as a busy shopping area, but today, it is the scene of a terrible bomb attack." The reporter then turned to a youth standing by his side. "What exactly did you see over there?" the camera panning over the wreckage.

"*Alors*, it was terrible. There were bodies everywhere. The screaming and groaning from the injured were terrifying," he said, suddenly revelling in this new-found fame.

The reporter finished by turning back to the camera and saying "Latest reports confirm that no deaths have yet been recorded here today but there are many who have been severely injured. Make no mistake. This was yet another example of anti-Semitism in Toulouse. We utterly deplore such violence against innocent French citizens. Remember, we are a secular nation but respect everyone's wish to practise their faith in private." Turning back to the camera, "We will bring you more about this heinous offence as soon as we hear directly from the authorities, but for now, back to the studio."

As Hanna Siskowsky was whisked away in the ambulance, just before she lost consciousness again, she was aware that she was still clutching her precious *meleke* stone.

CHAPTER FIVE

MOSHE WAS IN a quandary until a thought suddenly entered his fevered brain, as it did sometimes. Eventually, he fell into a deep sleep where first his wife, and then his long-gone father, mother, brothers and sisters all appeared to him in a dream, imploring him with their eyes but not spelling out exactly what they wanted him to do.

A bright light woke him in the morning, the rays of a distant rainbow glistening in the damp early morning air. With a struggle, the old man washed and dressed before stumbling along the long hallway to the salon. Simon was still there, having decided to keep an eye on his father whilst the shock was still evident in him. Simon was sitting, head in hands, after reading yet another news report on his cell phone.

Suddenly, Moshe knew what he had to do. It was the sight of his son that brought everything into sharp focus. He didn't know why he hadn't thought of it last night. The solution was staring him in the face.

HaShem surely worked in mysterious ways.

Simon worked for a film company.

Moshe knew he must talk more with his son.

Simon was sitting silently in the kitchen, his fingers as usual racing over the keys of his iphone. His thick black hair was now slicked back with oil, his habitual T shirt and worn jeans hanging loose around his slim body.

The old man turned to his son and began to speak earnestly. "Son, you must listen to me. So many of my old friends from Shul must have been injured in that terrible blast. I've just had enough of it. I simply must do something."

Leaning closer, he said "Simon, what do you know about our history in Palestine?"

Simon, brought up in a world of breaking-news stories and sensationalist global reporting, often biased towards whomever is considered the world's underdog at that time, could only spout what he habitually heard on TV. Like most young people, he rarely read a newspaper. He didn't see a need for it, as all the stuff he needed he obtained from the internet or TV news channels. "Well, of course I learned something about it years ago at Sunday *cheder* classes. Everyone did, especially when I was learning my *barmitzvah* portion, but not much at my normal school. I always got the impression that my history teacher didn't want to cross the line into non-secular areas for fear of complaints from parents. This is France after all."

Moshe grunted. "That's the problem. It's always been the same. Every generation, the real, historic truth always shifts according to the fashions of the day or which country you live in. And don't even mention the media. The tragedy these days is they're all full of those who are brought up to seek our people's demise, so yet again we are under the cosh. Historically, you know, Palestine has never been a nation. It was simply the name of the whole area, stretching from Jordan in the east to the Mediterranean in the west."

Simon nodded, seeing the truth in what his father was saying.

"I know. A friend of mine's actually just come back from Jordan, where he picked up a gift in the duty free shop at the airport there. It wasn't until later that he looked closer at the receipt, and the address listed on it wasn't Jordan but Palestine! Doesn't that show that even Jordan seems to recognise that the name Palestine refers to the whole region?"

Moshe nodded.

"But Papa," continued Simon, "our problem's always been the same. What can anyone do about it?" shaking his head. "Isn't it better if we keep our heads down and just get on with our lives?" Recalling his *cheder* classes in his youth, "Isn't that what biblical Queen Esther used to advise – never deny your religion but you don't have to shout it from the rooftops either?"

"Oh Simon. That's what we've always done and where does it get us? *In ergets nit* – nowhere!" bringing up the Yiddish from his childhood. "Son, our history has been long, our enemies constant, despite the fact that all we have ever wanted was to be left alone to live our lives in peace and to practise our religion in private. I just get the feeling that the time has finally come to actually do something about it. Remember, we're talking about three thousand years! Can you imagine that? No other people have had to suffer such an injustice for so long, being forced out of their homes by tribe after tribe, century after century *ad infinitum*, and then being castigated by more recent settlers in their land."

Head in hands, Moshe's thoughts collided within his frantic brain. "You know what, son? It's a bit like when Hitler stole all those valuable artworks owned by German Jews, the paintings then being sold on to new owners, who then refused to give back *their* possessions to the original owners! You really couldn't make it up, how unfair it all is."

"But, Papa. How can *you* do anything? You're old and defenceless. Just one man against the tide," shaking his head.

Moshe leaned closer to his son, pointing his finger. Ah, but that's where you come in Simon. I have an important job for you to do, a task that will be important for all time."

The old man started to pound on the thick oak table which commanded the centre of their kitchen, the knuckles of his long bony fingers cracking loudly with each resounding thud. The noise echoed against the ancient wooden cupboard in the corner of the room, rattling the dusty glass in the panes.

Moshe continued, as he walked painfully over to the window and stared vacantly outside. "Simon, you must listen to me. I have pondered long and hard. All night I was tossing and turning. Our people must do something before it is too late. However, first we must right a terrible wrong, a continuing unfair stain on our integrity. As we know only too well, this illogical persecution which we have to suffer is perpetually passed on down the generations. I was reading something about it the other day by some psychology fella. He said it's imbued in each individual's psyche via its own osmotic genetic code. I'm not sure I understood everything he said, but what's important is that we actually do something about it."

Moshe sighed deeply before continuing.

"All around the world the people are failing to understand. Everyone desperately needs to learn how to love one another. But first, they must be educated as to what actually happened to people like us and is still happening unless someone does something."

He paused before saying in solemn voice.

"Finally I've come to a decision. I'd like there to be a film produced and distributed in every language around the world, which shows the real truth of what has been happening to our people over the centuries. Such a film would need to show where and when the Jewish people first originated, complete with archaeological evidence, then how they kept being forced out of their homeland again and again via tribe after tribe.

Simon thought for a moment before asking "But, Papa, there have been many films covering biblical stories over the years, and not much has happened to change things afterwards. Why would yours be any different?"

"You know, Simon, it is mothers who pass on knowledge to future generations. What better way, therefore, than to direct some females to help us in our cause? Your task would be to tell the story of several heroic women – for this very special mission. It won't be possible to cover all our history, of course. But if you pick say three particular times when we were attacked by various tribes, that should work. So, I need you to produce a film set in the holy land covering different biblical eras. Remember: it is always the females of the species who influence the great deeds of man, so choose your actresses carefully."

Simon scratched his chin, trying to work out if it could be done and where the funds might come from. Buzzing through his head was how he could start a crowd-funding project through his film connections on the internet.

"Well, even if I were able to get enough funding for your project, and it's a big if, where should I start with the plot lines?" Simon asked, before adding, "and what will connect each girl through the centuries of their misfortunes so that the watching audience know that this is the same continuous story?"

"Ah," replied his father. "Do you remember my friend Hanna from *shul*?

"Of course, Papa. She loves Leah as though she were her very own daughter. We made her guest of honour at our wedding. She told me afterwards that it was the best day of her life. A wonderful woman."

"*Nu,*" replied Moshe. "Hanna told me a secret a long time ago that no-one else knows. She has a special stone that her late mother bequeathed to her. It's a *meleke* stone. Have you ever heard of that?"

Simon shook his head.

"Well," continued his father, "It's said to be part of the original temple built by King Herod in biblical times, but the stone was probably present in the ground long before then. It has been passed down through the ages via Jewish women. I would like you to use this *meleke* stone in your film."

"But Papa," replied Simon, somewhat agitated. "We don't even know if Hanna is still alive. She may well have been in *shul* during the explosion."

"She's still alive, son. I called the hospital and they tell me she's weak but should recover."

"But, what of her stone, Papa. What of that?"

"She still has it," replied his father, smiling. "The nurse told me. Whilst still in a coma, the staff tried to release the stone from her bony fingers, but she kept clinging on to it so as though her life depended on it, so in the end they left it where it was. They figured that if it were that important to the old woman, they should leave her be. But, son, I want you to get your wife to visit Hanna in hospital. If anything happens to poor Hanna......"

Simon understood, agreeing to ask Leah to visit the hospital as soon as Hanna felt a little better. He would ask his wife to gently talk to the old woman about her *meleke* stone.

Simon had grown up listening to his father's stories, some of them too bizarre to be acknowledged. But this idea? It might just work, and with the story of this special stone? That would be the link he as a filmmaker needed. He began to get excited, something he rarely did these days, listening to his father's voice.

"But what we clearly now need to do," said Moshe, "before it's too late, is to show the world how wrong they have been about our people. They should not have been persecuting us for thousands of years but allowing us the freedom to use our talents for the good of everyone. Like everyone else, we're not perfect but we have so many talents which keep getting shunted aside. Also, we're good people. Think about it. Think of all those terrible things done to us over the centuries. Did we ever harbour any hostilities against our attackers? We never have and never will. We always offer hospitality to strangers at the gate. We see only the good in others and merely wish for this to be reciprocated. Just once would be nice."

"Yes, you're right Papa," replied Simon thoughtfully, "whenever there's a sudden tragedy in the world, you never see Jewish people dancing in the street, celebrating the tragic deaths of others. What we do, and have always done, is send in task forces to help those poor people how ever we can, sending goods, medicines, helpers and food to places all over the world."

Shuffling up closer to Simon, his father concluded "As you rightly say, Simon, I'm now far too old to achieve this dream myself, but you Simon still have youthful vigour. Go back now to your production colleagues and see if you can progress this immense task, because you must not fail. Everything depends on it."

"Well, I'm not at all sure I can do it, but I will promise you this Papa. I will do whatever it takes," Simon replied, not wanting to worry his father at this stage about the immense complexities he faced. "And," almost forgetting, "I won't forget about Leah's role in all of this. I intend to use the *meleke* stone. It will be the very catalyst we need. Not only will it prove the archaeological truth of the film's message, but also act as a valuable link between the different historical eras I intend to portray. Oh, by the way," a thought suddenly hitting his brain like a thunderbolt, "what was Hanna's mother's name and who actually gave the stone to her?"

"Well," replied Moshe, "I can certainly tell you the first bit. Hanna's single, as you know. Her surname is Siskowski, the same as her mother's. But, I've a feeling Hanna never knew how her mother came to get the stone in the first place. Those bastard Nazis murdered her before she had a chance. It would be wonderful if we ever found out…."

Simon agreed with him but privately thought it might remain a mystery for ever. "Right then, which hospital did you say Hanna was in?"

Meantime, there was something else. Simon had never really known what had happened to his father during the war. He knew, of course, that Moshe had been in the Warsaw ghetto with his Polish friend Hanna, but never really understood how they'd managed to survive or even end up in France. If Simon was to achieve his father's aims, he felt he really needed to know more about what happened to him back then.

"Papa, a friend was telling me the other day how he regrets not asking his parents about their time during the war and now it's too late. So, do you feel able to tell me about how you and Hanna escaped from the ghetto? It would help me to understand and also set the tone for the film. But I understand if you feel you're not yet ready to talk about it."

Moshe felt the pain in the pit of his stomach but knew he had to relate what happened at some point so agreed that now was the time.

"You know, son, what I think today? It crossed my mind when I saw some of those Nuremberg trials on TV after the war. All the Germans standing in the dock displayed a similar demeanour. At first I couldn't put my finger on it, but now I'm certain. They all showed a complete lack of empathy. That's what the underlying problem was, from Hitler downwards. Absolutely no empathy towards their fellow man at all."

But now, how to remember what happened? How old was I when that remarkable man.....what was his name?.....ah yes, Gabriel... saved my life? Very young, that was for sure, but I was later told much of what at the time I couldn't possibly have understood.

CHAPTER SIX

Warsaw
1943

"MY LIFE AS a small child in Krakov was familiar to me. Every Friday, my mother would prepare our usual Friday night meal. I can still see her lighting the candles and saying the prayer that introduced the weekly *Shobbos* routine. I would try to emulate my father by mouthing the grace for bread and wine that I already knew by heart. But what happened next was a complete shock. Men were kicking down the door and forcing us into the ghetto. My mind became frozen. Everything moved so fast. We were all starving. My mother had already given up at that point, I think.

But then, like a miracle, came Gabriel….."

Moshe remembered it like a dream, even though he was still a small child. The recollection became a parable to his very soul. Much, much later, he learned what that wonderful man had done. Gabriel had marched into the commandant's office in the ghetto and somehow persuaded them that a number of people were actually Catholic and had been imprisoned wrongly. Moshe, being blond, had been selected as one to be saved. Another girl, Hanna, was ten years older than Moshe and had acted like a mother to him on their crazy journey to salvation. He remembered with fondness how her warm arms had enfolded him every time he cried out for his missing *Mamo*. He could still feel the roughness of the man's jacket Hanna had worn, its harsh fibres scratching his baby cheeks as he desperately sought comfort in the hard place they had been transported to. Not for a moment back then did he realise that Hanna was but a child herself, an orphan just like him.

It was only much, much later that Moshe discovered how Hanna had come to be in the ghetto.

Hanna Siskowski leaned against the wall on the corner of Żelazna 70 and Chłodna 23 and glanced furtively around. She was cold but steely-eyed. She had to be to survive. On her head was a crazily-tilted man's cap doing a poor job of covering up her long hair. The men's trousers she wore were far too big, hanging baggily around her knees and tied tightly around her slim waist with a length of rope. The black coat that hung limply from her scraggy shoulders at least helped to ward off some of the cold. Although she felt a pang for the corpse from whom she'd filched it, it could no longer keep him warm and she still had a job to do. Nevertheless she still whispered a silent *kaddish* mourning prayer for him.

It had been four years ago that the German occupational authorities had begun to concentrate Poland's population of over three million Jews into a number of extremely crowded ghettos located in large Polish cities. The largest of these, the

Warsaw ghetto where Hanna lived, concentrated hundreds of thousands of people into the densely packed, central area of Warsaw that she knew so well. It was only a few kilometres wide so conditions for Hanna and everyone else were terrible. She already knew that thousands of Jews had already died due to rampant disease and starvation under that bastard *SS-und-Polizeiführer* Odilo Gobocnik's rule, and his henchman *SS-Standartenführer* Ludwig Hahn was no better.

Hanna had only just managed to avoid the mass deportations from the ghetto that both men had conducted last September. It was pretty much an open secret that the destination for all the deportees was a camp to the east called Treblinka. Warsaw, sitting as it did on the mighty Vistula river, the river that had helped so many small tradesmen market their wares all along its route towards the northern port of Danzig, or Gdansk as she preferred to call it – just look what had happened to it. It was caught yet again in the stupid follies of man. Why, as someone once told her, Germany itself only existed as a territory because of Napoléon who had decreed, back in the eighteenth century, that the Holy Roman Empire should disappear and that the original Habsburg crown lands be transformed into a completely new 'Austrian Empire', the kingdom of Prussia being reconstructed as a separate place. Of course, after 1806, man being what he was, the Habsburgs and the Hohenzollerns became independent competitors for control of a future 'Germany' that was still some way in the future.

Hanna, contemplating her own life, thought back to that time, long ago, when she was five years old. She'd been small for her age, short and terrified. She remembered walking from her home at 22 Pilsudski Street, eventually standing in a crowd at the *Umschlagplatz* assembly point, right next to the Great Synagogue of her town, *Piotrkow* in Poland. Her father, with his impressive beard and black rabbi's suit, was in the centre of the square surrounded by Jews, men on one side, women and children on the other. She was there with her mother and older brother Schmuel. Another brother, Naphtali worked at the Hortensia glass factory nearby. Even now, years later, she wasn't sure why they'd taken her brother away. Nor did she know why a man with a *maikeh* three foot long rubber club had beaten her father. Again and again, the *maikeh* had come down on her poor father's back, but he hadn't complained. It was years later that Hanna had understood. The man was from the *Piotrkow* Gestapo and had ordered all the men to shave off their long beards, but her father had refused. Even as a child, Hanna knew such punishment wasn't unusual. No-one spoke of it, but everyone knew. It was never to do with anything they'd done. It was simply because of who they were.

They were Jewish.

When a young girl sees her father beaten by a Gestapo captain with a *maikeh*, attacked by snarling dogs, kicked with nailed boots, stumble from the sheer force of the blows and then suffer from being shamed in public, she can't help but carry that awful scene with her for the rest of her life. But, coupled with that, she saw the innate courage of her father, who submitted to the unjustified punishment with dignity and an amazing spiritual strength despite his frailty and weakened state due to lack of sufficient food. Over and over again, Hanna kept asking *dlaczego*, why? What had her family done to justify such cruelty, crushing their dignity and very souls in such a way?

Even at that young age, Hanna knew that men had to find a scapegoat for all their inner irritations. And that scapegoat, throughout millennia, always seemed to be her group. The Jews. *Why did they see us as evil?* she thought. *We never hate others; we don't commit crimes, as others do; we just want to get on with our lives. But others never, ever leave us alone.*

She knew that when ordinary people are worried and anxious, minor scuffles often arise. Complications began to arise from the fact that a number of Poles of mixed ancestry were classed as *Volksdeutsche* or ethnic Germans, who received special privileges and higher rations. So, unsurprisingly, those Poles who had signed the *Volksliste* and those who hadn't were strained, causing many unpleasant incidents.

Hanna heard of one girl called Anna who, after she'd been put on the *Volksliste* because of her German-sounding surname, then reported another to the Gestapo for defeatism and why? The other girl had innocently said to her 'no-one knows how the war will end'. However, luckily for the accused Polish girl, she spoke better German than Anna and was also fortunately supported by her employer, known localled as a *Polen- und Judenfreund*, who simply told the authorities that the two silly girls had had a spat. However, as Hanna knew well, situations like that were a close shave. Informers like that stupid Polish girl could easily get people sent east on cattle trucks to concentration camps.

Daily came news of what appeared to be happening in these camps. Inmates had no rights and no hope of release. They were fed on starvation diets, clothed in ragged, striped uniforms and housed in makeshift shacks. All were covered in lice and subject to every form of physical and psychological abuse. Inmates were drawn from every nationality of this Europe that was now German-occupied, victims of the policy – well-known to their counterparts of the Soviet Gulag – of final extermination by labour. All this was but a symbol of Nazi ideology, which said, with neither shame nor fear, that the 'master race' held the total and absolute right of life and death over those of 'inferior' breeds.

Whether these strong rumours were true or false, Hanna didn't know. But what she did know was that there were informers on every street corner. Hanna knew the best plan was to disbelieve everyone. That was her motto.

Trust no-one!

Now, as Hanna ducked into an alley to maintain her low profile, she wondered how long her luck would last. At least she was young and still relatively fit despite all the hardships. She knew that if she was ever going to survive, she'd need every ounce of strength and female wiles to help herself. God knows there was no-one else. It was every man for himself these days. Quickly Hanna disappeared into a house halfway down the alley and ran up the stairs to report to her friend Leon. Together they had amassed a group of Jewish warriors who were determined they would no longer submit willingly to the dictats of the Nazis. The room they used was dark and shuttered, but Hanna knew her way well enough not to need much light.

Growing up on the outskirts of Warsaw, despite the growing troubles, she'd been a budding violinist. Music had been her life, her bow floating over the strings as she soared like a bird up and down the cadences of her life until it fluctuated ever downwards to the current despair. Ever since her country was invaded in 1939, all cultural activities came under the control of the General Government's Department of People's Education and Propaganda *(Abteilung für Volksaufklarung und Propaganda)*. This meant that, for a musical girl like Hanna, opportunities for her to continue to experience the wonderful Warsaw culture were now severely restricted: no theatres, cinemas or cabarets; no education nor access to radio or press. Instead, she and her family were forced to watch films highlighting the achievements of the Third Reich, eventually only being addressed via megaphones.

Soon, her Polish school was closed, as were her favourite theatres and music clubs. The only Polish-language newspaper published in her now German-occupied district was also closed. Soon after, her Polish intellectual parents were arrested. It was only by the skin of her teeth that she had evaded capture so far. To further the tensions all around Warsaw, specific German leaflets had been distributed which contained propaganda which sought to create and encourage conflicts between ethnic groups, fueling yet more tensions between Poles and Jews, and also between Poles and Ukrainians. Some reported that in a nearby town, the Germans had forced Jews to help destroy a monument to a Polish hero, *Tadeusz Kosciuszko*, and then filmed them committing the act. Soon afterwards, the Germans set fire to a Jewish synagogue and filmed Polish bystanders, portraying them in special propaganda leaflets as a 'vengeful mob'.

And so Hanna survived, dodging the bullets of her circumstances as best she could.

By the time Gabriel arrived, by nefarious means, into the ghetto, he had noticed Hanna from the start as someone feisty and intelligent. Just what he needed if he was to accomplish his mission to rescue as many of these poor people as he could. No-one seemed to know why Gabriel was there. Some of the inmates, whispering in the alleys whenever the guard wasn't looking, said he was an English spy. Others said he was working for Churchill himself but no-one really knew. In truth they couldn't understand why anyone who didn't need to be in the Warsaw ghetto would actually want to be there. He was either very brave or *meshuggenah*, the latter being the most likely in their opinion.

A shout from the guard. "You there," his heavy jackboots crunching into the mud as he announced his arrival. "Stop talking now and get on with your work," the officer's hand resting on the gun nestled in his leather holster. His steely blue eyes looked wary as he glanced around, constantly on the alert for any signs of escape. Quickly, the inmates rushed to do his bidding. They'd learnt in the worst way possible the price of disobedience. So many had been gunned down for no reason whatsoever. Others were given demeaning tasks to do. One old man, a rabbi, had been made to kneel down and strip off all his clothes whilst a grinning guard had roughly sliced off his long wispy beard with a pen knife.

Daily their numbers had been diminishing as, following a roll call, large groups of them had been pushed into cattle trucks and taken away, never to be seen again. The rest of them lived from hand to mouth, the youths meeting secretly to plan out what to do. The language many used was a Polish variety of Yiddish, which quickly evolved to become their *lingua franca*.

But then, suddenly, the man called Gabriel arrived, joining the group meetings and discussing his plan with them. At first, several boys said they could not trust him.

"He's a foreigner," said one.

"How can we be sure he's on our side?"

"Look," said Hanna, whom the boys had allowed to join their meetings as, in truth, with her men's clothing and rough cap, looked little different from themselves. They'd all had to grow up fast. In the ghetto, only the quick and clever ones lived to fight another day. "He's Jewish, isn't he?"

"Yes. We made sure of that from the start," said their impromptu leader, amidst dry laughter.

"Well then," continued Hanna. "We've no choice but to trust him. He says he's here to help us so we shouldn't look a gift horse in the mouth."

"It's not in his mouth we looked," snickered another boy.

"We've no time to make jokes. If he says he has a plan, we should listen to him."

"I agree," said their leader, asking for a show of hands.

So it was decided.

Every evening, the main German guard changed shifts. This always took some time so a meeting with Gabriel was arranged at the precise hour of the guard changeover.

True to his word, Gabriel arrived at the secret hideaway in Niska Street, located in the furthermost building from the German sentry post. The inmate at the door quickly admitted him, and after prising open a floorboard, directed Gabriel to jump down to the cold, concrete cellar below, before replacing the loose plank and positioning himself at the entrance, ready to sound the alert at any sound of approaching jack boots.

As his eyes quickly adjusted to the gloom, Gabriel was pushed down to a sitting position. In front of him was a boy called Jacob and the girl called Hanna. A taper was lit so he could see their faces. After brief introductions, Gabriel took a stick and began to draw a diagram in the dust of what he planned.

Jacob and Hanna leaned forward as Gabriel whispered in heavily-accented Yiddish what he considered to be their best plan. "Jacob," said Gabriel, turning towards the leader of the group, "I'll be frank. I won't be able to rescue everyone. My plan is to convince the German commandant here that a number of you have been brought here by mistake, that in fact you are Catholic."

"But," said Hanna, "how are you going to convince the guards of that when so many of us look Jewish."

Gabriel passed a hand over his own blond head, his mind working feverishly. "I know, Hanna. We're going to have to be very clever. Look," turning to Jacob, "pass me your pen knife."

Jacob looked worried, but did as requested.

Leaning sideways, Gabriel carefully slit the side seam of his trousers, extricating a small thin package secreted there. Opening up the brown paper, he spread the contents on the floor in front of them. The light from Hanna's taper reflected off the line of small silver crucifixes and rosary beads.

There was a sharp intake of breath from both Hanna and Jacob.

"Wherever did you get those," asked Jacob.

"Never mind," responded Gabriel. "There are always means if the will is strong enough."

"Now," addressing Jacob again, "I need you to select about a dozen inmates, including the two of you of course. Wherever possible, choose those strong enough to withstand an escape. I suggest you choose men, women and small children so that the group looks like a normal large family outing. And, if they are blond, all the better. Now, my intelligence is that a senior Nazi official is visiting the ghetto next week."

"But," interrupted Jacob, "how will that help us? Surely, more Nazis about will make any escape harder."

"Ah, but that's where you're mistaken my friend. It's exactly what I need. Also, I've managed to get some guns from the *Zydowski Zwiqzek Wojsko*, which you'll know about as the right wing resistance group here."

Jacob interrupted. "Oh yes, we know about them," spitting on the ground to indicate his feelings about the group. "What makes you think we can trust the Poles?"

Gabriel smiled. "Sometimes, my friend, you have to do deals with the enemy if you want to get anywhere. It wasn't easy but I was able to do a trade off, bartering some western luxuries I brought with me. Just leave everything to me."

Hanna had been staring at Gabriel, finally coming to a decision. "Look, Jacob. What have we got to lose? This man is offering us a way out. I vote that we take him at his word."

Reluctantly, Jacob nodded, staring down at the rough diagram which Gabriel had drawn in the dirt.

Now turning to Hanna, Gabriel scooped up the Catholic jewellery lying in the dust and handed them to her, saying

"Now Hanna, once the escape group have been selected and have agreed, on the day when the Nazi VIPs arrive, I need you to distribute these crucifixes to the women and children and the rosary bead bracelets to the men. Tell them to wear them, ready to be shown when demanded by the Germans. Also, do you know any Hail Marys?"

Hanna said that, in fact, she'd spent a time in a convent before being captured.

"Good. Give the group a quick lesson on how to be good Catholics. That will help to convince the Nazis when the time comes. So," turning to both Joseph and Hanna, "is everything understood? Joseph, your task is to select a willing group of blond men, women and small children, and Hanna, you must distribute the jewellery and ensure that everyone keeps absolutely *shtum*. On no account must anyone say anything about this plan, on pain of death. OK?"

They both nodded.

"I will alert you to bring the group forward when the time comes. Any questions?"

Their silence confirmed it.

After quick handshakes, Gabriel was soon gone.

That night they all had a lot to think about.

Hanna hoped that her prayers would be answered, as she stuffed the jewellery in a slit she'd made in her thin, hard mattress. As her eyes finally closed, she knew she was very afraid but had steeled herself to never show it to the outside world. She was so young but life had changed for ever since she had been forced from the only home she'd ever known.

The ghetto guards were on high alert. Shoes and guns were given an extra polish and uniforms were brushed to an immaculate standard. German scouts were positioned along the road leading to the ghetto so that as much notice as possible could be given to the senior command. The Nazi VIPs were to be presented with an efficient report of how the Jewish menace was being effectively contained. Absolutely nothing must go wrong or they, themselves, were in danger of being shot.

Soon, the roar of an advancing cavalcade of vehicles approached the high walls. It was unmistakably the officials from Berlin. Sentries were detailed both sides of the entrance, guns pointed into the ghetto, to prevent any inmates making a run for it.

"Heil Hitler!" cries greeted the VIPs as they exited their vehicles, their salutes reciprocated and heels clicked. With much fawning, the ghetto commandant led the men to his office, positioned strategically on high to give a panoramic view of the ghetto's narrow streets.

"*Guten Morgan*," said SS Oberführer Hummel, walking into the commandant's office unannounced, his boots ringing over the hard floor, his arms clasped behind his back. "I have a message for you," throwing a piece of paper onto the desk.

The commandant felt his stomach tighten with fear. You never knew what these ruthless officers from Berlin's high command would spring on you next. Trying hard not to show his nervousness, he unfolded the paper and read that a Catholic priest with excellent credentials sought an immediate audience with him. *What on earth was all that about?*

The Oberführer indicated that Father Guiseppe, a colleague

and friend of the Pope, was a leading theologian, who was visiting them with an urgent request from his ministry. "Wouldn't do to upset the Pope at this critical juncture in our battle, now would it?"

The commandant felt beads of sweat running into his eyes as he nodded meekly. He couldn't afford to upset the Oberführer either. "*Jawohl*, Herr Oberführer," clicking his heels. "I'll personally see to it that this….what was his name again?…oh yes, Father Guiseppe, is invited up to my office so that we can listen to his request and help him out as best we can."

"*Gut,*" replied the Oberführer, "let me know when you have him here and I'll attend in person."

"It shall be done. *Heil* Hitler."

CHAPTER SEVEN

A MAN WEARING A long robe stood in the office of the commandant in the office overlooking the Warsaw ghetto. Around the back of his neck was draped a long narrow strip of cloth, its position denoting his position as a priest ordained into the Roman Catholic Church.

The man's expression was calm and benign, despite the obvious agitation of the commandant, who kept nervously crossing the room to search through the window for the arrival of the Oberführer. The priest waved away all offers of refreshments, saying that the needs of man paled against the requirements of the Lord Jesus Christ.

At first the commandant had difficulty understanding the priest's heavily-accented German until it was explained to him that those from Rome, as with all people speaking Romansch languages, found it hard to speak Germanic languages.

Nevertheless, they understood each other as they awaited the arrival of the Oberführer. Suddenly, the Nazi officer marched into the office, a broad smile on his face as he schooled his expression into one that was seemingly both charming and beneficent as he greeted the cleric.

"We are honoured to welcome you, Reverend Father. We

apologise that, in these times of war and amongst the depraved, we are unable to offer you a full German welcome. However, we would be only too pleased to offer you what assistance we can," bowing slightly from the waist. It was clear that Hummel was loathe to offend this representative of the Axis clergy. The way the war was going, Italy was an important ally at this difficult time so he felt honour-bound to try and help the Father in whatever way he could.

Hummel turned to the Father and asked humbly how they may help.

"First," Herr Oberführer, "as I explained to the commandant, I must apologise for my poor German. It is a language which all Italians find very difficult," said Guiseppe.

Hummel waved away the Father's apologies and bade him continue.

"*Danke*," said Guiseppe, "but I have a special request which I hope you can help me with. It has come to my notice that a group of Catholics, originally from my bishop's diocese in Rome, may have been wrongly grouped with a Jewish family and brought to this ghetto." Now turning to the commandant, Guiseppe handed him a piece of paper which, written in Jacob's best handwriting, listed the names of the chosen group.

"Yes, yes, I recognise some of these names," said the commandant to the Oberführer.

"Well," said Hummel, "send someone to fetch them here at once. We don't want to keep the Father waiting."

Half an hour later, a group of inmates stood in the commandant's office. The women all wore a crucifix around their necks, and the men fingered the beads of their rosary bracelet around their wrists. One girl held a small boy in her arms, who was mercifully asleep. None of the group said a word.

"Is this all of them on the list?" asked the commandant to his underling.

"*Jawohl*, Herr Commandant," said the man.

"*Gut, gut,*" smiled Hummel, turning to Guiseppe. "It seems you were right, Father. There's no doubt these people were wrongly kept here. We have no problem with those of the Catholic faith. No problem at all. Do you wish to take these people with you right away?"

Guiseppe paused a while, scratching his beard. "I think that would be best, Herr Oberführer. I promised His Excellency The Pope that I would endeavour to bring these good people home as soon as the good Lord allowed."

"Well then. The problem is solved," shooing the group away through the open door, and telling the commandant's underling to ensure they were not disturbed as they passed through the gates of the ghetto to the road outside. "*Auf Wiedersehen,* Holy Father," the two Germans called as they bade him a hearty goodbye.

Marching in formation, the group headed by the Holy Father walked silently through the gates and along the road outside until they came to an intersection. With a finger to his lips, Gabriel hid behind a bush as he disrobed himself of his outer garments, revealing his ordinary civilian wear underneath.

Whispering to Jacob and Hanna, he told them to tell the group to continue their silence until they reached the Vistula, the major river running through Warsaw, at which time further instructions would be issued.

In truth, they made a ragged group. They were all starving, malnourished and tired. Gabriel fished inside his voluminous coat and pulled out some bread and cheese which he asked Hanna to distribute. Everyone grabbed at the food and devoured it far too quickly, making the younger ones nauseous. As they walked on, Gabriel stopped at a stream, running with cool, clear water. He bade them all to lie down on their stomachs and to cup the delicious water in their hands before quenching their thirst. All the time, Gabriel kept a wary eye out for anyone who looked suspicious. No-one was about, which was normal in Poland in these times of war. Everyone kept themselves to themselves and only ventured out on urgent business. No-one wanted to be apprehended by a member of the occupying forces.

But Gabriel knew that although his elaborate ruse had worked amazingly well so far, the Germans were so efficient that it was only a matter of time before they were rumbled. It was imperative, therefore, that no time must be lost before they reached a position of relative safety.

At last, the group reached the Vistula. Gabriel ushered them all into an ancient, ramshackle barge which was tied up near the water's edge.

Hanna was so grateful to at last rest her weary legs. Although young Moshe was a toddler, the further she walked, the heavier he became. But even she was amazed at the comparative luxury inside the vessel. Behind the wheelhouse, there was a kitchen and a toilet. She couldn't believe it. She'd never seen such a thing. Her old apartment, where she lived before she'd been captured, had no running water nor indoor toilet. Everyone in their tenement block had shared one old toilet shed, situated in the yard at the back.

Jacob kept running his grimy fingers over the hull of the vessel.

"Yes, it's steel, Jacob," said Gabriel.

"But, how does it run?"

"Ah, that was my problem Jacob. I knew it had an engine. The days of vessels like this needing a horse are now mostly gone, but I had the devil of a job finding fuel. There's none to be had anywhere."

"So, what did you do? Did you get any?" said Jacob, suddenly panicked. He was starting to look at Gabriel as a saviour. There was so much more to him than met the eye. It seemed that there was nothing he couldn't do. Jacob couldn't believe how the man had managed to completely fool not only the ghetto commandant but also the Oberführer himself.

"Well. Where there's a will there's a way, Jacob. I found a man who was willing to do a trade. He had a Romanian source who, for a price, could import synthetic fuel. All other forms have become increasingly in short supply due to the war effort, so I grabbed whatever I could get. All I needed was enough to get us to the outskirts of Bialystok."

"Bialystok? But that's the wrong way isn't it?"

"Yes. That's my plan. Once the Germans get wind of how I've hoodwinked them, they'll assume we'll all be heading north west towards the English Channel. And, they'll think we'll be going by road, driving a large truck or similar. So, what better way than to navigate an old barge along the river Vistula and to be heading in the 'wrong direction'?"

Turning now to Hanna, Gabriel asked her to take the group down below and to ensure they all got some rest *en route*. She didn't need asking twice. Little Moshe was exhausted and she, herself, was falling over from tiredness and stress.

"Right, Jacob. Have you ever manned a river barge before?"

"Well, no. But I'd like to try," said Jacob.

"Good, good. We'll take it in turns. I'll manoeuvre it out first from its moorings and set it in the right direction heading north-east, while you get some rest."

Jacob agreed and followed the others to the lower deck.

Soon, the engine was running and the boat successfully heading away from the reeds, surging forth. As the soothing ripples ebbed and flowed in v-shaped patterns on both the port and starboard sides, and the pointed bow nosed the vessel ever forwards, the group slept soundly at last, whilst Gabriel yawned at the helm as he contemplated the next stage of their ambitious plan.

True to his word, Jacob hadn't demurred when a tiring Gabriel asked him to take over at the helm. "Wake me up when you see the outskirts of Bialystok come into view. It's important we don't miss the target I'm aiming for."

Jacob nodded as at last Gabriel managed to get a few hours of well-earned rest. He'd need all his wits about him if he was to successfully manage the next stage. Best he didn't tell the others yet. He didn't want to panic everyone.

It seemed like only five minutes had passed, but already Jacob was shaking him awake. "You told me to tell you when a town appeared and I can see it in the distance. Come quickly."

Yawning, Gabriel followed Jacob up the narrow stairs and stepped outside and walked up to the bow. Sure enough, in the far distance there were unmistakable signs of a large city looming on the horizon. An old wooden sign on the starboard sign indicated that the Vistula had now become the Narew River, so clearly the buildings dotted on the port side must be Bialystok suburbs, the provincial capital of the region and the largest city in the region. He'd heard that there was a concentration camp somewhere within the conurbation so it was imperative he didn't take his group anywhere near. If they knew, they'd throw a fit.

Hanna stuck her head outside and asked what she should do next. Gabriel told her to gather the group together and to line up just inside, ready for instructions. Quickly, she darted downstairs to do as she'd been bid, only too happy to do something for this man, who had been sent by *HaShem* himself.

Manoeuvring the vessel to the port side, after a few bumps, Gabriel finally managed to tether the barge to a steel pole alongside the grassy bank. Quickly, he jumped ashore and helped the group to exit the barge safely. Hanna handed the sleeping Moshe to Gabriel as she jumped ashore, then took the toddler back into her arms.

Finding a bit of flat grass that was reasonably shielded from any onlookers, he told everyone to sit down whilst he searched the area. He knew what he was looking for but didn't know whether they would have arrived yet.

Amazingly, several hours later, he heard the unmistakable sound of a jet flying low over the river. Rushing to the waterside, Gabriel strained his eyes skywards. Yes! He could just make out three blue letters on the side of the plane: RAF. Frantically, he stretched his arms up, intermittently crossing them to try to alert the pilot. But, had he seen him? He wasn't sure.

The Wing-Commander ducked down through the wispy cloud cover and steadied his machine before dropping down to a level above the Narew river, just short of the major conurbation of Bialystok. Adjusting his brown leather cap, he looked down to the port side, grabbing his field glasses in one hand and searching the terrain either side as best he could.

The Wing-Commander adjusted the flight controls so that he was flying as quietly as possible directly above the moving waters. At last he spotted someone waving his arms frantically, so he edged lower. Inside the plane, a commando was busy donning landing gear before sidling up to the sliding door. In his nostrils was the unmistakeable whiff of strong fuel and noisy rivets in his ears.

Now, as he adjusted the co-ordinates to fly as low as possible, alternately dipping the wings before re-routing itself more precisely, the pilot hovered above the place where he'd seen the man. He gave the signal and opened the hatch. The commando edged to the outer rim, dangling his legs over the side. No matter how many times he'd practised this manoeuvre, the fear never lessened. Instinctively the man tested the cord that was attached securely to the plane, knowing that once he'd jumped clear, the weight of his own body would snap the wire at the end of the cord, forcing open the parachute on his back. He jumped as far away from the moving plane as he could. The pilot checked his instruments to make sure that all looked in order before sighting a line of trees that fringed the waters of the river. Two swans were momentarily frightened as a very large 'bird' suddenly flew down at speed over their heads before expertly skidding onto a wide, straight avenue running parallel to the river.

The commando managed to avoid the panoply of leaves networking across the top of the forest before rolling safely onto the ground near the river bank. Quickly cutting away the strings of his parachute and disposing of it, he searched for Gabriel.

Hearing the crunch of boots on the forest floor, Gabriel ran towards his fellow kinsman and embraced him. "Thank God," he breathed.

"Where are they?" asked his compatriot, aware that time was of the essence if they were ever to escape and head back on the long journey to England before nightfall.

Gabriel led the way, signalling to Jacob that he and Hanna should follow the commando and to keep as silent as possible. Hanna again put Moshe on her sore hip as she struggled after the group, heading for the roadway. First, the commando signalled they should pause behind the trees whilst he did a reconnoitre of the surroundings.

Now signalling that all was clear, he beckoned the group to where the RAF jet was idling. Seeing their approach, the pilot quickly threw down some steps as, one by one, the tired, ragged, careworn, starving and frightened group of Jewish people, climbed up into the safety of the English flying machine.

Suddenly, there was a shout from the roadway "Halt, Halt!"

Gabriel, as the last man, pulled up the steps and slammed the door to. "Get down, get down everyone," he shouted as bullets started to pound against the fuselage. But already, the pilot was careering at full pelt along the roadway before, with a beautiful bird-like grace, the RAF jet lifted up, up and away into the blue yonder.

There was only one way they were headed and that was north west, over the blessed English Channel towards the welcoming arms of the white cliffs of Dover.

Looking back now, after all those years, Moshe had a tear in his eye.

"Thank you Gabriel. Thank you Hanna. Without you both, I would not be here now."

Chapter Eight

Toulouse
2019

"At last Papa has opened up about his past," Simon told his wife. He knew, of course, that his father must have suffered considerably in the ghetto, but he'd never known the remarkable story about how a brave Englishman and a remarkable woman, Hanna, had saved him from certain death. *No wonder Papa's been so choked up over the years,* he thought. *Without all that happening, I wouldn't even be here today. The least I can do now is to try and achieve Papa's dream.* It was beyond reason, but now was his chance to do something.

Simon studied his film notes.

First, scene I, way back in Jewish history.

Why, simply looking at the date, two thousand years before the Christian era, should concentrate minds, surely? How could the Jewish people be 'usurpers', when archaeological evidence proves that this was their land long before others even existed?

"Well, it's up to me then, love. No pressure then."

"Lights, camera, action"

Sodom and Gomorrah
1900 BCE

Admah was feeling exhausted. Every little thing these days was proving a drain on his strength. So many years of the Lord had passed since he was a young boy, but yet the world had not improved. There was so much sin abroad. He saw evidence of it all around his dwelling place and felt an urgent need to pass on this knowledge to everyone in his tribe.

Admah's house and outbuildings were relatively modest in style. The house itself was humble but sufficient for the family's needs, its walls made of rough stone and tar. There was one living space with a curtained off area for sleeping. The whole family worked hard in the fields every day, the gathered grains being the main source of sustenance in the hot arid plains in which they lived. Additionally, Naarah, his only daughter, looked after the family's precious goat flock and was responsible for collecting water. When not working in the fields, a large part of Admah'sday was spent serving the Lord. He was a humble man and decreed that his family and tribe should live by his example.

The house was located at the southern end of a stretch of salt water, over one thousand feet below sea level. The lake was divided into two basins, the northern basin being significantly larger. A peninsular separated the basins at the lake's narrowest point, which was used as a lucrative crossing point for shipping salt. It was because of this dead-end location that the lake was too salty to sustain life. The water was sufficiently viscous though, that mortals could float on their backs without any effort. In fact, the lake water and the mud were regularly used by the females for treating skin problems.

That night Admah dreamt that something was coming, something so traumatic that there was no knowing if anyone could survive. In his youth he remembered the wise men of the village warning him that when he dies many years in the future, it shall come.

But what was this 'it'? He didn't know but was very afraid. As his death must surely be approaching, so his fears increased. As he looked out towards the city near where he dwelt, he could see the moon's reflection off the distant, shallow waters of the *Al-Lisān* peninsula, which lay just to the south of his dwelling.

Over the years, Admah had learned to his cost to keep a low profile. More and more people were settling along the route to *Sodom,* and daily he saw evidence of how little these newcomers cared for his values. For him, giving alms to the poor and offering hospitality to strangers were second nature, but it wasn't even the lack of these things that gave him such cause for concern. It was the public lust, freely on display for all to see that was like a dagger to his heart. He'd brought his children up always to be pure in mind, spirit and body but when confronted daily by such wanton exhibitionism? As an Israelite, Admah felt heartsick, but what could he do but keep himself and his family out of the way of the infidels as much as possible?

So every night he prayed to *Adonai* to protect them from the hell fire that was coming.

"My family are righteous," he prayed, his eyes closed, his hands in supplication, "please Lord save us."

The Almighty must have heard his words for a message came to his brain. "If no-one welcomes you into his place of dwelling nor listens to your words, then shake the sand from your feet as you leave. Gather together your family and evacuate the city. Long, long after you have passed, your people will return to the land. But, by then, new, successive heathen tribes will establish themselves. The enemy will change but the troubles will continue. Your people will fight successive tribes again and again in order to return to their land of Israel. All of this is decreed. So, it will be necessary to build up your strength of will, in body and mind, in order to survive. This land is all important. Your people are my people and must be strong enough to overcome all obstacles in their path. Patience is of the essence. Remember my words."

Admah felt overcome with emotion as the words resonated in his brain. As with most people, Admah hated to leave his dwelling place. There was a comfort in the familiar, but he realised he now had little choice. The words of the Almighty were so powerful, his body quailed at the thought of resisting them. Yet, up until now, he had been able to live adequately by using the fertile land in this place he called home. There was enough fresh water nearby in the *Siddim* valley to sustain his work in the fields whilst his family tended their flocks.

But now? Admah was in a quandary. It was said that much of the ungodly habits of the newcomers happened in *Har Sedom,* a place he'd heard of but never visited. Some said it was a place established at the southwestern shores of the mighty sea.

Admah lay back and closed his eyes a moment, better to force some clarity into his thinking. The words of his own father of ancient memory (*Oleva Shalom* – peace be with him), came to his mind. "Son, at the blessed birth of a new child, our people give the name of a family forefather so that the new child can follow in the footsteps of his ancestor and continue his good work. So, I gave you the name of Admah. It signifies that you and your descendants will be as roots to the ground, each red tap-root establishing a network binding you to this land. Eventually, way into the future, this network will grow stronger and be impossible to uproot.

I would, therefore, beseech thee that whenever troubles lie heavily upon you, as they surely will, ask *Adonai* for strength and guidance."

Clearly, divine guidance had come to Admah and he must now deliver his people out of the danger that was daily encroaching on their lives.

Admah had always been treated with reverence by his tribe, a respect that sometimes bordered on fear. They knew there was a special aura surrounding him but were frightened of where it would lead them. But, nevertheless, Admah was certain that his people would follow him wherever the path should lead.

The following night, in order to follow the divine guidelines he'd been given, Admah focussed on what he knew so far of the heathen people. News abroad was that there were salt-water baths at *Har Sedom*, the water gleaned and heated from the barren, low-lying dead sea or from the hot mineral springs which were discovered high up in the mountains. Some said that the baths were being used for licentious purposes in *Har Sedom* and another place called *Gomorrah*.

An Israelite scout reported on a man called Zeboim, who was the chief tribesman of both places. Zeboim used the baths to legitimise his nefarious activities, activities that had escalated alarmingly during his reign. Stories were abroad that the people of the region were being led to terrible misdeeds and orgies, something that was abominable to Admah and all that he had instilled in his village tribe. So far, the Israelites had kept their heads low in an effort to distance themselves from the troubles all around them, but the latest news had kept Admah awake night after night. Something had to be done, and soon, before it was too late. The Lord had already prophesied that it was not enough to hide and do nothing; it was necessary to fight evil, tooth and nail.

But Admah knew that his people had been through enough. All they ever wanted was to live a good life in peace and harmony with their fellow men.

It was always the same. What could they do when others seemed to feel an irrational need to persecute them for no reason other than the fact that they existed? As soon as one enemy was finally vanquished, another would come along. Even the Lord, blessed be he, had said the same. When would it stop, so that his people could finally live in peace?

As the following day dawned, the sun already bright and clear in the heavens above, Admah decided that today was the day that he would call the youngest of the tribe to him. Young Naarah was a sweet child, honest and true, and now of an age to understand much of what Admah had to say. Admah clapped his hands and called for young Naarah to be brought to him.

It was true that Admah's village had encountered troubles with neighbouring places many times before. But they had survived by forging friendships with those who shared common practices. In this way, when one of them was attacked, their allies would help. However, both Admah's tribe and their allies were originally semi-nomads who had emerged from the areas surrounding the hot desert plains. As such, Admah knew they would be at a considerable disadvantage if they attempted to fight Zeboim and his highly trained henchmen. Also, the scout reported that Zeboim lived in a strongly armed city.

It was clear, therefore, that a very different plan was needed. On the plus side, Admah had built up much wisdom in his long years and he knew the strengths of his own people.

A young girl was tending to her goats, pushing and encouraging them towards the cool waters of a stream, which trickled down from the hills. In truth, the goats didn't need much urging. Already the sun's rays were hot on their scrawny backs and they trusted this girl. Instinctively, they sensed that she would never hurt them, her small hands gentle and loving as she guided them.

Naarah knew that the family was lucky to live in their village. Not many places enjoyed the natural resources available to them, so she was happy. Resting awhile, she tented her hand over her brow and peered southwards. She could just make out on the horizon the spot where the broad sands had evolved to become this now well-irrigated land. Turning her head, she gloried in the sight of rows and rows of wondrous olive trees, vineyards and orchards, all growing on the land which had been terraced to prevent erosion. At first she had found the fruit quite bitter but now loved the oily tang on her tongue. She was glad they didn't live amongst the rocky hills further north.

As soon as the goats had slaked their thirst, Naarah manoeuvred them back towards the land her father had cultivated to enable the family to eat meals rich with nutritious grains and vegetables.

Feeling the heat on the back of her neck, Naarah checked on the essential, water bags that she kept on a yoke around her neck. They were robust, sewn from tough goat skin. She may have been young, but the young goat-girl knew that careful hoarding of the precious water was imperative. Without it, all living things die. Some said that man could survive for quite a long time without food but not without water.

Thank the Lord for the winter rains which regularly brought life to the arid, parched land, flooding the wadis with torrents of rushing water. Nevertheless, it was always prudent to hoard water in catch basins and cisterns.

Now gently guiding the goats to the foot of the hills, Naarah turned to take the familiar route homewards. Naarah breathed in the deep scent flowing down from the hills. She loved working outside, away from the hustle and bustle of other people. Being on her own, with just the goats for company, was all she asked of life.

I wish I were grown up though, she thought longingly. She wiped her dirty hands over her tunic and adjusted her headdress in a vain attempt to straighten it. She knew that her father wouldn't be too pleased to see her in such a grubby state.

Alongside her, the youngest of the goats was frolicking in the wild grass, turning his head from side to side as sharp spikes tickled its chin. Naarah sighed. The kid was oblivious to the cares of the world. His coat was straggly and unkempt, but little did he care. *Why couldn't she be more like the goats*, she thought.

Feeling tired, Naarah sat down on the rough, stubby grass and gazed longingly over towards the horizon. *What will I be when I am grown?* she thought. She had a sudden premonition of disaster and she shivered uncontrollably in the heat of the day. *Oh I hope nothing happens to my family,* she thought. *I just couldn't bear it if the evil ones attack us. What will I do on my own?* Tears momentarily glistened on her young cheeks before she hastily brushed them aside. What would her family think of her? They'd say she was a baby. She shook herself and looked again over the distant hills.

Suddenly, she heard her name being called. "Naarah, Naarah, where are you? Admah is looking for you."

With a sigh, she stood upright again, rubbing her fingers to get the blood coursing again. As she herded her goats along the long straight river valley to her home, she was careful not to speak to anyone on her route. Her father had warned her many times that there was much sin in the world, so she must be extra careful on the road.

But Naarah was suddenly fearful. It was unusual for her father to seek her out when she was tending the goats in the hills. Friends often told her of troubles in other villages. Her mother told her only yesterday that when washing pots and pans at the river, some of the old gossips had told stories that had horrified her. She wondered if this was why she was being summoned now.

The sun was now high in the sky and she was hungry. But she must first obey her father. As she turned onto the sandy track which led to their modest house, she tightened the rope cord which held her headdress in place, in a vain attempt to keep her head cool. But beads of perspiration were running down into her eyes, which she quickly brushed away with the back of her hand. Stooping down to the animals, she untethered them and pushed them into the cool barn at the back of the family's dwelling, clicking her tongue at the recalcitrant ones in the language only they understood.

Quickly, she rushed inside.

"I'm here *Abba*. I'm sorry I've been so long. Amber and Black Foot just wouldn't behave, no matter what I did, so I had to tie more rope around their necks to stop them straying too far from the rest of the herd."

Admah shooed her quiet with an abstracted wave of his hand and bade her sit on the straw floor next to him. Naarah dropped to a cross-legged position on the straw and waited for her father's words of wisdom. At least he didn't appear to be unduly annoyed with her, which was a relief. So, if he wasn't angry, why had he called her and not an older member of the family? She idolised her *Abba* and knew that his wisdom far exceeded that of her friends' fathers.

Admah looked down at this young girl and knew that what he was going to ask would demand much of her. But already Naarah was showing signs of a maturity far above her years and reminded him of a time way back when he too ran and jumped with the goats in the hills. He sighed again with the long-suppressed memory, an agonising pain in his innards jolting him back to the present. Admah knew he did not have much time left. He feared an apocalypse was about to descend after his death: something he had always known, a divine intuition. He remembered his father, of blessed memory, telling him why he, Admah, must listen carefully. It had been decreed that he, Admah, had become a living testimony that there was a divine spirit and that *Adenoi* was calling him and warning him as to what was coming, should the evil in the world not abate. It appeared that the divine one was willing to wait by extending Admah's life, but after that.....

Admah's eyes had glazed over but suddenly everything became clear. Looking down on the child, whilst absently stroking his long white beard, he spoke.

"Naarah, my child, although you are young, you must surely be aware that there has been much trouble lately," looking at her questioningly.

"Yes, *Abba*. Mama has told me."

"That's good, that's good," relieved that he did not have to go into too much detail about activities he found personally repugnant. "Now listen carefully. I fear that something is about to happen and it won't be good. Some evil men have been rampaging and killing our people and it is only a matter of time before they reach us here. Recently I have watched with mounting alarm but nothing I say or do has any effect on them. In fact they laugh at me and call me a foolish old man!"

Naarah was shocked. Her hand flew to her mouth. *How could anyone talk to her Abba in this hateful way?*

"I'm afraid the people of the two big cities near us have become increasingly sinful, their behaviour becoming an abomination to all that our tribe holds dear. I have therefore sought counsel with the other elders of the village. Now," stroking Naarah's curly head, "be not afeared my child but we have decided that we must gather our people together and leave at first light."

"Oh *Abba!* But, what about my goats?"

Admah thought this was typical of his daughter, thinking of her beloved animals before anything else. "I understand your concerns but this crisis outweighs all other considerations. There's a reason why I called only you here today, and for that you should feel very proud. We need a messenger to alert our people: someone who can move silently and swiftly, without causing much consternation in the enemy camp. Naarah, I would like that messenger to be you. Are you willing to take on the heavy weight of this responsibility?" looking at her keenly.

Despite her initial feelings, Naarah trembled with excitement, oblivious to everything but her pride in being selected for such an important mission.

"Of course, *Abba*. Whenever you want me to begin, I shall be ready."

With that, Admah sighed with satisfaction and bade Naarah to go away and rest. She should be ready to leave at a moment's notice, whenever the call came.

Buildings constructed of *meleke* stone surrounded the square of one of the five large cities in the region. A series of majestic pillars supported the roofs, their statuary acting as sentry duty to the masses. In front of the building which housed the saline baths was an area which now heaved with mostly young citizens, frolicking and joyous after their adventures within.

Radiating out from the central square of the city were many newly-constructed buildings, the most prominent comprising a magnificent tower and grand apartments, elaborate baths and beautiful courtyards. The tower served as the official residence of the city leader, and was large enough to accommodate up to six hundred of his men at any one time.

The Jews of the city had been forced to live within the court of the temple so that they could be guarded, and that their strange festival practices and barbarous way of living could be kept under control.

The sound of hundreds of voices still echoed from within the bath house. The entrance was approached via wide steps, leading to the cool interior. No expense had been spared in its internal decoration, a panoply of vine leaves covering both ceiling and walls and acting as an instant antidote to the heat outside. Further inside and down more steps to cellar level brought more noise, loud voices resounding from inlaid tiles on opposite walls and floor of the bath house and off the stone rafters above.

Zeboim, chief tribesman of the two main cities, immersed himself further into the heavy saline waters, his white feet extended out before him like distant ships in the steamy, green opulence. His bloated stomach swelled on the water like a giant sperm whale breasting the waves before its sudden jet of water spurts upwards before submerging again. Zeboim's hairy arms were stretched outwards as he attempted to float in the salty water. The air above the waters was steamy and humid, clinging to the damp walls like slimy algae and obscuring sight lines like a sepulchral fog.

Zeboim sucked in his breath momentarily as the salt water stung his skin where he had cut himself the day before. Clapping his hands to alert a nearby slave girl, Zeboim indicated that she should massage away the tiny needles assaulting him. Closing his eyes, he visualised the sinful pleasures ahead.

Now looking across the water, Zeboim was always amused by the antics of his soldiers' cavorting with the slave girls in the water. However, he himself had rather different thoughts as he wafted in the humid air. He closed his eyes again and let himself completely relax as he recalled the first time he had encountered young Adonis. He couldn't contain a sigh of satisfaction at the boy's exquisite beauty, his head of golden curls, and eyes of such a clear blue that he was totally smitten. His limbs were hairless and straight, his body as soft and yielding as a girl's. The boy was clearly a virgin, his whole body trembling at Zeboim's first touch. Zeboim knew what he liked, those things that gave him pleasure and this boy encapsulated his cravings.

Other *Sodomites* enjoying the waters were of a similar mind. There were so many young males there with beautiful bodies, they couldn't stop themselves. Nothing gave them greater pleasure than to have the boys swim underneath the water and lick their gonads before enjoying them in moments of such frenzy that the water boiled and foamed over the rim of the baths, swirling right over the painted floor tiles to the cold showers and cubicles beyond.

Zeboim was a vain man, totally consumed by his own authority. His ego governed his whole life. To him, what he did wasn't sinful; rather, it was his absolute right. After all, hadn't he been named after a major city? Many were the occasions when he would say to his men "My needs are paramount. As Chief of two major cities, it is my due. I have little regard to what the Gods may say, nor how my behaviour affects others. They have to understand that a man in my position is of a higher status than they. My needs, therefore, are all the greater."

Of course, Zeboim had heard the whispers that his behaviour was 'unnatural'. In the private homes of many, the belief was that Zeboim could be both cruel and ruthless. Many of Zeboim's conquests were forced into slavery, their initial fairness of face eventually counting against them as they were continually exploited.

An old male servant loitered near his master, carrying over his arm a bolt of thick, absorbent material. Zeboim used his arms as paddles as he dragged his heavy body backwards towards the steps at the end of the bath. Swivelling around, he staggered up the slippery steps and waited whilst his servant swathed him in the absorbent cloth. Zeboim then walked to his own, specially-constructed, wooden cubicle where he flopped heavily onto the seat whilst his servant knelt down to swathe his feet. He was reminded that it was essential he remain completely covered in order that the health-giving salts could dry onto his body.

As he waited, his thoughts returned to the hated tribe who lived further down the valley. *By the Gods, what am I going to do about old man, Admah? Who does he think he is, usurping the role that he, Zeboim, had devised? I am the Chief around here, no-one else. Why, these days, old Admah's acting so arrogantly that his people are now refusing to obey my strictures or to take part in what I've devised for them! Both men and women too. The females refuse to obey my men, and Admah's tribesmen treat me with disdain. Time I showed them, once and for all, who's the leader around here.*

Suddenly mobilised, Zeboim hurriedly dressed and instructed one of his henchmen to call a senate meeting for the following day.

"What matters of importance will be discussed?" asked the man

"Tell the senate members that there will be only one item: the complete eradication of the downwater tribe led by Admah."

"Very well. It shall be done," replied the man, bowing deeply in obeisance.

Naarah awoke to find her mother Sariya urgently tapping her shoulder. "It is time," she said. 'Dress quickly. Oh, and Naarah, I was going to give you this when you reach maturity, but I think now is the time."

Puzzled, Naarah felt a small, round stone being pushed into her hand.

"Close your fingers around this stone, child, and never lose sight of it," said Sariya. "And, when *your* life nears its conclusion or the future suddenly becomes uncertain like now, you too must pass the stone on to another worthy female."

"But, I don't understand Mama. What am I supposed to do with it and how will I know when to pass the stone on?"

Sariya smiled. "You'll know, child, just as I did. For now, just remember. It's vital that you keep the stone safe."

After saying her morning prayers, Naarah jumped off her straw pallet, rubbing her eyes. She ran out to the earthen mound in the surrounding copse to complete her ablutions, first checking all around that no-one was about. Privacy and purity were essential attributes for all females. Her Mama was always telling her so. Feeling reassured, she splashed cold water on her face to wake himself up. This was the most important task she'd ever been given. It was imperative she did not let *Abba* down.

Running back inside, Naarah pulled on her boy's tunic, tying the cord tight around her slim waist, and secreted the special stone underneath. She then adjusted her head cloth before pulling on her rough leather sandals, binding them closely around her narrow ankles. As soon as she was ready, she ran outside to where Admah was waiting to instruct her.

The sun was just rising in the east, its first morning rays slanting down to give a pale golden glow. To the young Naarah, her father looked like a sepulchre in the early eerie light. Momentarily she shivered at what lay ahead, before admonishing herself. She must not show her father any weakness.

Admah knelt down stiffly and with his rough, age-mottled hand, smoothed a flat wide surface on the ground. Picking up a stick, he sharpened its end on the roughened exterior wall of their dwelling. Once he was satisfied that the point was sharp enough, he traced a circle on the flattened ground and proceeded to indicate by sharp indentations firstly the position of their house, then the dwellings of all the tribespeople in the village. He instructed Naarah to make sure she ran swiftly to each family, ensuring they all understood what was required of them. Every family must keep these plans secret, promising they would tell absolutely no-one or all would be lost.

Naarah studied her father's sketchy map carefully, already memorising the route she would follow. She decided she would take in the wider areas first in a circular route, moving progressively inwards until every family had been informed.

"Listen carefully," Admah whispered. "You have been selected because you can move silently and no-one would suspect a small child. If something unexpected happens, for instance if you find yourself challenged by one of Zeboim's men, you must say that your mother is in childbirth and that you are fetching some help. No man would want to be involved in such a thing, so you should then be allowed to continue.

"But now to the actual message you must give to our people," Admah continued, "tell them they must prepare to leave by first light tomorrow. They should gather together only the most essential personal items. Tomorrow morning, every man, woman and child should be ready, toting one knapsack on their backs. Babies should be tied securely into a sling on their mother's back. That's it. Is everything understood, Naarah? Everything depends on you," uncharacteristically pulling his daughter to him in a quick embrace.

With tears in her eyes, Naarah replied "Yes. You can trust me, *Abba*. I will not fail."

With that as her parting response, Naarah ran swiftly off into the gathering dawn, ready to fulfil her mission, family by family. She was determined, like never before, not to fail.

Zeboim clapped his hands and called for his trusted old servant. Despite a back bent with age and brow much furrowed,

nevertheless the servant knew from long experience it was better not to delay in answering the summons. He rushed through
into Zeboim's presence, throwing himself down into an elaborate bow.

"I am at your command, sire."

"Right, get the chariots hitched and full battle dress made
ready. I knew the senate would concur. The whole chamber was
silent with collective awe. To a man they know I will not be satisfied until our cities are cleansed of all those who stupidly continue
praying to some spiritual deity. About time they learned. I am their
leader, the one they must bow down to in reverence, no-one else.
It's time they were taught a lesson, one that has only one ending:
Zeboim, the mighty, is their supreme leader. So, I instruct you to
amass all my soldiers together. At dusk this very day, we will ride
through all five cities, obliterating all who would defy me."

Zeboim dismissed his man and immediately set about his
plans for the coming onslaught. He felt exhilarated for the first
time in aeons. There was nothing he liked more than a bloody
conquest, one that would exhibit his superiority throughout
the land. Who did these people think they were, anyway? He
reiterated for the thousandth time. He couldn't wait for the
evening, preening himself ready for the ultimate glory that
would surely be his.

As the hours progressed, Zeboim squinted up at the sun,
now high in the sky. There was just time for him to seek personal salvation for the battle ahead. He therefore made his way
to the town's central amphictyony, located near to the saltwater
baths. Kneeling down painfully, he glanced up into the green
eyes of the golden idol. Carefully anointing himself with the

water from the fountain beneath, Zeboim prayed for the idol to help him win in the coming battle. Nothing but a resounding success would do. He considered the downwater tribe as nothing short of heathens for *their* amphictyony was centred in the so-called *Ark of Yahweh,* a moveable shrine.

The heat of the afternoon was unrelenting in its severity. Everyone, man and beast, sought shade, wherever it could be found. The stubby hillsides were deserted of anything that moved. Not even the usual swarms of biting insects could be seen or heard.

The earth was stilled, waiting.

Admah groaned on his straw pallet. The pains in his belly were daily becoming worse, making him double over in agony. Lately there was such an odour coming from his body that not even his trusted aides would draw near. The potion Sariya had prepared for him for many years no longer worked. The medicine, like himself, had outlived its usefulness.

He must prepare for the endgame. He knew he was dying, the prophesy he had lived with all his life seemingly about to come true. Lately the fat had fallen from his bones, leaving his skin hanging grey and lifeless on his wasted, spindly frame.

At this juncture in his long life, as he waited for the return of young Naarah, he reflected on his tribe's many successes. With their flocks of sheep and goats they would have been at the point of moving into a more settled way of life, if it were not for the *Sodomites.*

As patriarch of his tribe, Admah's sole wish was that they could live in peace among their neighbours with whom he would gladly enter into covenants. Admah had long known that from the beginning of time, emerging tribes had linked to one another via ancestral blood ties. Such bonds established a unique existence, establishing a new loyalty amongst each tribe. Individual members learned their particular responsibilities. Any injury happening to another member of the group inferred injury to all, demanding repayment by the next of kin. Any blood shed became tribal blood requiring redemption by the next of kin. Other integral tribal laws included such things as when a man died without offspring. In such cases, his next of kin was required to bring the widow to fruition, but the child born to her became the child of the dead man, the one carrying his name. And, when a man died, leaving a widow and children, the tribe would look after them.

As each father was the head of the family, so too the tribal chief and elders were required to lead the larger group, the ultimate aim being the well-being, peace and spiritual health of the members. Everyone recognised that these laws were good things because they afforded great protection. What a relief for everyone, knowing that wherever a member went, he was backed by the strength of the tribe to which he belonged. But everyone also knew that if they deliberately sinned, the wrath of the whole tribe would be upon him.

Admah checked the sky outside as he waited impatiently for the return of Naarah, that he could die in peace knowing that his people could escape in time.

He must have dozed off because he was soon centre stage in what seemed to be an all-too-real dream.

A voice resonated in his head, ringing throughout his senses. "Listen carefully. I am on a mission of the utmost importance. I have come to save your people."

Outside, a loud noise rumbled. Admah could hear it clearly as it echoed ominously from hill to hill. He must have opened his eyes because suddenly there were lightening flashes zig-zagging down like silvery daggers, their hilts buried deep in the ground. Admah shivered, seeing them as portents of doom. The heavens darkened still further to an angry red hue as the voice continued.

"There is very little time. Already the forces of nature have begun – an outcome that has been foretold and cannot be changed. Zeboim and his soldiers are at this very minute making ready to attack your people, an attack that could only have one outcome."

As he spoke, the walls of Admah's dwelling started to shake as if in league with the future, something Admah had never experienced before in his long life. He was afeared like never before.

"Are you still listening Admah? Do not fall asleep. You must select a *minyan* of your most trusted people: men, women and children. They should be young, healthy and strong. These ten will be led to safety through all that is about to happen. Make sure that Naarah is one of the ten."

The pain in Admah's belly had now become agonising and it took all his strength to concentrate on the words echoing through his head. Were the words real or a dream? He wasn't sure. Writhing on his bed, his thoughts feverish, he weighed up every option. He knew that he had been asked to make a terrible choice, his selection was between life and death for his people. But ultimately the future of the tribe overrode everything else, so he had to think very hard. Every breath was coming now in painful spasms as he struggled to hold on to a beating heart that was inexorably slipping away. He had been given just one task to complete, but it was the most difficult in all of his long life: how to choose the ten who would live.

Dawn was on the horizon as Admah awoke from his vision, his choice finally made. He knew that he must act quickly. He prayed that his life blood would hold firm for just a while longer. His resolve remained unshaken.

Zeboim felt exultant. Dressed in his finest battle dress, his helmet was polished to a point which reflected his own face. At its apex was a white plume, its feathers standing proud. His tunic was white with gold edges, the straps of his leather sandals wound tightly around his muscular calves. In his right hand was a whip, its leather thong looped around his wrist. Now sitting astride his favourite horse, his left hand clutched tightly to the loop of the reins.

He glanced behind him. Beautiful, prancing Arabian horses, nostrils flaring as if in anticipation of the ordeal to come, pawed impatiently in the dry, red dust. Zeboim's chariot was the finest his carpenters could make, the wheels strong and robust as they nestled momentarily in the dust.

To the rear were the horses of his main cavalry, each animal hitched securely to a chariot. His soldiers waited impatiently for the command to begin. As they talked animatedly to each other, it was clear they expected only one outcome from the evening's exertions. Outright victory was surely assured as their numbers, efficiency and armaments would outclass by far the opposition.

At last Zeboim raised his right fist into the air. There was an expectant air of excitement before his arm came crashing down again, signalling the assault had begun. In a crash of skidding wheels, neighing snorts and swirling dust, Zeboim led his men into the affray. None, in the ensuing maelstrom, seemed to hear the eerie rumblings thundering from hill to hill on the horizon; nor did anyone notice the skies darkening overhead.

Zeboim whipped his horses into a hard gallop, white flecks of foam spraying from their nostrils as they were forced to run faster and faster. Behind him, the thunder of his following army masked the distant thunder in the hills as chariot wheels carved giant, red tracks into the barren landscape.

Suddenly Zeboim's leading horse shuddered to a halt, almost throwing him to the ground. He swore as he attempted to remount, but his horse's fore legs were raised in fright. He tried whipping him even harder, but nothing would make him move. There was a crazed look in his eye and a glistening sweat dripping from its broad flanks. Zeboim was used to seeing the kind of sweat that horses produce after running hard, but this was altogether different. It was as if the horse had encountered something so terrifying, nothing in this world could move him.

Not sure what to do, Zeboim raised his arm and called a halt to his army, as he loosened his grip on the reins and jumped heavily down again to the red soil.

Even he, with all his battle experience, was surprised at what he could see in the distance. There was an enormous crack in the rocks, a gap that alarmingly was growing with every second that passed. With his sandalled feet now on what should have been firm ground, it was only now he felt it. The earth under his feet was moving, jagged fissures growing wider and wider in the reddening dust. At last, now that his army had quietened somewhat, he heard the low, distant rumble. Frightened, his men began scattering to the hills, but there was no escape. The roaring became ever louder as the very ground beneath their running feet shook uncontrollably. Even Zeboim's most loyal servants had now dismounted and were running in panic for the near hills, their route made ever difficult by the *ad hoc* way the widening, vein-like fissures were spreading.

As Zeboim glanced upwards to the nearest mountain, he was astonished to see flames and smoke suddenly shooting from the apex. Squinting, he peered up into the suddenly dark red sky. Despite the gloom, he was certain he could see giant black boulders and what looked like flaming ash pouring down from the fire and smoke of the mountain top. He shouted out, but no-one could hear him: "The smoke of the country is going up like the smoke of a furnace. We are doomed."

Ahead of him, those soldiers who'd been the first to run in the panic, found themselves bent double, racked with uncontrollable coughing from a mighty increase in eolian dust and aridity. Others too were also experiencing terrible coughing fits.

In a last desperate effort to save himself, Zeboim struggled to release his goat-skin water bag which had been tied securely to the chariot wheels. However, the pull-cords which anchored the bag together had withered in the intense heat, sending the precious water supplies into the dust beneath.

Enormous explosions were now happening all around them, as with a terrified scream, Zeboim and all his men, chariots and horses disappeared into a cavernous hole that opened up beneath them. Back home, at least two of their magnificent cities were also completely destroyed, along with their complement of human inhabitants.

It would take aeons of time before anyone would be able to chronicle what happened that night. For the meantime, all that was known was there'd been a dramatic and stunning increase in windborne dust and brimstone. Although wise men said it was this which eventually led to the end of Zeboim's tribe and surrounding civilizations, others felt a strong spiritual presence in everything that had happened.

Naarah didn't know what had caused the devastation, only that the very earth had moved mightily. Some said it could be felt even as far south as the big river valley and other lands far away.

It was a phenomenon which was to persist for another three hundred years, the absolute destruction and total obliteration of two cities so profound as to erase all but minimal evidence that they ever existed.

But for now, downwind from the abomination, there was still time for the ten righteous people to move to safety, their precious possessions tied securely onto their backs as they'd been told. But Naarah was tearful. She would never see her beloved *Abba* again, nor most of her good neighbours. The elders had spoken the last rites for Admah, who was no more. They interred him according to their rites, within twenty-four hours of his death, and spoke out loud the special *Kaddish* prayers – prayers for the living, as their tribe dictated. Admah had indeed lived an inordinately long life and was revered as only those of such age can be, but now he was gone.

Naarah cried at his passing. She didn't talk to anyone; she couldn't. Why did anyone have to die? She didn't understand. She wanted to live for ever. She couldn't imagine what it must be like to lie underground, your body slowly crumbling into dust. But then she remembered what her dear *Abba* had told her. She could still hear his voice in her head, clear as a bell. "The body is but a shell, Naarah, When a person dies, the soul within is released to rise up to heaven again, to the place whence it came."

Naarah thought about that. So, did that mean that her living body was like a magic machine with herself living inside it, her task being to fix the various parts when they went wrong? And when her machine becomes too old to continue, would it rust up just like their old plough? And then would her soul whisper 'goodbye' and fly up to heaven, leaving the rusty old machine to be buried in the ground? If that was so, what would happen to everything she'd achieved in life? And, and…was there someone in heaven who would congratulate or scold her when she arrived in heaven? Her father had said "Yes, Naarah, that person is G-d almighty, the creator of all things."

The distant rumbling of the land had made the group of ten speed up in terror. But they were fortunate to discover a hidden cave in the mountains of *Zoar*, a cave that no-one else had discovered before, not even Naarah who knew every inch of the surrounding countryside.

The mouth of the cave was partly obscured by bracken and large, heavy rocks, but the strongest of the group were able to heave it all away. They crawled into its small, dark interior, brushing away hanging stalactites of bracken that threatened to strangle them at every turn. Eventually reaching a circular inner cavern, they were able to rest. High above their heads was a lofty but airy ceiling and enough flat ground on which to squat and relive their miraculous escape. After a while, they unloaded what few possessions they had managed to carry with them whilst they were shielded from the outside terrain which was disintegrating. Fortunately they couldn't hear the distant screams of people who had succumbed to the terrors unleashed by the exploding countryside. Fire and brimstone continued to rain down from the very heavens in eternal damnation of the evil that had reigned beneath.

At first, Naarah's tribe felt doomed because there were simply not enough men to beget children. However, they knew that as long as there were females, there was always hope. Previous inhibitions must now be forgotten. The ultimate goal of continued life must always overcome every objection. Life was of necessity difficult but the tribe would continue.

Naarah looked through the opening of the cave and absently fingered the smooth, round stone which still resided under her tunic. She saw that outside, the blood-red sky was changing from the colour of a fresh bruise to swiftly passing clouds. Her eyes glazed as in a frenzy, the heavens zoomed across the mouth of the cave faster and faster.

Naarah thought she must be dreaming. She closed her eyes and felt herself floating, floating with the clouds. Up above five crashing claps of thunder jolted her as she held her hands forward as if reaching for something or someone. In her hand, her fingers were still clutching the small stone.

CHAPTER NINE

Toulouse
2019

"Y OU KNOW, *coucou*," said Simon to his wife, as they sat on a low wall in *Place Capitole,* "After what we believe happened in the cities of Sodom and Gomorrah four thousand years ago, HaShem predicted that no-one would ever live there again. And you know what? This has turned out to be true. The cities do not exist today."

Leah shook her head at how long ago all that was. She couldn't even contemplate the enormity of how long four thousand years was and the journey man had made in all that time as she looked around her.

Toulouse was looking wonderful in the summer sunshine. They were taking a break from filming and feeling like tourists as they wandered around *Capitole,* as everyone called the famous central square, stopping to listen to the itinerant musicians to build up an appetite for lunch.

But there was no avoiding the police posters on every corner and building.

"*Étiez-vous présent dans la région d'Esquirol samedi matin dernier? Avez-vous vu quelque-chose de suspect? Contactez le police.*

"Haven't they caught anyone yet? asked Leah, reading that the police were asking whether anyone had seen anything suspicious on the day of the explosion. "Can't believe it. Someone must have seen something, surely?"

"Apparently not," said Simon. "Best thing we can do is carry on with our plan and let the police get on with it. I'm so glad that no-one was killed. It's a miracle. TG Hanna's all right. I don't think Papa could have coped if she hadn't survived the blast."

"I know. After all she's been through, I can't believe she's had to suffer that too. She's such a lovely lady," shaking her head and trying to take her mind off things. "Can we take a look around the *Hotel du Grand Balcon*?" asked Leah. "That would cheer me up. As a child I loved reading *Le Petit Prince,* and there's a gallery in there all about him." It wasn't so much a request as a demand as she pulled her reluctant husband along a lane just off *Capitole*. But Simon didn't mind. It was all welcome relief from the stresses and strains of filming.

But Simon was worrying again about the techniques he was using. Had he followed all the guidelines to make the film work?

Simon scratched his head. He knew that the first part of the film was coming along very well, but he needed to concentrate if he was to bring this immense project to the kind of conclusion and reception that Moshe craved.

The crowd sourcing idea had surprised him, many people from all over the world seeing the merit of his story. His whole problem now was to ensure that the breadth and scope of the narrative didn't exceed the funds he had available. He smiled. Story of his life.

Now back on the métro towards their home, Simon used Leah as a sounding board. Quickly, he ticked off the essential elements if he were to pull this thing off. First: did his film have a beginning, middle and end?

Check.

Had he kept the expensive visual effects to a minimum?

Check.

I must think about the potential audience of this film. Have I given them what they need to appreciate my fundamental motive and rationale for the film?

Check.

Have I agreed with the screenwriter a suitable fee?

Check, after some negotiation.

Has Leah, my artistic wife (buttering her up), produced a suitable storyboard, depicting each scene?

Check.

Now, the next task was to ask local French traders in the Toulouse area for permission to use their premises for scenes taking place in present day France. Already, there had been a queue of local people fancying their chances of becoming a movie star.

He'd managed to save money by recruiting friends and colleagues from the *Espace de Judaism* building in the city, who'd been only too willing to assist as crew once they heard of what he was trying to achieve. Simon and Leah had taken the opportunity to talk to them after watching a film show about *Hanukah,* one of their festivals celebrating that time when a little oil lasted a full eight days. So it was said. It was their colleagues in the EDJ building who asked whether there'd be a scene telling the story of the Maccabees. Simon told them he would see what he could do. His people's fight against King Antiochus certainly fitted the film's remit.

Meantime, his mind was flitting over all the obstacles in his path. He surmised that dressing the actors for the Jewish scenes would be easy enough, his own knowledge of his faith being sufficient.

But his biggest future headache would be the scenes set in Egypt. Did he know enough about the Egyptians to accurately portray the dress, culture and activities, particularly during later scenes set in 1967?

Simon decided to discuss all of this with his father's friend Menes, who'd be the perfect choice. They met up in a sports café on the main road in *Varen*, the medieval village where Menes' house was situated. As the bar tender put coffee cups in front of them, Simon's eyes roamed up to the TV on the wall, showing the live rugby game happening in the nearby *Gaillac* stadium.

"This village is such a lovely place, Menes," said Simon, trying to put the old man in the right frame of mind. "How ever did you find it?"

Menes' eyes glazed as he thought about the past. So much easier than focusing on the future.

"Oh I remember it as if it was yesterday. Layla and I were so excited. At last, we were ready to put down roots in this new country and bring up a family. But it didn't turn out to be as easy as expected. You know," shrugging his shoulders, "nothing is in this world. So often, you start off with such high hopes, only to have them come crashing down on your head before you know it. Oh, if only I'd known back then how hard it would be, I'd have done things very differently."

Simon interrupted, sympathising with his friend "But you have your lovely children. You don't regret that, surely?"

Menes sighed. "No, of course not, but I admit I should have done more to help our eldest, Sami. He was the first and the apple of my eye. There's nothing I wouldn't have done for him. Nothing. But, as he grew out of babyhood, it was clear that something was wrong with him. Oh, he looked well enough physically but it was how he acted. I blame myself. I should have had him assessed when he was young but you know….life was hard and once the other four boys came along, I simply didn't have the time to do anything but try to earn enough for us to live," wiping his eyes.

Simon sympathised. "I know what you mean, Menes. We have a saying 'should've, would've, could've…. But, I'd still love to hear about how you came to France in the first place."

Menes took another swallow of the hot, bitter coffee whilst he cast his mind back.

"Ah, back then Layla and I were so young. We didn't really know what we were doing. Somehow we were caught up in the general wave of people leaving Egypt, for all sorts of reasons. The government were actively encouraging emigration, whilst some groups like the large Jewish population were expelled *en bloc!* At least we weren't in that position, but it was still very stressful."

Simon leaned forward, intensely interested. "So, who else was leaving Egypt at that time? And what did the Egyptian government have against the Jews?"

"Oh, Simon. You needed to be living in the thick of a place like Cairo and to be an Egyptian citizen to understand the mentality. The papers were full of it. The enforced expulsions of those whom they considered foreign applied to what they called the *Mutamassirun* population. For centuries, there had been various foreign communities in Egypt. The government wanted them gone because they were considered to be taking control and power from 'real' Egyptians."

"I see," replied Simon. "So, who exactly did they hate the most, though I can guess!"

"Well, the Jews, of course, but also those considered alien by Nasser and his supporters, like the Italians and the Greeks. But I also remember others leaving the country around the same time as me, like the French, the Belgians and the British. Many of us, you know, were only allowed to take one small suitcase and a little cash. Not much at all. Oh, and many had to sign legal documents, 'agreeing' to have their remaining property confiscated by the Egyptian government, and to guarantee they would stay silent about their treatment."

"Terrible. Awful. But, Menes, what about you personally. You were not a Jew and an Egyptian citizen. Why did you and your new wife decide to leave?"

"Oh, living on the streets of Cairo was difficult for so many people. Ever since France, Israel and Britain invaded the Suez

Canal, Nasser was cracking down on everyone. I remember when he decided to introduce all those new laws abolishing our civil liberties. Yes, it got to the stage when he was staging mass arrests of innocent, law-abiding citizens on trumped-up charges. It was about then that Nasser became more of a dictator, removing people's Egyptian citizenship on a whim. Even professional people suddenly found themselves out of a job.

"So, Layla and I started thinking the unthinkable. We both felt that we needed to get out, but where? Eventually, there was only one place. Like everyone else, we both spoke a form of French, it being our second language after Arabic. And France was in Europe, a modern country which was actively seeking and encouraging immigrants from North Africa. So, despite every kind of hardship, we arrived, pretty much penniless, but we managed it. Thanks to *Allah*, we were still young, healthy, and had our whole lives ahead of us. At last we could look forward to a new life in which to bring up our family.

"So, Simon, does that answer your question? That's how Layla and I came to live here all those years ago," sighing with all that had happened since then.

"Thanks, my friend. That was really interesting. I just wanted to know how someone from Egypt had ended up in France, because I'm currently making a film about Egypt and Palestine as a whole. I was actually wondering," pausing to find the right words, "whether you'd do me the honour of attending the set when I get to the scenes about the Six Day War between Egypt and Israel? Your input would be really invaluable, so please say yes. Oh, and of course I'll be asking my father too."

CHAPTER TEN

Albi
2019

T HE *HOTEL DE Police* in Albi was its usual hubbub of noise
and mayhem. Outside, the distinctive red tiled façade of
the building normally acted as a formidable deterrent to visitors. However, inside at the counter, the *agent de service de police*
was fighting hard to contain a loud argument which threatened
to overwhelm the whole of Albi. An overlarge man, dressed in
dark blue overalls, stained with murky substances of unknown
origin, shuffling from foot to foot in his heavy wellington
boots, was strongly criticising everyone and everything in the
place, intermittently calling on anyone in earshot to side with
his version of the story. The little man standing alongside him
sporadically raised his voice a decibel above his in continuous
opposition.

"*Messieurs, Messieurs!*" shouted the officer at the counter.
"One at a time, please."

A standard neighbourhood dispute, but now completely
disregarding rules. Gallic disdain for others was evident
everywhere.

Outside the reception area, a man somewhat the worse for drink lay on the bench smiling happily to himself, an empty bottle of Gaillac wine lying beside him. That was the only way to live these days. If problems seemed insurmountable, reach for a bottle. In this area, a decent bottle of wine could be obtained for less than three euros. Far better than the so-called anti-depressants from the doctor. And cheaper too, as no *médicin traitant* doctor in the vicinity would ever prescribe such a thing! The man congratulated himself, seemingly oblivious to the comic opera all around him. Nothing seemed to change.

C'était la France.

Back inside the building, heavy black phones from yesteryear were ringing non-stop. Despite the air-conditioning running full-blast, the shirt-sleeved occupants were losing the battle against the heat. Sweat patches appeared at their armpits, and beads of perspiration threatened to run into their eyes. In the far corner a woman non-commissioned officer was busy tapping away at a PC, every so often tearing up a sheet of handwritten notes before screwing it up into a ball and targeting a nearby wastebin with the considerable accuracy that comes from constant practice.

In a tiny office at the back of the building, well out of sight from the main counter, Détective LeBrun was feeling harassed and in a foul mood. His superior, acting under direct orders from the *Préfet de Police,* had left him in no doubt. His Toulouse superiors had instructed him to progress this part of the bomb enquiry. Albi was *mi-chemin*, mid-way between Toulouse and the village of St. Antonin Noble Val, and as such was best-placed to co-ordinate the enquiry.

LeBrun's superior wanted results. *Immédiatement*. As if that wasn't enough, the media had somehow got hold of his name and was now constantly at his throat, demanding instant results about the Toulouse bombing. They were coming at him from all sides but, despite his blithe assurances that their investigations were going well, in reality he'd hit a brick wall.

A veritable impasse.

LeBrun leaned back in his cracked leather swivel chair, arms behind his head, as he looked around the office for inspiration. On the wall was a rogues' gallery of photos, all stuck slightly askew with an array of colourful pins. As his eyes once again roved over the blurry faces of known past criminals, he knew he hadn't a cat in hell's chance of nailing any one of them to this crime. What he needed was inspiration, something lateral that he hadn't yet thought of.

On a whim he decided to liaise with the president of the Central Consistory of France, the representation of Jewish worship in France since the time of Napoléon. After all, the *Consistoire* was the organization responsible for religious Jewish life in France, so if anyone knew about how the Jews of Toulouse went about their daily lives, it should be him.

Maybe that's what I need, thought LeBrun. *Someone who knows inside out how the Jewish community ticks and who, maybe, just maybe, could shine a light on what would motivate someone to target a synagogue in the heart of a major city like Toulouse.*

It was worth a shot. God knew, he had very little else to go on, despite his pseudo confidence when facing the merciless French media.

LeBrun picked up the phone on his desk and checked the

area code for Paris. Not for him the modern craze for cell phones. When in a jam he always stuck to his old and tried methods. They hadn't let him down yet, in all his thirty years in the force.

"Allo? Is that Monsieur le Président? Détective LeBrun here, from the *Hotel de Police* in Albi. I'm investigating the bombing of the synagogue in Toulouse and would like a word with you, if you could spare me a few minutes?"

A slight pause,

"*Oui, Détective. Naturellement,* anything I can do to help the police solve such a terrible crime I'm at your disposal. In fact, we were discussing the bombing only yesterday at a meeting I convened of Rabbis from all over the country. We all agreed. A terrible business. Simply terrible, but what can we do? It's always been the same."

LeBrun pondered for a moment before responding. In his present situation, he needed more information on how the Jewish community ticked in the hope of hitting on any clues as to the perpetrator of the bombing. At this stage, even tiny, insignificant factors might help him put together a credible line of investigation. "I understand completely, Monsieur. I think what I need at present is to find out more about how the French Jewish community thinks and acts. You never know. You might just trigger a new line of enquiry in this case, so please feel free to tell me what your thoughts are."

"Well, let me think," replied the Jewish president. "At our meeting yesterday, I was having a conversation with the Chief Rabbi. He was arguing that the Jewish community is basically inseparable from the wider French society, insisting that we can overcome our many challenges, including the on-going anti-Semitism that has driven so many French Jews to seek an *aliyah* emigration to Israel. But, I am sorry to tell you that there were many at the meeting who disagreed with the Chief Rabbi. They accused him of failing to recognise the bitter reality we all face, as so clearly evidenced in the tragic Toulouse bombing. You know, Monsieur Détective, it's what goes on behind the closed doors of every Jewish home in France that really concerns me. Everyone is pessimistic. All that the bombing has done is bring into the open the deep resentments and irritations that every French Jew feels. Security has always been fundamental to us, Monsieur Détective, because of our history. I myself recall being harassed for wearing a *yarmulke* skull cap on the Paris subway. I'm sure it's the same in Toulouse. My own opinion is that Jews live in France for reasons that are essentially practical. They love the culture and, of course, support la France at football matches, but increasingly their children are leaving in their droves for Israel, the only place where their neighbours aren't going to harass them at festivals and on holy days. You know, contrary to what many non-Jews think, many of the Jewish community in Toulouse live in rough areas, so they've seen at first hand what anti-Semitic incidents look like. It's especially true on holy days, when they go to the synagogue on foot. It's they who you need to talk to, you know, rather than communal leaders who tend to live in more upscale areas."

LeBrun thanked the Jewish president most sincerely for his thoughts, telling him that he would keep in touch as his investigation progressed. Gently putting down the phone, LeBrun pressed the off switch on his old recording machine, thinking that another listen later to what the man had to say might help.

With a sigh, he grabbed his jacket from the back of his chair, closed the office door and headed home to his apartment in central Albi.

Bone weary, exhausted, he desperately sought a lead.

Perhaps tomorrow it would come.

CHAPTER ELEVEN

Toulouse
2019

DUSK WAS FALLING over the pink city as Simon and Leah sank thankfully into two facing métro seats *en route* for their home in an outer suburb.

"At least we didn't have to use the car today. I dread driving into the centre at the best of times, but during rush hour? No thanks," he said to his wife, feeling weary. Looking across at his wife, who looked rather tired "How are you feeling, love? Was all this too much for you? I don't want anything to happen to that baby of ours," looking with concern into her eyes.

"Oh, I think the baby's fine, if all this kicking has anything to do with it. Feels as if I've got the next Thierry Henri in there."

Simon smiled.

"Look love, I know I've been neglecting you lately. I promise I'll make it up to you once this film's over. I promise."

Leah looked over to him. "I know how important it is to you, love. Don't worry about us," patting her protuberant stomach, "we're happy to wait, aren't we *coucou*?"

Simon was mentally going through all the things he still

needed to do before the next scene, set in the time of the Maccabees, could go ahead. Sometimes he just needed to do things from the seat of his pants. Such was his energy and dedication to the whole project, his heart and soul were dedicated to this enterprise. He just hoped that, once finished, the watching public would share his enthusiasm.

Time would tell.

The following day, at the studios, everyone was ready.

"Lights, camera, action"

Jerusalem
167 BCE

It was the seventh day of the sand storm. Out on the desert plains, not a thing moved. Not even the desert cat, its distinctive pointed ears sharply raised against all known enemies. Not today would it appear on its usual nocturnal prowls across the smooth sands of the Judean desert. A sixth sense told him to sit it out in the dark mountain caves nearby.

Hadassah, now an old woman, couldn't remember a storm like it. Even the donkey keeper, who was himself an old man, agreed with her. Holding her borrowed *ghutra* close to her face, she struggled across to the tent of Mattathias, the leader of the group. She had something important to say to him so refused to be gainsaid.

As a woman, she would need special permission to enter his tent, but knew that his wife would allow it. Hadassah had brought each of Mattathias's five healthy sons into the world and, as such, demanded respect. As she crossed painfully towards their tent, she struggled to peer out of the narrow slits of her face covering. The sand was blowing so hard she couldn't see a thing in front of her. She knew that in such weather, if she became lost, the searing, swirling sand would consume her in no time. Despite her best efforts, sand stones hit her skin like fiery ammunition, pelting her like a million locusts as she sped along, head down.

She didn't worry about her appearance, wearing a man's *ghutra*. Of course, as a girl, her skin had been like fine alabaster but now? All that mattered was to survive, help to look after this precious family and promote the interests of 'her' special five boys. Nothing else mattered but their survival in this harsh terrain.

"Welcome, Hadassah," said Mattathias, beckoning her into the dim interior of his tent. He was leaning to his left, just like the *Haggadah* prayer book instructed during Passover, his body resting awhile on a low divan. Every so often he would hawk stubborn phlegm into a bowl lying on the floor under his chin, but instead of moisture, only the grainy dryness of sand forced itself through. Carefully he dried his mouth with a cloth he kept tucked into his tunic.

"Hadassah," he said, smiling, "it's not often we see you in our tent these days. My wife's days of child bearing are, sadly, long gone. But it's through your special care that my precious sons were born healthy and strong. For that reason alone, we owe you an eternal debt of gratitude."

Hadassah bowed her head, in deference to the great man.

Mattathias, a descendant of the Levite tribe, was always priestly in his dealings with others.

Hesitating a moment, Hadassah wasn't sure where to begin. She had lived a long, hard life. They all had, but never had she experienced a dream such as the one last night. But was it a dream? She didn't know. It was more of a divine revelation. She was sure of it. For that reason, she felt an urgent need to transmit its message to their leader so that he, in his wisdom, could understand and interpret it.

"Last night I had a dream," she began, "but it was like no other I have ever had in my entire, long life."

The old man moved painfully to sit upright, better to heed what Hadassah was saying. In truth, he had been searching for days for an answer to their problems. The Jewish people were being persecuted mercilessly by King Antiochus Epiphanes and his hordes, assisted by an increasing mob of men made up of Seleucids, Hellenes and Samaritans. So many Jews had crossed over to the king's side, preferring to take on his *traife* unholy ways rather than be killed in the process. By so doing, they had chosen life over death, but at what cost? He waved for Hadassah to continue.

"My dream was very odd. I felt as if I was being granted an exclusive view of a life way, way in the future. Although it was hazy, I remember seeing hordes of people wearing strange clothes being pushed into large wagons on wheels. The men and the boys had *tzitsit* strings dangling down. The people were very thin, pale and were crying out for food and water, but brutal men kept shoving them into the wagons, one person on top of another, until they could not breathe."

Mattathias leaned forward, eager to hear the rest. "Go on, Hadassah, continue."

"Well, then came the strangest thing of all. The wagons, full of these poor people, seemed to be linked together in some way. Maybe it was with the kind of hemp we use for our oxen, I don't know. But, suddenly, without horses to lead them or donkeys, there was movement. The lead wagon, now sealed from the outside, giving the people inside no means of escape or air to breathe, sprang forward. It was a bit like the way our camels rise up from their prostrate position on the hot sand, before suddenly lurching forward. But these wagons in my dream had no visible means of movement. Nevertheless, they all very quickly moved in a straight line away from my line of sight. My lasting impression, before I awoke, was the terrible cries slowly receding as the wagons moved towards the far horizon. There was no doubt in my mind. Those poor people were being led to an appalling death. Just before I awoke, I was sure I could smell smoke. In fact I sprang up, thinking there was a fire in the camp, but all was quiet and still."

Mattathias stroked his chin, trying to make sense of Hadassah's revelation. For surely, this had been a message from *HaShem*. Why hadn't those people fought against their oppressors, as he and his family would have done? The description of them seemed to fit with their being Jewish, so why hadn't they rebelled? Ever since *HaShem* had granted his people their promised land between the west bank of the Jordan to the mighty sea, enemies had constantly battled and forced them out. No matter whether they were the Babylonians, the Philistines or any of the numerous other tribes which kept springing up against them, the enemies of the children of Israel kept coming, generation after generation. Maybe Hadassah's dream revealed some future tribe bent on yet more persecution of his people? Aware that Jewish women often have a special spiritual gift quite separate from the men, he turned to the old woman "What do you think Hadassah? What do you think *HaShem* was trying to tell you?"

Hadassah raised her bowed head and lifted her eyes to the roof of the tent, noting how it swayed subtly in rhythm with the desert winds outside. "I believe that it was indeed a divine message. How has our faith endured through aeons of time? There is no doubt in my mind. Despite our being forced again and again out of our promised land, our faith has survived because we have no idols to carry with us as a false god. What we carry with us, wherever we go, is our love for the Torah. This we carry in our hearts, where no man can put it asunder. And why have we, the people, survived this long, Mattathias, despite tribe after tribe attacking and killing us for no reason other than they hate the Jewish people? We have always fought back. But this dream I had? It worries me greatly. I saw none of our people attempt to fight their aggressors. They meekly stepped into those cattle wagons. A big mistake. That's what I think, Mattathias. That's the message I received from *HaShem*. Always defend ourselves. Never give up. Always uphold the only law we recognise: that of *HaShem* alone."

Mattathias looked up at Hadassah, astonishment writ large in his face. His right elbow supported his weight on a small table at his side as he struggled with the intense emotions that flooded his brain. Intermittently, an oil lamp flickered, lending shadows in the darkness. He did not speak for a while. A giant of a man in his youth, he was not much given to words.

At last, turning to Hadassah "I grow despondent. Why does He keep giving us such trials? Sometimes I think there must be sand in the eyes of *HaShem*," he said. "He is blind and has lost sight of us."

Hadassah was shocked. Maybe the old man's thinking, so long famed for its sharpness, had succumbed to the disease of forgetfulness.

"Oh Mattathias," she said, her voice showing concern. "Now that we've made our journey this far, do you think He would lose sight of us just when we're on the verge of victory?" She couldn't believe that this great man, someone she had revered all her life, could fall into melancholy just when their people needed him the most.

"There is death in the air," Mattathias said stubbornly. "Even the donkeys can smell it. For the first time they are nervous."

"Donkeys are easy to deal with," she replied. Unlike mere men, she thought to herself. "Put blankets over their heads," she told him. "If they cannot see, they will think it nighttime and doze a little."

"It's still a bad omen," he replied. "What we need is a miracle to fight Antiochus. They say that Jerusalem is in ruins, our temple desecrated, our sacred scrolls defiled. And that's not all," he shouted, drowning out the desert winds which continued to blast sandstones against the tent. Everything trembled. The donkeys were at last silent. Even the oil lamp, usually so true, flickered nervously, first to the east, then to the west. "Our people have been murdered for refusing to stop circumcision and even forced to eat the *traife* flesh of swine. We simply cannot let this barbarism continue, but what can I do?" reacting in anguish to his own spoken words.

Hadassah sat listening, quietly waiting for his wrath to subside, as it always did eventually. She had learned much in the long life that *HaShem* had granted her. Whilst the men were always contemplating war, expecting their women to bear children, cook their meals and tend to the wounded, little did they understand how women like her really felt. Hadassah had always been amazed how little men knew of what she really thought. Did they think that she had no brain, no wisdom? Could they not see that whilst wives were capably stirring pots of meat stew, washing clothes at the oasis stream, and tending to their children, all these many tasks were accomplished in synchrony and harmony? But, more than that. Whilst juggling their many physical tasks, women's minds were actively crisscrossing truth, lore and love. In contrast, she thought, men seemed only capable of doing one single task at a time and heaven help a wife who interrupted him whilst doing it!

"Listen, Mattathias," she said now. "I have never failed you in the past, have I?"

He nodded, his head still in his hands.

"You may be old, and approaching the end of things, as do I," replied Hadassah. "So, it's time you appointed one of your fine sons to lead our tribe. Think very carefully as it's not always the eldest of our children who are the most suited."

Mattathias suddenly looked up at her words. "So, wise woman, you know my sons very well. You brought them into the world and have observed them as they grew into manhood.

Whom would you choose?" his eyes piercing her with a sudden steely light.

Hadassah thought long and hard. "Let's think of why *HaShem* chose Moshe to lead our people. Some say that, as a young man, Moshe chased after a young lamb who had run away from his flock. Moshe hadn't understood how thirsty the young creature must have been until he saw just how much the lamb drank from a distant brook. Moshe spoke to the lamb, saying that if he had known just how desperately the creature sought water, he would have carried him to the brook on his own back. *HaShem*, on hearing this, decided that Moshe was therefore worthy of leading His people."

Mattathias stroked his chin thoughtfully. "So, old woman, what you're saying is that *HaShem* didn't look for the strongest man to lead our people, but the one who showed genuine compassion and kindness?"

Hadassah smiled into the now strong glow from the oil lamp. At last, the old man was beginning to see sense. It wasn't for her to pronounce which of his sons should lead their tribe to victory. As a woman, her mission was to lay all the facts bare so that, in the end, there could be no doubt.

It was now clear who the old man should choose.

The five brothers stood waiting outside their father's tent. They knew he was about to make a pronouncement, which would involve them all. It was clear the old man was dying and could no longer command their people with the same force as in his youth. It was therefore clear that he would choose one of them to be his successor, but which? JoHannan, as the oldest, expected the call as he stood, arms folded, alongside his younger siblings. Simon, his head always in the scribes, was unsuited to open warfare, whilst Jonathan was surely too young to take on this man's challenge. Of the others, it was either Judah or Eliezer. Judah was certainly big and strong, many calling him Judah Maccabee or hammerhead because of his physical presence. But Judah was often meek and timid, so how could he lead so many men?

They waited, their eyes focused on this land they loved. Beneath their feet was the multi-coloured red and brown soil, which had formed from a melange of different types of limestone chalk. In the near distance, amongst the craggy hills, hundreds of plant species forced their way beneath the splintered rock. They knew that in the spring, masses of wild flowers would emerge on the slopes and in the crevices. And up above, they were often startled to hear the calls of the swift, nestling in old walls, together with the hooded crow and jay.

But everywhere, as venomous as any enemy, was the viper, who would lurk camouflaged amongst the hills and in the undergrowth.

Life was a constant struggle against man and beast. They'd need all their ingenuity to survive.

Their thoughts swirling around their head, at last Mattathias appeared, pulling open the flap of his tent and blinking in the strong sunlight. His eyes flickered over each of his sons, giving no indication of which one he would choose.

Now standing on top of a ridge, finally he spoke. "My sons, I am dying so it is time to choose one of you to lead our people in the long fight ahead. Each of you have special talents, which in the years to come you should hone and refine to its upmost. Our people have long given their lives for the covenant of our Fathers. Now is the time for us to do the same. Love *HaShem* and always heed his advice, though His ways are not always easy to follow. Turning to Simon, he said "You, Simon, have already shown how wise you are in counsel, so I urge the rest of you to listen to your brother and imbibe his wisdom whenever you can. But wisdom alone is not enough." His eyes roved over them once again before coming to his final decision. "I have thought long and hard over this, taken counsel myself from a surprising source. As *HaShem* chose Moshe to lead our people, so I too have learned from this. We need the one who not only has the necessary physical strength but also a tender heart. Therefore, there is but one who encompasses both these essential traits."

Almost falling with the urgency of his task, all five of his sons rushed to his aid before he brushed them aside.

Our new leader will be Judah."

CHAPTER TWELVE

Modein
167 BCE

H ADASSAH WAS IN trouble. The other wives were gossiping about her as they sheltered in the caves of Gophna. Was it true that she and Mattathias had once *known* each other in true biblical sense? It was well known throughout the camp that the old woman was allowed privileges that no-one else was given and she was often to be seen in his tent giving advice on what the family should do. It was even said that it was she who had told the old man to pick Judah as his successor.

Who does she think she is? they all said.

None of the women liked her. They simply didn't trust Hadassah and kept their distance at all times.

Of course, everyone knew and understood that Judah had chosen this place as being the best way to keep the women and children safe and hidden whilst they trained on the scrubby plains, awaiting the coming fight. But what the men hadn't re- alised was what happens when you place a lot of women to- gether in a small place.

They bicker and argue.

Although Mattathias' widow tried hard to keep them all sweet, there was no gainsaying the women's different personalities. It was hard having to live in such cramped conditions on stony ground, not being allowed to light a fire during daylight hours and to practise escape routes through the maze of caves surrounding them, should the need arise. Judah had been clear. They must all work together to keep themselves safe, fed and watered. But Judah was a man, knowing little about the workings of a female mind.

But what the women all knew was that their men were about to go into battle yet again and they were afraid.

The man who called himself Governor of Samaria was preparing to eradicate, once and for all, those pesky people who called themselves the children of Israel. Apollonius had gathered his immense army of Gentiles and Samaritans, ready for what should surely be an easy battle. As soon as the enemy saw the might of his army and the strength of their armour and weapons, they would flee. He was sure of it.

Judah, now commander of his people after the death of his father Mattathias, was preparing for what was to come. He knew that Apollonius's army would contain a large group of Samaritans, a people who claimed to be descendants of the Israelites but who had become apostates after intermarrying with other native people and taking on their heathen practices, something forbidden by the law of Moshe. Despite the fact that enemy Seleucids had previously defiled the Samaritans' temple as well as their own, Judah had never trusted them. The Samaritans could be fickle, as was proven now.

But first, he was persuaded, against his own feelings, to send a few of his men to negotiate with the commander.

The following day three of Judah's men went up to the enemy camp and demanded an audience with the Samarian governor.

"Governor," said one of Apollonius's men. "The Jews are at the door."

"Good," he replied, rubbing his hands in glee. "Find an inn that has a solid door on the front. Then admit the Jews, and afterwards bolt and bar the door behind them.

When approached by the governor's man, the leader of Judah's group spoke up. "Please be assured that we mean your men no harm," he replied. "We merely wish to discuss the situation with your leader. We are unarmed and expect you to respect our wishes and good intentions."

Eventually, after checking that Judah's men were unarmed, the inn door was opened and the three men were ushered inside. "The governor is in the room at the back," the soldier told them.

But Apollonius was becoming increasingly irritated by the stubbornness of the Jews throughout the region. They were always complaining over injustices and the fact that they couldn't perform their rites. What did it matter whether their sons weren't circumcised or their temples destroyed? It was about time they understood that it was he, now, who was in charge. Not some spiritual being who lived on high. It was well nigh time to make an example of these Jews once and for all.

As soon as Judah's men had entered the inn, someone outside slammed the door behind them, locking and barring it.

Annoyed, Judah's men walked briskly through the inn looking for the governor. But there was no sign of him. Suddenly they were seized from behind, their mouths gagged with foul-smelling cloth, and flung to the ground, where they were stripped of their clothing. Next, as their muffled shouts were drowned out, their legs were shackled with chains and they were whipped mercilessly with corded ropes.

"Let's see your god help you now," their oppressors said, grinning to each other. Eventually, the punishment stopped. Blood dripped onto the straw beneath them as they writhed in agony.

When Apollonius received the news, he was mightily pleased. "Throw them onto the streets of Jerusalem, so that the other Jews can see what happens when they tangle with me," he said.

On receiving the news, Judah rode into Jerusalem and rescued his men, vowing revenge. His men had approached the governor unarmed and this was how they'd been treated. Well, now was the time for revenge.

He wasn't called Hammerhead for nothing.

Before long, one of Judah's scouts came running into his tent, breathless with haste. "They're coming, they're coming. I saw thousands of soldiers marching on the horizon and a huge pall of dust was wavering like a giant cloud over hundreds of men on horseback!" he breathed.

"So be it," announced Judah, racing outside and climbing to the pinnacle of the large rock in the centre of their camp. All around, thousands of Judah's men emerged from their tents, eager to hear what their new leader had to say. To many, Judah was their saviour. He was the one whom *HaShem* favoured. "The time has come," shouted Judah, his arms outstretched to the heavens like Moses before him. "The enemy are marching towards us. Though they outnumber us, we will not fail. We, and only we, have *HaShem* on our side. So, go with strength, faith and determination in your hearts. We may only have our slingshots and swords against the enemy's might, just as David did against Goliath. But, just like David, we too will prevail."

A mighty roar rose over the camp. No matter whether they were boys, young men or the old. All would be ready on Judah's signal.

For many days Judah had been preparing for the fight. He had decided to split the men into groups, each with its own commander. Now addressing his commanders, Judah instructed them to be sure each of his troop had their slingshots full of pebbles, their swords sharpened, even their pitchforks from the fields, strengthened and straightened. No matter. The enemy were still days away. Time enough for Judah's army to march towards the familiar territory of Lebonah where each man would lie flat and hidden behind the grassy hills, his weaponry alongside.

Apollonius had decided to make camp a little to the north of where Judah's men lay waiting. A scout reported that he had never seen such luxury. Their tents were emblazoned and embroidered in gold thread, the finest horses he had ever seen were pawing at the ground, and many fires were set. The aroma of roasting meat assailed the senses. Judah counselled his commanders to ignore the enemy's outer trappings, for what the children of Israel had was the guidance of *HaShem*.

Judah looked up at the black sky, its stars twinkling their eternal message. The most important thing of all was for the children of Israel to continue. No matter what afflictions or minor defeats lay ahead of them, eventually his army would march on into the future and on this same precious, tiny piece of land. That's all they wanted. Coveting nothing else, it was all they would ever need.

Dawn arose to the sound of snorting animals, the chink of heavy armour and the steady pounding of a thousand feet. Apollonius rode in the centre, just behind a legion of archers, all heavily armed. Those at the fore approached in a loose formation, eight to ten feet separating each man. Several men manned each bolt thrower, another group carrying a basket of extra bolts.

A night-time scouting party had surveyed the terrain ahead of them, a range of hills and narrow gorges giving the governor a headache. It would be very difficult to accurately assess where the enemy's main force were hiding. The governor decided to move forward on foot, behind his archers, so as not to give the enemy a target to aim for.

As the noise grew louder, still Judah lay flat behind a hill. His men breathlessly awaited his signal. The time had to be right, not too soon and certainly not after the enemy was so close they could unleash their weaponry. Judah knew he had the upper hand, despite their comparative paucity of men and arms because he had the benefit of the high ground.

Suddenly, with a loud whistle, Judah stood up and raced towards the enemy. His men roared behind him, a steely glint in each man's eye, an uncanny strength coursing through their veins. Whilst his men fought tooth and nail with the enemy foot soldiers, there was only one man whom Judah sought. Racing towards Apollonius, Judah forced the man down onto the ground where they could fight man to man on the barren plain. As frightened horses behind him reared up before racing off wildly in to the distance, Judah and Apollonius faced each other.

"You will not last long, Jew," said Apolloneus, baring his teeth. He liked to set his men an example by leading from the front. "I will despatch you just as I did your fellow Jews in Jerusalem. You will run just as they did before I put paid to them and your God. Soon I will have your men eating swine just like I do. You should try it. Delicious," grinning.

Behind Judah, spurred on by their leader's shout, his men unleashed a violent storm of pebbles, arrows and missiles towards the enemy. From their hidden vantage point on high, Judah's army caught the enemy unawares. Apollonius's men quickly began to brandish their weaponry and machines, but despite their sophistication, they were just too slow. Before they could arm and utilise all the armaments they had at their disposal, they were felled, one after the other. Each time a man fell, Judah's army would roar on in celebration.

But the enemy was not finished. Again and again they employed the tactic of passage-of-lines, whereby fresh ranks of men would surge forward to replace losses in the front ranks. It was something that the enemy has trained hard for, but in

practice – out on the actual field of battle – it proved very difficult to achieve. For one thing, the Jews were simply too clever.
What they lacked in numbers, they gained by cleverness. They
knew this land better than the enemy and Judah had given considerable pre-thought on how to utilise its natural habitat to aid
their mission. That, combined with his old adage of always taking the upper ground, proved of incalculable worth now.

But first, Judah had to deal with Apollonius himself. Judah
gritted his teeth at the effrontery of his opponent. "For what
you have done to my people, you will pay a thousandfold,"
he shouted at Apollonius as he lunged towards his heavily-ar-
moured opponent. Long had Judah trained using his small dagger and sharply honed sword in perfect synchrony. Now was
the time to put this training into practice. As the other man
lunged and parried in foolish self-confidence, Judah leaned a
little to the left before kicking his right leg high and hard. There
was a satisfying crunch as his enemy's jaw broke, causing him to
crumple into a heap on the stony ground in agony. Then, with
the use of both his weapons, Judah dispatched the governor
with his sword, a fountain of fresh, red blood suddenly spurting
up from his innards. Apollonius looked surprised at the sight
before closing his eyes for the final time.

Everywhere, the bodies of Apollonius's army lay dead and
vanquished across the barren land.

"All we want is to be left alone and in peace," Judah whispered before shouting out the single word "victory" to his men.
Everywhere they looked, enemy foot soldiers and the remaining men on horseback retreated at the sight of their leader's
death.

Judah's battle was won.

Thanks be to *HaShem*.

The children of Israel had won this battle, but there would be many more to come.

In the caves of Gophna, another very different battle was being waged by the women. Someone had poisoned Hadassah's drinking water. The old woman lay dying, being tended by the only one who loved her. It was Esther, the daughter of the man who tended the donkeys.

"Is there anything I can do for you, dear *Safta*?" asked Esther, using the familiar name she had grown up calling her. Hadassah had been the only grandmother the girl had ever known. Always she had been treated with love and kindness by the old woman. Now was the time she could repay her, as best she could.

Hadassah's eyes fluttered open as she beckoned Esther nearer to her. She stretched her arms upwards in an anguished attempt to allay the pains in her neck and shoulders. She was old and knew she lay dying as she reflected on the life. *Why me?* Hadassah thought. *I was never meant to be old.* What was it *Abba* used to say: 'age doth not come alone.' *And he was right,* she thought, rubbing her neck again. It wasn't fair. Age had always belonged to other people. *I used to be young and beautiful. There were so many things I wanted to do, but always I thought I would do them tomorrow. Time is so fleeting, a mere breath away. Why, it was only yesterday when I was so beautiful, the whole World was before me.*

First, with supreme strength, she needed to do one last thing before she quitted this world. Hadassah had no fear of dying. Indeed, she had lived long and now looked forward to meeting *HaShem*. But now, with her last few breaths, she un-clasped her bony fingers from around an object and thrust it into young Esther's hands. "Listen well, daughter, for that's what you are to me. I will say this only once. You must guard this precious stone with your very life. Tell no-one you have it. It comes from the ruins of our mighty temple..." Hadassah's words trailed off, leaving Esther perplexed.

"But *Safta,*" looking down in consternation at the small round object in her hand, "what must I do with this stone?"

The last words Hadassah spoke before her final breath rasped from her dry throat were "keep the *meleke* stone safe always. Then, you must pass it on to another female, with the same message. Can you do that for me, Esther?"

Esther nodded.

With tears raining down her cheeks, Esther stowed the precious stone under her tunic where none of the other women would ever find it.

Within the statutory twenty-four hours, Hadassah was bur-ied amongst others under a mount of olives.

And a young girl remembered the important task she was given.

Chapter Thirteen

St. Antonin Noble Val
2019

S AMI'S FATHER MENES was in a quandary.

Something had to be done about his eldest son. He knew he was up to no good and feared the worst.

Last Sunday, after a busy but profitable market day, as usual Sami was nowhere to be seen as Menes and his other sons packed up all their remaining, unsold, goods into their old van ready for the short drive home. After his sons had hopped into the back, ready for the bumpy journey, he turned the ignition waiting for the familiar coughing start from the engine. But, Pfft. Nothing.

P'raps it needs some water. It's been standing in the heat all day," offered one of his sons. "There's a standpipe over there," pointing across the street to the carpark in front of the Mairie's building.

"OK," said his father, grumbling as he lifted the red-hot bonnet of their ubiquitous white van, trying to ignore the various graffiti messages scrawled in the dust along the sides. "Give me a break," he muttered as he lifted the cap of the water tank, just avoiding the blast of hot air which immediately burst upwards.

As the boy sprinted off across the main street and around the corner, he spotted his brother Sami deep in conversation with his friend Seth, the latter looking very worried. Both were smoking like their lives depended on it. He decided not to interrupt and pretended he hadn't seen them. Sami was always up to no good and he wanted no part of it.

Now back at the van with a bucket of water, the boy handed it to his father. Menes poured the cooling water into the hot tank and tried the ignition again. Thankfully, the engine sprang into life. Cigarette dangling from his lower lip, Menes did a three-point turn in the next side street before turning left towards the road bridge leading to their home village.

As he drove along, sunlight dappling through the trees fronting the river, Menes thought of that other sunny time when he married Layla. Ah, how innocent they's both been. The memories came flooding back.

The clay house in a village just outside Cairo, like those surrounding it, consisted of a few rooms opening into a courtyard and accessible only from the front. It seemed like a million miles away from the bustle of the capital, the largest city of Egypt. Some said that there were over nine million people living in poverty there, but for those in the poor outlying areas like Layla's house, they simply focused on their daily lives.

"One day at a time, Menes," said Layla to him. "That's the best way to live. Why worry yourself about people living different lives in the big city? We have enough to worry about here, so we just have to get on with it."

And she was right, thought Menes. The air was certainly cleaner out in the countryside, despite the village's lack of facilities.

Menes remembered his first visit there and, in particular, his future mother-in-law, Fatima. He'd had to be on his best behaviour because Layla's mother was formidable. She had this way of standing, her fists on her hips as she looked him up and down. He always felt discomforted when she was around, even though he soon realised she had a heart of gold beneath.

Menes was just a child, really, and had grown up in Layla's village. He remembered Fatima's cooking skills, in particular.

Inside the big old farmhouse, Fatima had been busy preparing the family's main meal of the day. After her work tending the flocks on the hills, Layla had rushed over to greet her mother and bring Menes to their home. He'd been there before but was still hesitant in a stranger's house.

Fatima had this trick of putting her elbow up to her forehead to wipe away the moisture that kept dripping into her eyes, no matter how hard she tried to stop it, and subconsciously to brush away the few errant wisps of her hair that kept escaping from the headscarf she always wore.

"Enter, enter, Menes. Don't just stand there on the doorstep. Come in. Will you join us for a meal? We do not have much but what we have you are very welcome to enjoy with us," said Fatima kindly.

Menes stood uncertainly on the threshold, not knowing what to do. Layla's mother at once recognised his feelings, and intuitively asked Layla to help with the preparation of their meal, whilst shooing Menes away. With some relief, Menes had smiled at Layla and said he would be back soon, as he ran gladly out again. *Better to wait for Layla's father to return,* thought Menes. He felt uncomfortable with only females for company.

As his wife later told him, Layla had been trying to learn her mother's cooking techniques, which she knew she'd have to perform herself when she was married one day. Her mother beckoned Layla forwards and explained that today she was making *mansaf*, a dish that everyone ate in their area. Layla looked troubled, thinking she'd never remember it all.

That day Fatima was using lamb, rice, and *jameed,* which looked to Layla like the milk curds she made from goats' milk.

Glancing at her daughter, Fatima said "I can see that you are puzzled by the *jameed* but don't worry. It's only goats' milk. See," pointing to a fine woven cheesecloth she kept in a cool wicker cupboard underneath the window, "that's where I make it. It soon becomes my very own mix of hard and dry *labane*, then all that I need to do is to add salt every day to thicken the yogurt even more."

"I'll never learn all this," cried Layla. "What am I going to do when I get married? My husband will leave me and then what?" wiping her eyes.

"Nonsense," replied Fatima. "It's easy. Remember, I didn't know anything either when I married your father but you soon learn. Everybody does."

Next, as Layla nervously watched by the table, Fatima rinsed the outside of the yogurt mixture with water to allow any remaining whey to seep through the porous cheesecloth.

'You see, child,' said Fatima, warming to her theme, pleased despite herself to see that Layla at last seemed to be taking it all in, "after a few days of salting the yogurt, it becomes very dense and it can be removed from the cheesecloth and shaped into round balls. It is then set to dry for a few days."

"You'll see that you need to dry the yogurt in the sun until it becomes yellow because if it's dried indoors or in the shade it stays white. I soon learned as a child that it is important that the *jameed* is dry to the core because any dampness can spoil the preservation process."

Fatima paused awhile from rushing around, and told Layla to sit down in the coolest part of the room, while they waited for the *jameed* to finish drying.

Layla was discomforted by her mother's searching look. She always seemed to know what was going on inside. It made her stomach form into tight knots, somehow, that wouldn't go away. She raised her eyes and looked tearfully around the room, a room that was familiar yet forbidding because of her mother's strict rules. Layla didn't really know what was the matter with her. They'd always lived like this, her mother and father had grown to be happy with their lives, however humble, and followed traditions and practices that they had learned from their own parents and grandparents before them. So what was wrong with her? Layla felt a foreboding that her own future would be very different from her mother's and that Fatima would not be happy about it.

But, for now, Layla came to realise that it was best to live according to her parents' rules. The future would take care of itself. She knew that her parents' simple view on life was to be happy, to be well and to offer the best hospitality to visitors like Menes that they possibly could. She realised that this was her chance to prove to her mother that she was no longer a dreamer, that she could make something of herself. All she had to do was remember what Menes had told her and to always do the right thing. She was sure, then, that everything would turn out all right in the end.

Layla smiled a watery smile at her mother and wiped her nose on her sleeve. Fatima didn't know what was wrong with the girl, but realised that she'd been young and innocent once herself. So, in an uncharacteristic gesture for her, she walked over to her daughter and put a kindly arm around her shoulders. "Look," she said to take her daughter's mind off whatever was troubling her, "I think the *jameed* is now dry enough, so we can move to the next stage." Fatima took a platter from a wooden cupboard and placed on it an enormous, thin layer of *markook* flatbread. It was very thin and almost transparent.

"You already are quite good at baking," said her mother. Layla smiled at this unexpected compliment. "I baked it this morning on our *saj* griddle. As you know, it's important to always flatten the dough of *saj* bread and to make sure it stays very thin before cooking," placing the platter to the side. "The shops that sell it up in the town usually fold it and put it in bags before being sold, but I have always made my own and I'm not likely to change my habits now." She clucked her tongue against her bottom teeth at such a preposterous idea.

Next, Fatima took from the stove an enormous pot of rice which she carefully poured on top of the bread, finally placing a lamb's head on top. She told Layla to fetch a bowl of shelled pinenuts and almonds from the windowsill and suggested she sprinkle these on top of the finished dish. Momentarily, Layla smiled, thinking of pictures of small animals nibbling on the nuts, their bushy tails flicking behind them as they ate.

"That's better," smiled Fatima, misinterpreting Layla's smile. "See, I knew you'd feel better helping me with the cooking. All we have to do now is to pour the yogurt sauce right over the *mansaf*. There now. Doesn't that look good?"

The front door suddenly burst open, and a large man walked confidently in, followed by a sheepish Menes. "I'm starving, Fatima. Is the meal ready?"

"Yes, yes, husband," replied Fatima, flustered. "Layla's been helping me. It'll be on the table as soon as you've finished washing." Her husband's eyes flickered at Menes. "I didn't know that the boy would be here today?" eyeing his wife.

"Yes, yes, Hamid. I told Menes you wouldn't mind him joining us, as his family is away…," finishing off her sentence uncertainly, as she didn't really know why the boy seemed to always be on his own these days. Menes looked down and kept himself to himself.

"Well then," said Hamid kindly. "The boy can stay here for a few days until his family return. What do you say Menes?" patting him on the back.

Hamid paused awhile, critically appraising the boy. Menes was growing up fast. Already he had bristles on his chin and had grown tall. But Hamid was a generous, uncomplicated man and he had always been of the opinion that at a time of need, *Allah* always instructed them to offer whatever hospitality he could.

"Menes, you are very welcome to join us in our home and for our humble meals."

Layla breathed out, and relaxed for the first time that day

as her mother ushered them all to the table. Menes waited until everyone was seated, then nervously slid into a place by the side of Layla.

The large platter of *mansaf* sat in its full glory in the centre of the table. Hamid beamed at Menes, remembering his own boyhood days, and told him that when he was a boy each one in the family ate their meal with the right hand instead of using a utensil and that they were supposed to keep the left hand behind their back whilst eating.

"Is that how it is in your house?"

Menes looked discomforted, but nodded to keep the peace. In fact, his family were far poorer than this one and they often went hungry.

Hamid continued. It was clear he loved an audience for his tales, and this boy seemed eager to hear more. He told Menes that in his home it was perfectly acceptable to use a spoon from an individual plate, as long as there were not more than six to seven people sitting around the table. He told him that when he was a boy it was always traditional for guests to eat first, but as he was as yet still young and seemed a little nervous, he should just follow what the rest of them did.

"As you will surely recall," said Hamid, warming to his theme, even though Menes clearly came from the same background as his family, "there are some things *Allah* forbids us to eat. We don't eat any meat from the pig, as it is considered an unclean animal. In fact, it's the one thing we have in common with the Jews," laughing at such a preposterous thing to say. 'We have nothing against the animal in itself, of course. It's just that we don't consider it fit for us to eat."

Hamid then started to cut slivers of meat from the lamb's head, telling Menes that this was the way that their family appreciated his company amidst them. Looking at the food, Menes realised just how hungry he was. To him, it all looked so strange. In his own house, they never ate anything like that but his hunger won in the end as he tentatively took a spoonful of the *mansaf* and raised it to his lips.

Between hearty mouthfuls, Hamid told Menes a little about his working day.

"Trade's good at the moment, but it changes a lot at different times of the year," he told him. "My business is with dyes. It's been handed down in my family for generations." He clearly enjoyed telling this boy all about it. "You see, er Menes, I collect pigments for the finest of clothes from southern Spain, but I take care to use only the very best carmine, vermillion, azurite, ochre and malachite. You probably haven't heard of these before, but believe me, they're quality materials. My father before me, *Allah* rest his soul, always avoided the cheaper materials such as saffron or indigo."

Hamid continued, forking more of the delicious *mansaf* into his mouth: "Of course, sometimes I get special orders. Then I have to get the royal purple of Tyre," Hamid continued, touching the side of his nose, as if telling him a big secret. "That's a material more costly even than amber, lapis or silk. What we have to do is crush and crumble thousands of rotting shellfish shells. It's hard work, don't I know it, but once the dyes are finally made, I can trade them with men in the major trading centres."

Hamid told him that the previous year he had even dealt

with tradesmen in the great ports of France, particularly Nimes and Narbonne.

Fatima noticed that Menes's eyes were glazing a little so gently chided her husband, telling him that the boy didn't want to hear about all this business, so he heeded her advice and changed tack a little.

"Tomorrow evening, in case your father didn't tell you, is the beginning of *Ramadan*," said Hamid. "As you know, our festivals start in the evening as soon as the moon rises and finish when the sun sets. During the festival we eat early in the morning, then fast all day, and eat again at night. It is a holy time, but I know you will like the festival that follows it. Everybody does. It's when everyone celebrates and gives each other gifts." He paused for a moment, looking at his daughter and the strange boy. "As both of you are still young, you are not required to fast if you don't want to, only the adults."

He turned to Layla: 'Daughter, when the holy days are over, why don't you show Menes around the town. I'm sure it would interest him and stop him from becoming bored."

Layla smiled and said that would be cool. His father shook his head. His daughter was a good girl but always seemed to be picking up western styles of speech. What was this 'cool', anyway? He never could understand young people nowadays. Now, when he was a boy.......

But Fatima wondered if this was a good idea. It was one thing having the boy stay in their home, where she could keep an eye on him, but quite another letting her precious daughter walk outside with him. However, she kept her thoughts to herself.

Early on the first morning of *Ramadan*, at a time when it was still dark but just before dawn, Menes was woken up by the sound of a distant monotonous tone. Layla crept in to explain that was the moment when the grown-ups had to get up every day during the month of *Ramadan* to eat the *Suhoor* pre-dawn meal followed by their *fajr* prayer. That way they wouldn't die of hunger before the fourth prayer of the day was due at sunset. Although Menes was of the same faith as Layla, he knew very little about it. His whole life, so far, had been spent in simply struggling to live. His father had no money nor prospects, being disabled, and his mother was of a depressive frame of mind.

"It's good that you arrived when you did," said Layla, "because the holy days are when the people are taught to have sympathy for those who have been cast off, like yourself." Somehow she'd gathered that his background was very different from hers.

Menes puffed himself up for a moment, wanting to show Layla that he was going to be a 'somebody' some day. He proclaimed that next year he would be a man. "That's when I too will fast," trying his best to impress this girl whose life was very different from his own.

"What do you eat when the fast is over?" he asked, thinking that it would be very late in the day for a big meal.

"Oh, nothing very much," said Layla. "Usually we have dates, maybe vegetable soup with pasta crackers and pitta bread. But only after the sun has set."

That night Menes lay in his makeshift hard pallet-bed, his arms behind his head, thinking about all that he had learned. This was so so different from his life so far. He just couldn't believe it. But whenever he started to panic, he felt the presence of someone or something, who soothed him and told him he was doing very well. All he had to do was bide his time in this new but temporary family home. The future would take care of itself.

He knew, deep inside, that he should follow his heart and his instincts. Lying back, he cast his eyes upwards and stared through a hole in the roof at the glittering stars in the jet black sky overhead.

Back in the present, Menes as an old man, drove automatically to their home in this new land called France. Life had certainly played a heavy toll on him, but one thing he never regretted, not for an instance, was the day he married Layla. It was the best day of his life. As his van turned the bend and proceeded up the hill homewards, he remembered his wedding day as though it were just yesterday. Later, much later, his wife told him just how she'd felt in the days leading up to their union.

Vine leaves decorated the doorway of Layla's childhood home, and the entrance was strewn with sweet-smelling herbs.

Today was a day of great celebration. Layla was getting married.

As a little girl she used to love playing with her brothers in the dust surrounding their dwelling. However she was far from being a dutiful sister. She was often annoyed because the boys kept shoving her away, saying that they were playing men's games which were not for females.

"It's not fair," sobbed Layla, "I want to play men's games and to wear what you are wearing, not these silly girls' clothes."

"Be quiet and obedient,' replied her brother Ahmed. "You must watch what our respected mother does in the kitchen and learn how to wash our clothes and bake the bread. You will then be considered a suitable wife for someone when you grow up."

Layla stamped her foot in annoyance and complete frustration. She didn't want to bake or wash clothes. She wanted to run in the hills and climb trees, just like her brothers, but also she wanted to heal the sick like the woman in their village. Whenever anyone was ill, they would knock on the old lady's door and whatever time of day or night, she would try to help. Layla would often pester the old lady to find out everything she could about all those strange potions which she kept in the back of the house. To Layla, they were mysterious wonderful liquids – brown with sediment at the bottom, but with a thick layer like cream froth at the top. There were also all manner of hand-made wooden implements, which she saw the old lady use to straighten people when their backs or their legs hurt. Sometimes she just used her hands. Layla remembered that time when her father, Hamid, had a terrible pain at the base of his spine. The old lady told him to raise the knee which was on the opposite side to the pain, then she would dig her finger tips into that dimple at the base of the back and do a simple flick with her fingers. It was certainly a miraculous cure, anyway.

But most of the time Layla had to help her mother bake the family's bread in a small, dark crumbling building that adjoined their main living quarters. Deep slits had been gouged out of the walls high above their heads, but these were mainly for ventilation. Most of the light was generated from a large oven in the centre of the room. Fatima was constantly irritated that Layla's head was always in the clouds over some dream or other. But her mother still persisted, as it was a girl's duty to her future husband to learn how to feed a family.

But Layla is as yet young, her mother reassured herself.

Fatima would still do most of the work herself and supervise Layla so that she didn't scald herself on the hot surfaces. After the bread had finished baking in their clay oven, which rested on smooth flat stones heated to a glowing red by the burning faggots piled beneath, a huge gaping hole acted as a chimney to vent out most of the smoke. However this same chimney also served to channel in gusts of rain, which hissed into steamy contact with the hot ovens on baking days.

But all that was a while ago, for today was Layla's wedding day.

Layla stood looking out far over the horizon. Like all the dwellings in the area, the house was shuttered up in an often futile attempt to keep the interior cool. Layla, though, had long ago discovered a chink in the front wooden shutter, which she often made use of to peer out at everyone else's lives outside. Today the sky was the kind of colour that comes with intense heat: a fiery white, too intense to look at with the naked eye. The sun beat down on everything in its path, its inexorable journey shot with glints of pure gold. The roadway was dry and rough with chiselled pebbles, their worn corners catching the rays of the sun in refractory rainbows of light. A lone cart suddenly rumbled past, its overloaded household contents almost overbalancing as the rough wooden wheels creaked over the old pebbles.

Layla reached up to the sky, stretching her fingers up towards the heavens, just like she used to do to show her brothers she was nearly as tall as they were. Today the gesture was more subliminal, an unconscious gesture to show not only that she was her own person, fully in control of her own body, but also that she had a hand in her own destiny.

Her destiny was clear. She was going to marry Menes.

Fatima was bustling away in the background, preparing with much excitement the wedding feast. She also had a tear in her eye for today she would lose her beloved daughter, the only daughter in the family, as she was to hand her over to her new husband. But at least Fatima knew the groom. It seemed only yesterday when he, as a young boy, would join them for a meal. She remembered how worried she'd been when Layla and Menes would play outside, but fortunately nothing untoward had happened. Praise be to *Allah*. Ah, how quickly time flew past.

Yesterday Fatima had excused Layla from helping with bread-making duties. After all, it was her wedding day tomorrow and she needed to be fresh and pure for her new husband. So Fatima had set about making as many loaves as she could for the celebration. She had already finished the first batch of loaves and was ready to start the second. Each batch made twenty black loaves, fresh and crispy just how the men liked them. Fatima was hot and floury, rolling and pushing the sleeves of her dress up past her elbows. The wood beneath the oven splintered and cracked in the heat, a choking cloud of smoke already reaching far up and through the roof chimney. She set to work on the second batch, kneading the bread in a huge pan and settling the loaves on the oven shelves to bake. She knew from long experience that the stones beneath the oven needed to be heated to exactly the right temperature. Too low a heat and the bread bakes sadly flat; too high and the dough would be scorched on the outside, but raw inside. Fatima was tired, but determined that nothing would spoil her daughter's big day. And at last the bread was ready, leaving her to drop in a dead sleep ready for the big day tomorrow.

"Layla, come away from the doorway. You have much to do. Go and wash yourself and your hair very thoroughly. I've some special sweet oils to anoint you after your bath, and cousin Anawara is coming over to do your hair. The dressmaker is due to arrive very soon with the clothes we chose, made from your father's special dyes, so be quick; there is much to do.'

As Layla, with a sigh, rushed to do her mother's bidding, her father was talking with his brother. They started off, as they always did, by talking business. Trade was good.

After their usual discussions about work, Hamid turned to the more pressing business at hand, his daughter Layla and her forthcoming nuptials.

"Abasi, we have done our best for the girl, although she was always wilful. Although I will be sorry to hand her over to her husband, in a way it will be a relief. It is always a struggle to bring up girls in the world today. How to protect their innocence, when there are so many dangers abroad?"

"I know what you mean, Brother," replied Abasi. "I once knew of a daughter who disobeyed her father and ran off with a boy who was totally unsuitable. There was absolute uproar in the whole community. No-one spoke to the family for years, and the girl herself had to leave the area for good, so besmirched was her reputation after that. There was even great difficulty years later when they tried to get the younger daughter married. So much depends on a family's good name and reputation that one bad egg can spoil the chances for everyone else."

"Well, at least," replied Hamid, "we have managed to arrange a suitable husband for Layla. I have always said that if a marriage is going to be successful, it should follow our practices by being arranged by both families. You know, a marriage is not just about the couple who are getting married, it is also a marriage between the two families joining together. By this method, there is always support for the young couple from both families and the marriage is so much stronger as a result and less likely to break up. And, you know Abasi, I have always tried to be a reasonable father. I always said to Layla that, after meeting her intended, she could still refuse him if she felt that the marriage would not work."

"I know, Brother. But I think it is a good match. They say that Menes, her intended, has worked long and hard, so he must indeed be a good man. And he is young and strong, even though his family have always been very poor. I remember a time when I was a boy when it was quite usual for men in all the Arabian lands to enjoy such licentious pleasures as dancing and drinking, but all that has changed lately. *Allah* has brought much good to our people and taught them the error of their ways."

The men walked outside to await the arrival of the groom's family and the *mukhtar*, chief of the village. Their village was considered one of the finest in the region, famous for its figs and grapes. It was important that only the best hospitality be offered, including the fare from their own village, anything less being considered an insult to the family's honour and prestige.

Layla was in a tizzy of something between excitement and dread. Yes, she knew that to achieve anything in life, it was necessary for a girl to get married. The only consolation for her was that, once married, she could concentrate on improving her cooking skills. Surely no-one could object once she was an old married woman and completely respectable in the eyes of the families and their community?

With a large wooden pail she fetched enough water from the well outside and heated it thoroughly over the fire. She then poured it carefully into the old tin tub and pulled a curtain around it for privacy. She had fetched enough lye soap and a clean cloth with which to dry herself afterwards. Once all was ready, she loosened her long, heavy hair from the pins holding it off the back of her neck, stripped off her old woollen day dress and stepped gingerly into the hot water. First of all she knelt down and, with a deft movement of the back of her hand, threw her hair forwards into the water and wet it thoroughly before soaping it with a careful kneading action of her fingertips. Once she was sure all the old oils and dust had been washed out, she rinsed it clean and threw it back off her forehead again. By now her knees were sore, so she shifted into a more comfortable sitting position and scrubbed all over her body, until her young skin was shiny and glistening all over. Once she was satisfied that her mother would approve, she stood up, parted the curtain and enfolded herself in the soft clean cloth.

She was just in time, as her mother was now calling her.

"Layla, Anawara is here to do your hair. Are you ready yet?"

"My hair's still wet, mother, so I'll have to dry it in the sun, first. Tell Anawara to come out to the back and I'll fetch a hairbrush and some pins."

"Good. We haven't much time. The dressmaker's already been and left our new clothes. Praise Be to *Allah* that we have been to so many fittings so we know they will fit us."

Whilst Anawara was busy arranging her hair outside, Layla was silent, contemplating her future. On the outside she appeared calm, but inside, her stomach was quivering like a thousand jelly fish.

"Oh, aren't you excited Layla?" asked the as yet unmarried Anawara eagerly.

"I don't know. I feel slightly strange, unreal almost, as though I'm in another world in another far off place," dreamed Layla.

As soon as her hair was ready, Anawara and Fatima helped her into her wedding clothes. She slipped on the new red shalwar trousers and tunic, accompanied by a cascade of gold jewellery given to her by members of the family. Once all this was done, Anawara told her to sit and extend her feet in front of her so that her feet could be painted with henna. Once her feet were anointed, her hands were also done. Anawara then commenced to paint Layla's face with some white powders concocted to create the illusion of an interesting pallor, considered to be more becoming, with a subtle black line around her eyes achieved with a stick made of kohl and burnt ash.

Pleased with the final result, her mother and cousin giggled as they led the 'blushing' bride to the altar in the village square.

Already the villagers were crowding around, eager to see the bride and groom and to be part of the festivities. Layla knew that there was no alternative but to go through with the ceremony, consoling herself that it could have been much worse. At least she liked her new husband and had known him for years.

The religious ceremony was performed by the *imam* (teacher), attended by her father and brothers as the adult witnesses. Menes insisted on speaking aloud the religious readings. They then exchanged vows in front of all the witnesses and read special prayers. The family and villagers then, one by one, came forward to give them their blessings and to bless their new marital home. All around them, villagers danced the *dabke* and listened to the *oud*, whilst the elders smoked their *narjeels* and played ancient strategic games with sticks and stones on the hard ground beneath.

This is it, then, thought Layla in a dream as she and Menes walked out into the bright glare of their new married life together. Little did they know how their lives would be turned upside down, war would arrive and they would move to a safer country.

As Menes drove past the old Lexos railway station, *en route* for home, a passing train bound for Toulouse jolted him back to the present. What on earth was he to do about Sami, their eldest? As a baby, Sami had been the apple of Layla's eye. It had taken them years to start a family, Sami's birth proving particularly hard. In fact, at first they didn't know if the baby would live, the midwife telling them he may have suffered oxygen damage during the twenty-four hours of labour. Because of all of that, and the fact that Layla had waited so long to raise a family, there was no doubt that she had spoiled the boy. Menes could understand that, but what was he to do now? At least, the four children who had followed in quick succession all seemed normal, happy go lucky boys.

Finally, as Menes pulled into their long driveway, he came to a decision. Menes had lived a long and difficult life but nothing compared to his time in the Egyptian army. It had been so harrowing, he hadn't even told his wife of all that he had endured during the Six Day War.

But now, he felt that Sami needed to be told a few home truths. He wasn't sure exactly what he would tell him, but a good start would be to talk about Nasser's war machine and the surprising face of the enemy. One thing he had learnt over his life was that nothing is as clear cut as the young seem to think it is. There was good in most people if you looked hard enough. Sometimes when you least expected it, but especially during times of war, people had a habit of surprising you, even the supposed enemy.

Yes, that was what he must impress on Sami. He'd try to talk to him soon before his resolve failed him.

What Menes didn't realise, though, was that it was already too late.

Chapter Fourteen

Toulouse
2019

"Have you started the Egypt scene yet, love?" asked Leah. "I've always been fascinated by the different cultures in the Middle East."

Simon had been contemplating just how he was going to tackle this next great challenge. He needed more insight, not just about the dress, the settings etc, but especially about how the people of Egypt were brought up as children and their thought processes. "Not yet, *coucou*. I was thinking of talking to Papa's old friend Menes." On seeing his wife's puzzled look "You remember. He's the one we met in St. Antonin that day when we went up to the Sunday market."

"Oh, of course. I remember now. Wasn't he that old man with the accent who was selling those lovely herbs and spices on the main street there?"

"Yes. He's the one. I've known him for quite a while. In fact he's actually an old friend of *Abba's*. He was telling me recently about how he came to live in France. It was a fascinating story. But, importantly, Menes grew up in Egypt in the '50s during the Suez crisis, so now I need to pick his brains about all things Egyptian."

"That sounds like a brilliant idea, love. We could go up to St. Antonin next Sunday. I love mooching around all those stalls."

Simon nodded, but added "There's something else I want to do too. I've been thinking about how the personalities of different cultures coincided in France. So, I'd first like to go back to *Capitole* when that African market is next scheduled to be there. Could you look it up for me?"

Capitole was its usual self. Throngs of shoppers and tourists intermingling, some sitting at pavement cafés, others perched on low stone bollards, watching the world go by.

Whilst the African market stalls were being erected, Simon and Leah decided to take the opportunity to grab some lunch at their favourite place. Walking past the large department store on the corner, avoiding the notorious ancient central gullies, where many a high heel had become unstuck, they meandered left into the *rue Puits Verts* to their favourite vegetarian restaurant. Just off the beaten track, it was a haven for artists and students alike, as well as those who for various reasons opted not to eat meat.

Now enjoying a strong black coffee, Simon was talking with Leah about their fellow Frenchmen.

"Do you remember, *coucou*, when we visited London and how taken aback we were by how different they seemed? I was wondering whether it's because of the differences in the weather? Certainly," laughing, "the English do nothing but talk about their weather all the time, I remember!"

Leah laughed. "Yes, but it's more than that, *n'est-ce pas*? Don't get me started on the French," she said, beginning to numerate on her fingers all the things about them that irritated and annoyed her in equal measure. Let's see. We know only too well how the average French person is a hypochondriac, a suicidal driver, flirtatious, racist(!), unhygienic, anti-American, a gourmand, sensuous, chauvinistic, chic, patriotic, proud, nationalistic, debauched, elegant, relaxed, completely unprudish about baring their bodies anywhere (particularly men seen everywhere urinating at the side of the road!), philosophical, unsqueamish, superior in their attitudes to other nations, unsporting and bureaucratic. And that's just for starters," she humphed in disgust.

Simon laughed in agreement but felt he had to stick up a little for his fellow countrymen. "Yes, but don't forget we're famed for our culture and especially for our food," eying the wonderful food now in front of them in the packed restaurant. All around them, groups of artistic people laughed and joked, as glasses of local wine were downed in quick succession.

Now retracing their steps back to *Capitole*, everywhere they looked was a delight. A sudden klaxon announced a wedding group, hooting its way through the maze of cobbled streets, brightly-dressed ticket sellers and packed pavement cafés every few feet.

But it was the market sellers that particularly caught their eye, setting up their weekly stalls.

"Now that's what I need to see, love," said Simon, tugging Leah's sleeve as he walked towards the aisle with north African wares. Wonder whether any of these stall holders are Egyptian?

"Yes, that's the bit I'd really like to see. I have a friend Mireille, who was born in Egypt," she replied eagerly.

"After a few enquiries, they were directed to a stall further along the narrow aisle, where a man wearing a long, floor-length white shirt with sleeves was arranging his stall.

"This," pointing to his shirt "we call a *gallibaya*," he said proudly. On his head was a white skull cap. Puzzled, Simon asked "I thought that Egyptian men wore a red fez?"

The man laughed. "Oh you mean the *tarboosh*? We don't wear that any more. My father used to when he was in the army, but that was abolished a long time ago."

Thanking the man, they mooched further along, relishing all the vibrant coloured kaftans and matching coloured turbans worn by the women, before making their way home again.

Simon's head was buzzing with ideas for the next phase, the Egyptian scenes. First, he needed to get the actors on set and have them go through a basic reading of the scenes in the Sinai. Following that, they'd need to actively act out those scenes. Thinking about his conversation with Menes, when the actors go through those scenes, he'd need to tell them specifically what he wanted them to do, how they should interact with the environment, and let them know of any changes that he wanted to see in their acting. This was important. There was a moral to this narrative, so it was imperative that the film portrayed exactly what he envisaged to bring his message across. This process was called 'blocking the scene.' Simon knew that the read through of the script could be done anywhere, but the blocking needed to be done on set.

Next would come the visuals of dressing the actors in realistic costumes depicting both the chosen era and country of origin. Because each of the actor's roles required either Egyptian or Israeli clothing and appropriate makeup, he wanted to make sure that each actor was in character before he started the shoot. So, first the rehearsal, then in full costume. And, because there were significant cultural and religious issues to be considered, whenever an actor was required to wear a cultural or religious piece, such as a *hijab* or *yarmulke*, he had to be sure he was getting it right. It wouldn't be enough for an actor to simply throw the piece on; they needed to be as accurate as possible in how the item was worn and how they moved around in it.

That night, Simon was discussing all the difficulties with Leah. "My budget's so tight, I just don't know how I'm going to achieve everything I need to do regarding the costumes, in particular."

Leah considered for a moment before giving her some ideas of her own. "Look, love, why don't you ask the actors themselves if they have anything in their own wardrobes that might do? What I mean is: if some of the cast playing Egyptians have Middle Eastern roots, they might well have something they could use. That would help enormously to bring the eras you're depicting into life."

Simon recognised the logic of what Leah was saying. He was so glad to have her. *A woman often comes up with a realistic plan when all else fails*, he thought with a smile. Now he just needed to prepare this bit of his storyboard and film as many scenes as he could within his time frame. He knew that he didn't always have to shoot his film in chronological order, so he planned to shoot the easiest scenes first, knowing he could then put them in the right order afterwards. At least living in SW France, he was able to use sunny days to mimic the strong sunshine of the Middle East, which had already saved him a lot of money on location scenes. South France was only the other side of the Meditérranean from North Africa after all. Clearly, if it was raining and cloudy in France, that wasn't the day for filming!

He knew, though, that the film's visuals were all important. In some ways, this and the lighting mattered more than the dialogue.

He certainly had much to think about and to arrange before the next phase of the film. But next, he needed to talk to friend Menes again. It was one thing looking at the clothes the Egyptians wore, but quite another to discover how they were brought up and their mindsets. In particular, Simon needed to tactfully find out just what Menes thought about the Jewish people. There was only one way to find out.

The following Sunday dawned sunny and bright as Simon drove towards St. Antonin. Leah said it would be better if he went alone, as her presence might inhibit the kind of confidences Simon hoped to evince from Menes. Simon agreed with her.

By the time Simon had driven under the overhead road bridge and turned right, the market traffic was already building. But always, the beautiful flower displays along the river bridge emitted a heavenly perfume to delight pedestrian tourists as they took selfies by the river. Knowing that the main *Avenue du Paul Benet* would be a no-go for parking, Simon pulled into a space on the left, opposite the boulangerie and under the shade of a plane tree.

Carefully locking the car, he turned right into the main avenue and squinted behind his shades. Approaching the many white vans parked kerbside on the right, at last he found Menes, arranging his wares in front of a local bank, set back behind paving slabs. The usual queue of tourists was lining up at the bank's outside cash machine, the tail end trailing to the other end of the avenue. It never ceased to amaze Simon that none of those tourists ever realised beforehand that market traders never took plastic, all demanding cash in hand.

Now facing Menes, Simon wondered how he was going to broach the subject, but decided to trust his instincts and blurt it out.

"*Bonjour Menes. Ça va?*" shaking his friend's hand across his wide stall.

"Ah, *c'est mon ami Simon,*" replied Menes. "*Ton papa, il va bien?*"

Simon nodded that yes, his father was OK.

"*Alors,* what can I do for you today? Perhaps some ripe black olives? I think that the lovely Leah likes these, *n'est-ce pas?*" proffering a handful and bringing them close to Simon's nose so that he could gain the full benefit of the pungent aroma.

It seemed only good manners for Simon to purchase something from this kindly man, especially if he was to gain an element of trust, so he threw some coins onto the counter and put the bag of olives into his capacious jacket pocket.

He launched straight to the chase.

"Um, Menes, could you spare me a few minutes, do you

think? There's something I need to ask you." Eying one of Menes' sons at the back of the stall, he suggested they might pop across the avenue to the *Gazpacho* café on the corner for a coffee. "Could your son perhaps look after your stall whilst we are gone?"

Menes thought for a moment but eventually agreed. It was time his sons took a more active role in the selling side of the business.

Now pushing open the stiff door of the café opposite, they found an empty table in the corner and ordered two strong black coffees. Easing himself painfully into the window seat, Menes turned to Simon inquisitively. "So, *mon ami*, how can I help you?" palms turned up in his usual way.

"You remember that I make films?" said Simon, tentatively.

Menes nodded.

"Well, my current work in progress involves some scenes set in Egypt and I remembered that you were born there. I wondered if you'd mind telling me a little about how the Egyptian people think about the Jewish people?"

Menes shifted a little in his seat, glancing around to see who else was within earshot. As it was still early, only one other table was occupied by a couple of locals, who were deep in conversation. "Well," trying to be tactful, "you've got to realise. There are a lot of countries that used to be lifelong enemies. Just look at France and Germany. They were always at each other's throats until after world war two, and now look at them. Bosom buddies!"

Simon nodded, but said "Somehow, though, *mon ami*, I don't think this applies to Israel and Egypt."

"Well, I don't want to upset our friendship, but yes, you're right; the same cannot be said about Egypt. In the country of my birth, Israel is hated so much that if you were seen carrying the Israeli flag, you'd probably get lynched!"

"But," responded Simon, "hasn't it improved since Israel and Egypt signed that peace treaty? I mean, that was years ago."

"Unfortunately, no," responded Menes. "I know for a fact that even today Egyptians still refuse to recognize Israel as a country."

"What do you think is the reason?"

"Well, there are many reasons. First, anti-Semitism in Egypt has always been dangerously high. This is why I always advise my Jewish friends not to show any sign of their Jewish identity when they come to Egypt. It's high because everyone thinks that Jews will stop at nothing to fulfil their true dream: to conquer the Middle-East."

"You and I both know that that's utter nonsense," said Simon, exasperated. "In any case, I didn't think there were any Jewish people still left in Egypt. They were all forced out in the '50s."

"I know. But that's what all Egyptian kids are taught these days in school. I'm the only one I know of who accepts Israel and their right to exist and considers them as my neighbours and brothers. The same cannot be said about the rest of Egypt, I'm afraid. Nobody there wants peace; everyone just wants war. It always makes me sad to know that it will take a long time for the people of Egypt to accept Israel, but I pray that it happens soon.".

Leaning forward, Simon grasped his friend's hands in his.

"Listen Menes. I'm thinking of depicting a scene from the 1967 Six Day War. What if both you and my father come onto the set? What I mean is: we could then portray a scene showing a fictitious Israeli character and an Egyptian! That way we can show the conflict from each man's point of view, but importantly at the end proving that friendship knows no barriers. What do you think? In fact, would you mind telling me a little about how you and your wife lived back then? Didn't you say you had an apartment in Cairo?"

"OK," said Menes. "Perhaps it would do me good to remember dear Layla exactly how she was after our wedding. She was so lovely, you know. I couldn't believe I had her all to myself. It was such a good time, you know. That is, until the war came. Then, everything changed."

Simon thanked his friend sincerely and promised that he'd treat everything Menes told him in as sensitive a way as he possibly could.

In response, Menes leaned across the table and kissed Simon on both cheeks.

With tears in his eyes, Simon embraced his father's dear friend, wishing him *Salaam*, Peace.

CHAPTER FIFTEEN

"Lights, camera, action"
Egypt
1967

THE NILE SNAKED lazily at a point just south of the metropolis, the river's meandering waters cooling the bullrushes growing alongside the river banks as it flowed steadily past the desert-bound valleys before entering the low-lying Nile delta area.

But today, there was no baby Moses floating in a basket near the bullrushes. Cairo had become a major metropolis, home to millions.

Despite Cairo radiating away from the river in every direction, the city was in fact located just on its east bank, home to foreign embassies. To the north, the Boulaq district houses many industries. But it's to the west that most inhabitants dreamed of living, their eyes glazing across wide boulevards, wondrous architecture and glorious open spaces. However, as with all major cities, there was poverty hiding behind the new facades. The eastern sector was overrun with crowded tenement buildings and narrow, cobbled lanes.

But everyone knew that the country constantly sought tourists, no more so than in the suburb of Giza. There was nothing that visitors loved more than to gaze in wonder at the pyramids and to ride on a camel, their heads covered with an old, traditional headdress.

Today Cairo was even hotter than usual. Damned hot. Sweat glistened under Menes' collar as, every day he sought to make a living. He so wanted to look after his new wife in the best way he could. Nothing would be too good for her in his eyes, but the country was in turmoil.

He still remembered when British troops were on every street corner. Even though they were now long gone, he still recalled their influence on the city. So many advances, he couldn't keep up with it all. In urban areas, new bridges and transport links had sprung up everywhere, even to all those high class areas he aspired to, like Zamalek and Helipolis.

Maybe one day, he told himself, one day.

But now the city was heaving with so many people. Some said the population had tripled since the last century. Well, if the streets outside their apartment were anything to go by, he could well believe it. People absolutely thronged the pavements so that, whenever he and Layla had to go out, it was necessary to push and shove simply to get anywhere at all.

There had even been riots a while ago. The papers had been full of it. Hundreds and hundreds of shops, theatres, hotels and casinos had been burned down and destroyed. No-one seemed to know who or why the initial touchpaper was lit, but once ignited, the crowds roared their approval as they rushed to be part of enacting their anger at the government.

The British, of course, left Cairo after the revolution in the early fifties, but still the city grew and still the masses gave vent to their anger. Sometimes Menes and Layla liked to walk along the Nile Corniche, taking advantage of the city's improved roads to get there. Only recently, the President had developed the waterfront, building some new desert satellite towns in the hope that the people living in poverty in overcrowded Cairo might be tempted to move there. But Menes had yet to be convinced. Cairo was certainly thronged, but it was so exciting to live there. It was also the place where people wanted to be, close to their family and friends.

Ah, that day when he and Layla first moved to their new home. Layla ran from room to room, glorying in all the modern fixtures and fittings. She was amazed. She was still only seventeen and, now that she had a husband, she was so excited at sharing her future with this man called Menes, well away from the rules and strictures of her parents and family. She couldn't believe her good fortune. Her husband was everything she had dreamed of. Good, kind and thoughtful. The only thing missing in their lives was a family. Every night she prayed that she would soon be pregnant but still her courses flowed, regular as clockwork.

In the early days, they used to love walking along the busy Cairo streets, looking at all the signs of how Egypt had progressed. Everywhere were bright lights, music, the latest fashions and groups of men on street corners, discussing the politics of the day.

What Layla particularly enjoyed was going to the cinema, where they could sit, hand in hand in the dark, watching how their country had managed to blend silver screen glamour with their centuries-old culture. Wide-eyed, she'd look up at the big screen and watch her idol Omar Sharif and his wife Faten Hamama.

Menes was interested in how their local film company, Studio Misr, seemed to be doing really well, launching the careers of many prominent Egyptian actors into international acclaim. But, privately, Menes preferred the thriller films that regularly came to their local cinema. He was sure they could easily rival that American Alfred Hitchcock in the use of special effects.

"All of this makes me proud to be an Egyptian," he told his wife with pride, even though secretly he harboured a fear about how his country was gearing up for war.

Trying to dismiss his own fears, Menes led his young wife to a pavement café, where they enjoyed a Turkish coffee whilst watching the world go by. Some restaurants even had belly dancers, but Layla didn't like them. They were much too crude for her.

"That's why I don't like going to the beach," she whispered to Menes. "I don't like the way so many young girls wear a bikini. To me, they look immodest." Layla knew she was now married but she couldn't erase all those years of deprivation and enforced modesty.

But Menes was again thinking of the times they lived in. There was no doubt that their country had changed under Nasser, its leader.

Layla's idyllic life started to fall apart when Menes was called up to the Egyptian army.

"I'm sorry, love, but I saw all this coming. I had hoped against hope that I wouldn't be involved, but it was inevitable. Despite my own feelings, you know I'm a proud man."

"I know love. That's what I love about you," squeezing his hand. "But do you really have to go?" cried Layla.

"You know I must, my dear. How would it look? I'd be vilified everywhere as a coward and I couldn't live with that. So, you'll just have to be brave, my dear, and I'll be back before you know it."

"Someone gave me an English newspaper the other day, and you know what they're saying? They actively fear Nasser, our great leader, noticing how he's raising our spirits and firing us up so that once again we become the leading nation we should be."

"Really?" said Layla, noticing her husband's worried frown. "But that's good news, isn't it? Doesn't it mean we're on the right path for victory? Someone told me at my sewing group the other day that once the enemy is frightened, our war is almost won."

But Menes still didn't look convinced. "But, at what cost? At what cost, eh?" his eyes staring vacantly at the far walls.

Layla didn't understand, so she did what she normally did in such situations. She changed the subject so that her dear man would smile again. That's all she wanted: just to make him happy. *Oh, if only she could find a way to get pregnant. She was sure that would finally bring a smile to Menes' face, especially if it were a boy.*

But the following evening, Menes was still reading as many newspaper reports as he could. Together they'd been watching the one Egyptian TV station, which was continuously portraying the streets of Cairo filled with flag-waving citizens, all shouting allegiance to their country and war to their enemies.

Menes felt sick in the pit of his stomach, but he daren't show his true feelings lest it worry his wife, so he kept silent.

"But I don't understand what it's all about," cried Layla.

"Well, as far as I can see," replied her husband, "it's been pretty much tit for tat reprisals by both sides. Guerilla groups based in places like Syria, Lebanon and Jordan have been attacking Israel, so of course they responded. And it looks like Nasser has been getting Soviet intelligence. They think that Israel is planning a campaign against Syria, but it may not be true. But I don't think Nasser cares about that. He'll seize on anything to justify war against the enemy."

Reading his mind, Layla said "Let's hear what the radio's saying."

Menes twiddled the dial to the Cairo radio station, which they preferred. Daily they received the all-day radio broadcast called The Voice of Thunder. The broadcaster knew that many of the enemy also listened in, having no TV station themselves.

"I think the broadcaster actually wants the Israelis to listen in," said Menes.

"How can you tell?" asked Layla, puzzled.

"Can't you hear all those terrible Hebrew words?" he said, having picked up the language over the years.

"But why would Nasser want the enemy to listen in? I don't understand," she said, shaking her head.

"Well, our leader doesn't care. To him, the most important thing is to spread the agreed propaganda as far and wide as possible to create a diversion. Everyone does it. If they can frighten the enemy, they'll do it."

Menes had reverted back to his newspaper. Page after page contained reports from correspondents with varied viewpoints.

"Just listen to what this man's saying," jabbing his nicotine-stained finger at the offending article. "For too long we have been at the mercy of other people like the French or the British. What right do they have to lord it over us in our own country? All our fathers hated the British in particular and always cheered on the guerrillas in their fight against colonial control. But, make no mistake, their faces soon changed when Egypt agreed to sign an agreement with them, even though it meant the British would withdraw within the following two years. I, for one, would never sign any agreement with a mad dog. Never!"

"I can hear the reporter shouting loud and clear from his printed article," said Menes.

"He's trying to stir us all up," whispered Layla, looking worried.

"Well," replied Menes. "Looks like he's succeeded. I and many more like me have all been called up. It's war for sure now."

By 14th May, Menai was mobilized just outside the Sinai, in support of Syria.

Now sitting in a tent, Menes was smoking hard, listening to one of his army colleagues. Abdul was feeling confident in his role as a foot soldier in the Egyptian army, as he shared a thin cigarette with another colleague. During a lull in their relentless training, they were taking a break in their tent.

"How can we fail?" Abdul boasted. "Everyone knows that the Zionists' state is only the size of a flea compared with us. Why, together with the twenty other Arab states, our land is more than a million square miles larger than the whole of the United States!"

His colleague somehow doubted that, but went along with it. Comparisons were good, boosting their confidence. "I reckon we outnumber them by more than forty to one."

Abdul's eyes were glazed, thinking, ever thinking. "We have to recognise our assets at this time. The Suez Canal and the Sinai region. They're ours. Don't forget: the enemies really need our canal so that their trading goods can pass through. In fact, any attack on our canal by the enemy would be their way of trying to goad Nasser into doing something stupid. But stupid, we're not."

"Yes, we'll be ready for them," said his companion. They say we've been massing weapons from Czechoslovakia and Russia to aid in our just battle."

Quietly sitting in the corner of the tent with Abdul and the others was a soldier called Menes. To them he was a bit of an enigma, preferring to puff huge plumes of smoke into the humid air rather than voice his opinion.

What's the matter with him anyway? thought Abdul. *Is he a Jew or something?*

But there was no doubting how the whole division loved their leader, Gamal Abdel Nasser. To them he was a God.

Nasser's vision, which had been drummed in to them all, was to form one Arab state stretching from central Asia, across the Middle East and Africa to the Atlantic in the west. His dream was for this new state to be modern, socialist and equipped with the latest weaponry and technology. Already Egypt and Syria had allied themselves with the might of the Soviets. Nasser knew that with the Russians' superior artillery, Israel couldn't possibly compete.

"Just look here," shouted Abdul, stabbing at an old, grimy newspaper. "Here's a picture of our leader, Look how delighted he is to have created the United Arab Command. Yes, we now have thirteen nations all committed to one purpose: to eradicate the Zionist entity. And remember, not one of our maps even bothers to include the entity called Israel. No Arab child learns of Israel's existence, nor should they".

To Abdul's mind, the war was already won.

May 15th.

"Men," cried Abdul, his chest expanding with pride. "I've received word. We're marching into Sinai."

A massive roar rang out. It was what they'd all be waiting to hear. Anything was better than sitting, day after day, waiting. Now was the time for action.

More and more Arab divisions followed over successive days. They all cheered when their great leader, Nasser, ordered the United Nations out of Sinai entirely. They knew that the Jews would be very angry about this, because Israel expected the UN to be a peace-keeping force. But how Abdul laughed when The Voice of Thunder reported that, despite the Israelis' pleas to U-Thant, the UN's Secretary General, the UN peace-keepers had been seen packing their bags and leaving the Sinai. The entire Arab world exploded in delirious joy, fuelling yet more Death to the Zionists' marches.

But Menes didn't know what to do. *Why do we always have to hate our neighbours? They only have a small bit of land whereas we have more than we know what to do with. If I were Nasser, I wouldn't fight the Israelis at all but talk to them,* he thought, knowing though that he mustn't voice his feelings out loud. He'd probably be shot!

So, even though Menes went through the motions of gathering his weaponry together, his feelings were very different from those of his companions. *Yes, that's what I'd do,* his inner voice continued. *I'd engage the Israeli leader in a deep conversation, negotiating peace in exchange for economic and technological help for our citizens. Allah only knows how the poor people are suffering. I'd do anything to help ease their problems.*

Oh, and I'd ask for help in changing what the schools teach our children. Instead of the current mania for hatred and misinformation about the history of our region, I'd ask for the Israelis' help in forming a new, more balanced educational syllabus, based on equality for the whole of the Middle East.

Closing his eyes for a moment, Menes already knew that sometimes you have to recognise when another person or nation has skills you need. But Menes was also realistic. He knew he didn't have a hope in hell of achieving his aims.

But still, I can dream can't I?

Menes knew, of course, that at present his ideas were an impossible ideal but his country could benefit so much from economic and educational assistance. He thought back to his own schooldays, where he'd always been a scholar, excelling in mathematics and science in particular. But his family was poor, so there was no chance he could achieve his dream of going to university. In any case there was all this talk of war. His father, disabled since childhood with polio, expected so much of his son and he didn't want to let him down. All Egyptian boys were brought up the same. It was imperative that, when the time came, they would bring honour to their family's name. He didn't want to let his poor father down.

So, night after night, Menes anguished about his life. He was a good son and loved his country but it was all this hatred. What on earth was he to do? It would be unthinkable and cowardly to refuse to join the Egyptian army just when it needed him so, in the end, he had no choice but to enlist.

Of course, all this had happened many times before. Even the year Menes was born, Egypt had joined with Syria, Iraq, Jordan and Lebanon to eradicate those "damned Jews" once and for all. And what had happened? Yet again, the Jews had prevailed. His father had been flabbergasted when he heard that his country had been attacked from the air by four Messerschmitt 109s, all with the Star of David painted on their flanks. The Egyptian army in 1948 had had no choice but to scatter to the east, ostensibly to link with other Arab forces. But they all knew the outcome back then. Jerusalem had been saved yet again!

But, now things looked different. Where were Israel's so-called allies? Egyptian newspapers reported with much glee how the US was still mired in Vietnam, France after an expensive battle in Algeria, had decided instead to befriend the Arabs, and Britain was not at all keen it seemed to engage in yet more warfare purely for a small number of Jews.

So, once again the Jews were alone in their fight but, as before over the centuries, this was not new. They had learned that, in times of trouble, their best weapon was themselves and their uncanny lateral thinking.

Whilst Menes was consumed with his feelings of indecision, another man on the opposite side had no such doubts.

CHAPTER SIXTEEN

Tel Aviv
1967

G ENERAL DOV COHEN lived in the suburbs of Tel Aviv. Soon every home in the town was emptying of Jewish men and young women, all called up for war within a moment's notice. The normally busy Allenby Street was soon absolutely deserted. Many of the older women, suddenly left behind, couldn't believe how easy it was to cross the street, something normally impossible in the middle of the day.

The stores in Dizengoff Street were quickly barred by roll-down, iron shutters. Elsewhere, those householders who hadn't fled to more peaceful climes, were busy taping down windows and sandbagging doors. There were no buses or even fire trucks. All had been mobilised for war. Every citizen re-membered what happened during other conflicts, so those with gardens dug zig-zag trenches, the gradient necessary to prevent sudden missiles from travelling the full length.

Quick thinking and ready planning weren't just for com-manders; it was essential for every war-weary person in this land they called *Haaretz* – or *Eretz Yisrael,* the land of Israel.

June 1967
Sinai Desert

Dov relayed to his team the instructions he had just received from on high. "This is Operation *Shlita*. Our mission is to destroy Nasser's forces in Sinai. Already other forces have joined him from Iraq, Jordan and Syria. But remember. We never have, nor ever will have, any intention towards territorial expansion. We have no desire to conquer any other people nor to take the Suez Canal, but we will always wage war against those who threaten our existence. Here are some of the stats," reading from a densely-packed sheet, "we will be allied against an estimated one hundred and thirty thousand troops, a thousand tanks and guns. But, be not afraid of their numbers. We can always outwit the enemy. Remember King David. Ingenuity always wins against might."

A soldier asked Dov "How long do you estimate our mission will take?"

Dov walked over to a map and, with a stick, pointed out their various positions. "If all goes well, it should take only three to five days. But, and this is a big but, if Nasser decides to bomb our citizens in Israel itself, then we may have to expand our operations towards sites in Syria, Jordan and Iraq. So, in answer to your question, soldier, let's see how it plays out."

Now turning to the whole section, their eager eyes lifted so as not to miss a word, "Remember, the term IDF – the Israel Defence Forces – is what the Americans call us. But we call ourselves *Zva Hagana Leyisrael,* or *Zahal* for short. In fact, I have a house in *Zahala*, on Joab Street, on the outskirts of *Tel Aviv,* to remind me. Joab in the bible was King David's nephew and commander of his army."

Dov looked his team in the eye. "We only fight when attacked. We are not interested in aggression unless sorely provoked by those who would be our enemies. To reiterate: we are not interested in land expansion or global interests for their own sake. All our people have ever wanted is to be left in peace, to live our lives in our own small land, as promised by *HaShem*. But today, as usual, yet another enemy is on the horizon who proclaims aloud that their sole intention is to effect our annihilation.

"So, men, yet again we must fight."

Before dismissing his team, comprising both men and women, Dov added the rejoinder "One last thing. Remember. Not one word to anyone about what we've discussed. Not your spouse, not your family, your friends. No-one. Our whole mission depends on secrecy. Do I have your word?" glancing around the room.

By 23.00 hours, Dov had finished his work for the day. After the briefing, he remained in the mess room, stubby pencil behind his ear, going over his battle plans. He preferred working at this time of day, when the intense heat had abated somewhat.

In front of him, spread out on the chipped wooden table, was a large, creased map of the entire region. Every so often, his eyes weary with lack of sleep, he would unpin a coloured peg and insert it somewhere else. Only he knew the significance of the different colours. It was imperative that this mission was successful. Everything depended on it.

Finally satisfied that there was not much more to be done, Dov drove home in his battered Deux Chevaux. Reaching up automatically, he opened the canvas roof to get a breath of the cool night air. The drive to his family's accommodation at the edge of the base didn't take long. He knew that his wife Sabra would still be awake, but their four children should be fast asleep by now, despite their worries.

Parking the car in front of their bungalow, he walked quietly to the darkened door and let himself in. Inside, he sidestepped the array of suitcases neatly lined up along the hallway. He didn't want to wake the children. Sabra, in her usual efficient manner, had been packed for days. She knew, of course, that something was coming, but never asked Dov for the details. She knew what he would say. Best she knew as little as possible.

Sabra had thoughtfully provided him with something to eat. Now watching him, leaning against the doorframe, her eyes were anxious. He kissed her perfunctorily before taking a shower to wash off all the desert sand before collapsing on the bed. He was soon out like a light. After watching him for a few moments, Sabra lay back and stared at the dark ceiling. Silently, she prayed to *HaShem*, as she'd done every night since growing up in the *kibbutz*.

Sabra's whole life had been dedicated to this land they called *eretz*, her whole childhood being focused on how to make it bloom and be fruitful. She and her friend Ruth, once they'd grown out of the nursery, were happy enough working on the land. This wasn't a place where individual farmers worked on their own plot. This was a collective ideal. A whole group settlement.

But life was hard at first, the terrain harsh and unforgiving. The Galilee area was full of swamps, the mountains in Judea were barren and full of rocks, and the Negev desert, to the south was inhospitable desert.

Many of the early young visiting students, like her friend Ruth Siskowski's mother, had their hearts in the right place, but unfortunately had little farming experience. They also found it difficult to adjust to the poor sanitary conditions. Sabra, so named because she was born there, could remember so many babies in the kibbutz nursery who had perished from diseases like cholera, typhus and malaria, which were rampant. The girls had grown used to the fact that all the children slept in children's houses and visited their parents only a few hours a day.

Security needed to be tight, as always. Every Jew had had to grow a hard skin, knowing that enemies kept coming, year after year. Some old-timers could be heard saying to one another "So, which enemy will it be today?" Such was life.

Sometimes it would be the *Bedouins* who would creep in during the night, raiding their settled areas and farms. Sometimes Sabra and Ruth would go outside and discover that their irrigation canals had been sabotaged or their crops burnt in the night.

But, like the other *sabras* living there, it was the only life they knew. Living together and working collectively was the best way they'd found to keep themselves secure in this land they'd lived in for thousands of years. And economically, the best way to increase the resources of their *kibbutz* was to farm collectively. This brought in far more money than individuals working alone.

But every night, Sabra and Ruth would collapse from their backbreaking labour. Their young bodies felt crushed, their heads hurt, their legs wobbling as the sun burned down on them day after day.

Many of the older members of their *kibbutz* had originated from Eastern Europe, fleeing from yet more pogroms and anti-Semitism. Sabra remembered that, in the early days, her friend Ruth in particular had enjoyed the informal meetings that were held outside in the evenings, everyone gathering around a camp fire to discuss the running of their commune. Ruth would often ask newcomers from Poland whether they knew her mother, as she was desperate to find out more about her family. All she had found out was that her mother's name was Adela, that she lived in Poland and had spent several months on the *kibbutz* picking grapes. Someone told her that many of the Polish women, brought up by strict religious fathers, liked the fact that those who wanted an easier life could still enjoy a Jewish life nonetheless. Friday nights were still *Shabbat* with a white tablecloth and lovely food and work was suspended wherever possible on Saturdays. And every *Yom Kippur,* the community would take the opportunity to discuss their fears for the future of the kibbutz.

Ruth had grown used to the way the women and men treated each other. Women called their husbands *ishi* (my man) rather than the standard Hebrew word for husband *ba'ali*, meaning 'my master'. By degrees, Ruth discovered what must have happened to her mother. During the evening discussions with the other young people at the time, the young Adela must have succumbed to the advances of another student. The lure of the *kibbutz* ideals coupled with the romance of the warm tropical nights had clearly brought the inevitable result. Early in 1932, Adela had found herself pregnant. No longer could she ignore the signs. As Ruth eventually found out, at first her mother had thought the nausea was because she'd been in the hot sun for too long, but as the months wore on, it became obvious.

As a collective, the *kibbutz* women helped Adela, of course. To them, it was as natural as breathing. This would be another *sabra* to be born in this precious land and so they were over-joyed. But for Adela, who had left her young husband at home in Poland for this student sabbatical, there was only one thing to do after the birth.

Baby Ruth Siskowski was left in the *kibbutz* nursery. The adults in the community did their utmost to make the chil-dren's house into a children's home. It was fully furnished to accommodate every age group. Surrounding the home was a courtyard, well equipped with everything that a growing child would need. There were also parks with playgrounds, flowering plants, hiding places and playgrounds.

But meantime, Ruth's grieving mother Adela went home to her Polish husband. A few years later, another daughter, Hanna, would be born. Later, as the Nazis moved in to Poland and forced the family into the ghetto, Adela was relieved that at least one member of her family would be safe: her secret love child Ruth. She also fervently hoped that a precious artefact, a *meleke* stone, that she'd left buried in the garden with a note, would explain everything should one of her daughters live to adulthood.

As Ruth and Sabra grew older, inevitably their *kibbutz* began to assume a more prominent military role, one forced upon them due to the constant attacks by Arabs living in countries completely surrounding their tiny country. Sabra could never understand why, when her country was the size of a postage stamp, and the Arab lands were absolutely massive in comparison, the Arabs still felt the need to covet it. The Arabs had more than enough land themselves. Why did they want yet more? So, to protect themselves, rifles had to be purchased or made and *kibbutz* members drilled and shooting abilities practised.

By the time Sabra and Ruth joined the Israeli army, and Sabra went on to marry her soldier husband Dov, their minds were set. Although they had loved the *kibbutz* life as children, lately their thoughts had hardened. Their sense of identification with the *kibbutz* and its goals diminished. It wasn't just their personal frustration with other members, it was the fact that they were part of a generation born and raised in the *kibbutzim* who hadn't inherited their parents' fiery ideological and motivational drive to 'settle the land'. So, joining the army proved a turning point for them both.

Recalling all the dreams and eventual disillusionment of her childhood, Sabra at last fell into a deep sleep. By the time Sabra awoke, her husband Dov was already gone. Their agreed signal was an old clock, which no longer worked, sitting on top of the wall cupboard, out of the children's reach. Every morning after Dov's departure, the first thing she did was check it. Her hand to her mouth, Sabra saw the inevitable. Both hands had been turned to twelve o'clock. The time had come.

"Hurry up children," she shouted as she roused each of them out of bed. "We have to go. Now!"

"Can I take Mischka?" asked Noa, the youngest.

"Yes, yes," ruffling her daughter's curly head before pushing each of them into the bathroom and laying clean clothes out on their beds.

In truth, the family was used to it. All their lives had been dominated by sirens and sudden curfews. Soon, Sabra was reversing their stationwagon out of the compound and driving the family to their agreed safe zone.

"Please keep *Aba* safe," said a small voice in the back, as skilfully Sabra drove quickly away.

Hours later, Dov's tanks were moving towards *El Arish*, the main base of the Egyptian seventh division. Dov knew that, whilst other nations at war could afford to lose a battle, recover and still continue, this wasn't the case for tiny Israel.

"If we fail this battle, our country will be overrun." he told his tank commander.

A simple nod of agreement came from his taciturn companion.

CHAPTER SEVENTEEN

Egyptian frontier
Sinai
1967

R UTH SISKOWSKI FELT tired. Her brow was dripping with sweat and she longed for the comfort of her own bed. She was thirty-four years old and had recently been promoted to the position of Lieutenant, one of the few women in the combat troops in her Company.

Fleetingly, she wondered about her childhood friend, Sabra Cohen, but knew that with several small children, and being the wife of an army General, Sabra had her own life to lead.

Ruth's fiancé, Lev, was platoon commander in the Division. "After this is all over," Lev had told her, "we'll get married. I'm weary of this life and long for some home comforts and would dearly love for us to raise a family."

It was what Ruth wanted too, more than anything. She didn't think she'd ever find out what really happened to Adela, her mother. But one thing Ruth could do was start afresh with her own family, well away from past horrors of pogroms and the Nazis.

Life was *b'shert*, decreed from above. That's what everyone said and she believed it too.

Meanwhile, she had a job to do if ever they were going to keep the Arabs at bay. Binoculars to her eyes, the panorama spread before her. All she could see for miles was their own armoured brigade, strategically positioned right up to the horizon. There were hundreds of half-tracks, tanks and support vehicles. All were fully alert, engines revving. Helmets were on, chin-straps tightened, and every ear was tuned to the radio nets.

All was ready for Nasser to attack at dawn. Ruth's job was to act as part of the reconnaissance force, to locate the enemy and to lead the tanks towards the enemy. She drove an American CJ-5 jeep which had been souped up by some of the guys. It was pretty makeshift, she knew, because if too much ammunition and food rations were loaded, the tyres would sink into the sand.

The latest scout report was that Nasser's Egyptian 7th Division awaited them across the border, plus further units behind it, snaking back to central Sinai. On another flank, to the northeast was another large task force, calling themselves the Palestinian Force. With a wry smile, Ruth wanted to shout out to them. "We're all Palestinian, brothers. Don't you see? Palestine isn't a country; it's the whole of this region, stretching across from Jordan in the east. Why can't we all live together?" But Ruth knew it was no use. She couldn't discuss anything with those of a closed mind.

It was decreed. Ruth's division would be the first to cross the border, ahead of the tanks. The project involved her brigade's two armoured battalions to strike north from their current position on the Israeli side towards the junction on the Egyptian side. Instructions had filtered down from high command. They were to make for *El Arish* in Sinai.

Back home, the newspapers *Maariv* (the evening) and *Haaretz* (the land) were all calling for the Prime Minister to appoint someone else as Minister of Defence because many wanted a unity government. But Ruth wasn't generally interested in politics; just what she needed to know to do her job to the best of her ability.

Ruth reached for a pack of gum, anything to ease the stress she was feeling. Every day rumours abounded that tomorrow would be the day they attacked, but every time, the sun went down and still they waited and waited.

Finally the day arrived. Ruth's jeep would be involved in leading out the tanks during the night. But, under cover of darkness, it would be easy for a lumbering tank to get stuck in a deep sand ravine, so she had to be sure she guided them away from such pitfalls. Every night, she preferred to sleep under a blanket on the sand. Inside the vehicle was just too cramped. And every time an alert arrived, she tried to mentally rehearse herself to face death when it arrived.

A friend was stationed in one of the half-tracks. She didn't like it, she told her. "It's like a coffin."

"Better that than a real one.".

Days later, and several miles from Ruth's division, there still remained enemy tanks within their sights.

General Dov Cohen ordered "fire".

His brigade's two tank battalions of Pattons and Centurions were positioned on high ground, three thousand metres from the enemy column. Dov shouted to his next in command "Just like Judah Maccabee did when confronting his enemy, always attack from on high, and always position yourself where the enemy has nowhere else to flee."

His team nodded as the onslaught began.

Several hours later, an enormous cloud of dust was spotted on the road outside *Jebel Maara*. Dov and his team were exhausted but their impossible mission was edging towards an incalculable victory. Military binoculars to his eyes, it was clear what was happening. Several Egyptian battalions were on the run, desperate in their rush west towards the Canal.

The scenes of destruction were terrible, mile after mile. Burnt-out tanks, trucks and other vehicles lined the route home for Dov and his team. Everywhere were Egyptian army trucks lying flat on bare rims at the side of the road. The air smelt of gasoline, burning rubber, cordite, mingling with the sunbaked smell of melting asphalt.

Dov felt sorry for the Egyptians.

"Look over there," he pointed, as more men were spotted in the distance, their bodies heaped at the side of the road. "Most of them were not even proper soldiers. Those poor men look like simple fellahin peasants from the delta. What did they know about war?" shaking his head.

"Sir," someone shouted at the back of their tank. "I think one of them's still alive."

Dov ordered a halt, whilst he jumped down to investigate.

"Be careful, Sir. May be a trap," they shouted. Dov nodded, trusting to his instincts nevertheless. They hadn't let him down thus far in his life.

A man in Egyptian army uniform lay at the side of the road, his hands bloodied, his legs positioned at a crazy angle. But there were signs of life. His team leader was right. The Egyptian's eyes kept fluttering open and closed involuntarily, as he lay in the sweltering heat.

Quickly, Dov reached under the prostrate man's armpits and pulled him sideways towards some bushes growing along the route. This would afford him some measure of shade whilst Dov checked for his vital signs. He pulled out of his top uniform pocket a small mirror which he held to the man's mouth. The glass fogged up. Now signalling to his team, together they lifted the casualty up and into the back of the tank where one of their medics could assess his injuries.

Dov unscrewed the cap of a small phial he always carried and, lifting up the man's head, he poured a few drops of brandy through his parched lips. Dov knew that in normal times, the man probably didn't drink alcohol. But, as with the Jewish religion, he suspected that in times of trouble, the pursuit of life supersedes all other considerations. Coughing, the man managed to swallow the fiery elixir before dropping into unconsciousness again.

Days later, after all hostilities were over and the six day war was finally won, Dov took some time off to find out where the Egyptian casualty had been taken. Eventually, after locating him in a field station, Dov pulled back the flap of the tent and ducking his head walked into the shady interior.

A man lay in an army bed, his head propped up on a pillow, his leg bandaged. Seeing the Israeli uniform, the man shrunk back in fear.

"Don't worry," said Dov in the Arabic he'd learned at school. "I come bearing gifts," putting a small bottle of whisky on the wooden table by the bed. "Thought you might be in need of some of this when the drugs start to wear off," holding out his hand as a sign of friendship. "Once you're well again, keep it hidden away with your other medicines. There'll come a time when you or your family will need it. Mark my words."

The patient was puzzled. He still didn't know who had rescued him from almost certain death on that road of destruction. "I don't understand," he said in a faltering voice. "You're obviously an Israeli. Why would you care about me? To you, I'm the enemy, and not even anyone important," his watery eyes eyeing the tall man in front of him. "Is this a trick? Do you want me to do something terrible?"

Dov tried to smile to put the man at ease, but he was never any good at smiling, so he let his words do the explaining. "No, no. Please be reassured. This is no trick. My name is Dov Cohen and I commanded a team of Israeli soldiers in the Sinai. On the sixth day of the war, my tank was returning when we saw you lying at the side of the road with signs of life. So, common humanity meant I had to do what I could to help you."

"Oh, so you were the one who saved me? I still don't understand. Why would you do that when you must have spent days shelling Egyptian soldiers by the thousand?"

At last Dov managed to form a smile. "You know, in my country we have to join the army when we reach manhood, so over the years I've learned a lot. Yes, unfortunately, my people have had to fight for ever to keep themselves alive, but one injured man in front of your eyes is very different to thousands massed against you. When I see one man in trouble, from whichever side, I just have to try to do whatever I can to help. It's my duty. So, that's what happened. For you, I was the Samaritan the other side of the road."

The patient couldn't believe it. Tears were forming in his eyes. "What can I give you in return. I'm just a poor man. I don't have much…."

Dov shook his head. "Just seeing you alive and getting better is all I need," he said. "We're all casualties of war, my friend. For myself, I'm in mourning for a fellow soldier, a young woman who was a friend of my wife's. Her name is Ruth and she died from Egyptian fire a few hours ago. I'm just on my way to tell my wife. She will be heartbroken to hear the news. I just hope I manage to find the right words to tell her that Ruth was a heroine to the last. She always thought of others before herself and now her life is over. It's a tragedy."

Menes looked abashed. *Why should I live, whilst this Israeli woman die? It doesn't make sense. We're all human.*

Dov could see that this Egyptian was sorrowful at hearing his news, so this was a good man. Turning to the patient, a sudden thought came into Dov's head. "What's your name, anyway? It would be nice to put a name to a fellow soldier."

"My name is Menes."

CHAPTER EIGHTEEN

Toulouse
April 2020

"I T'S FINISHED, AT last!"

Simon couldn't believe it. He'd just wrapped a long shoot that was totally upended by a growing world pandemic. Right through the final scenes, he had to continually shout over the public address system, reminding cast and crew to change their masks. Wearing them too long meant that the masks became too moist and therefore ineffective. And the TV news kept insisting on social distancing. That had been the hardest part. "How am I supposed to keep everyone apart when the film requires the actors to liaise?" he agonised.

Simon was glad that he wasn't starting his film right at that minute. At least he'd managed to keep within his crowd-funded budget during the months before the virus. It was the Egyptian scenes that had caused him the most headaches. At least now he could forget all those daily safety briefings and his newly-devised colour-coded zones for the crew and the cast.

After thanking his cast, crew, costume and set designers, including Leah, after the shoot was finished he'd sent the film to post-production for editing. He'd even paid for pizzas all round to show his gratitude to their individual dedication to his project. After all, it wasn't just his project, it was Moshe's life-long idea too.

Already he had uploaded the film to special editing software and made some cuts and amendments. He'd found an editing programme that was particularly easy to use, but still needed to make sure that its flow and continuity were logical and that the story as a whole made sense. His team had also added the audio tracks, matching them up with the film, and adjusting the biblical background music, as appropriate, so that it wasn't too loud or soft at critical moments.

Now the all-important thing was to show his film to the right people. Moshe had been adamant. If the film was to make any sense at all and to make an impact on how the general public viewed the Jewish people, then it had to be distributed all over the world.

So, his biggest decision now was how to distribute his film when so many standard cinemas around the world were closing. In the end, he decided to bypass cinemas and go straight to VOD, which would hopefully appeal to frazzled families desperate for entertainment options.

"Actually, Simon," said an industry colleague, "handled correctly, your film could be an amazing digital debut. Think about it," his eyes glazing, "online distribution could recoup far more revenue than cinemas ever could!"

"That's interesting," replied Simon. "I was worrying that I'd need cinemas to be at least half full for my film, to make sense financially."

He'd put so much work into the project, he just hoped the public would understand what he'd been trying to achieve.

Even Moshe looked excited when his son spoke to him after all the filming was put to bed. "I'm really proud of you, son," he said. "It's what I've always dreamed of."

"I know what you mean," said Simon, "It's a good job you don't do social media. Every day I read discussions fuelled by people who have never been educated fully about the history of the whole area of Palestine. It drives me crazy. So many have built up opinions based on unsound knowledge and biased media reports. At least I've finished the film now. We can only hope that it redresses the balance a bit, for the sake of the Jewish people at least," wiping the sweat off his brow. He'd worked long and hard and needed a break.

Moshe noticed how tired his son looked, so changed the subject. "When's the baby due, son? Can't be long now, surely?"

Simon smiled. "No, it won't be long now. The doctors have given her a date at the end of April."

"And, how is Leah?"

"Oh, she's absolutely blooming. Once the nausea went, she looks really well.

"*Nu*, and is it a boy or a girl? Doctors can do amazing things these days, I understand."

"Oh, both of us agreed early on. We didn't want to know. As long as the baby is well, we'll be happy. Don't worry Papa. You'll know soon enough. Not long to wait now," hugging his father in a sudden rush of fondness. He'd lived a life full of difficulties. At least, the coming birth should give him a bit of *nachas* he deserved.

"Papa, now that the film's finally finished," said Simon, trying to turn his father's thoughts in a different direction, "I'd like to invite Menes, his wife Layla and his sons round to see how we celebrate *Pesach*. Yes, I'm sure he'd be interested to see how we incorporate all those old traditions into our festivals." Thinking of his film, he continued "We could even discuss the interactions between the Jews and the Egyptians all those years ago. I mean, our festival's all about our people's flight from Egypt, so it seems appropriate somehow. What do you think? Could you cope with that? I'll help with the arrangements."

"Not sure that older boy of his….what's his name?……. would want to come. I'm usually good at reading behind people's outward appearances, and with him, I'm not so sure," said his father in his usual stoic manner.

"Oh, you mean Sami?" replied Simon. "Yes, I know what you mean. The other boys all seem nice, likeable lads, but him? He's always so morose. He never looks you in the eye when you talk to him. But, it's only right that we invite him anyway. Let's see what happens."

"OK," said Moshe. "I haven't done any entertaining in a long while. It'll be good to blow the dust off my *Hagaddah,* the old Passover book that I brought with me from *der Heim,*" he said, showing a growing enthusiasm for the idea. "But, what about your wife, Simon? Will she be well enough to attend? She must be near her time by now?"

Simon smiled. "Oh yes. Not long now. I've never seen her look so well. Thank G-d she's recovered from all that sickness in the early months. It's strange but as soon as that first magical heartbeat could be felt, the nausea vanished never to return.

I'm sure she'd love to come round and meet up with Menes and his family again. It'll give her something else to do other than her endless knitting!"

So Simon called Menes, who said, after a moment's hesitation, they'd love to come round. "What day did you say it was? When should we arrive?" calculating how long it would take to drive down to Toulouse from St. Antonin.

Simon checked his diary. "The *Seder* night – that's what we call the beginning of the Passover – is Wednesday 8th April and it comes in around 20.45h. All our festivals start in the evening, when the moon rises. You probably do the same. People say that Passover is the oldest continuously-observed celebration in the world, you know. Anyway, I suggest you plan to arrive at Papa's house for 20.00h. Do you remember where his house is? Have you got GPS in your van? Basically, you need to take *Sortie 1* off the A68 autoroute towards *L'Union*, and Papa's house is in the road behind the kosher butcher's shop. Oh, and one more thing, would your youngest boy agree to read the bit which asks 'Why is this night different from all other nights'? I'll understand if he feels he doesn't want to, but it's traditional for the youngest in the room to read that line. Tell your family that we'll be serving lamb, but there'll be plenty of vegetables in case anyone's vegetarian."

Despite himself, Moshe was feeling quite excited. Increasingly lately he found himself thinking about Israel. When times were good, Jerusalem was always thronged with people who had come to marvel at the temple service and to celebrate together. But he also knew, only too well, that at other times,

Jews had had to hide in cellars or attics, sometimes trying to make the service seem to be merely a family gathering in case of discovery.

Increasingly, lately, he found himself becoming more spiritual. *They say everyone's the same when they become old,* he thought. *It's like a bet,* chuckling, *when the time comes, better to be safe than sorry.*

It was so different when he was young. Life changes you. He thought back to when his dear wife Naomi, of blessed memory, was alive. It had always been a chore preparing for *Pesach* beforehand. His eyes glazed as the memories kept flooding back. Why was it always easier to remember events which happened years ago than it was to recall what he did yesterday? Yet further evidence of his age. He pictured again how Naomi, every year, had always been rushing round looking for *Chametz* (bread and other yeast products) and cleaning the house from top to bottom. She had been brought up in a much more observant family than he had. He wiped a tear from his eye, remembering always remembering, how his family had been murdered in the Holocaust. But Naomi always knew that there must be no sign of any bread, yeast or products containing these things anywhere in the house. For the duration of the eight-day festival, everyone ate *Matzoh,* which was a special flat crispy bread made without yeast, as it was symbolic of when the Israelites had to flee from their land, leaving them no time to bake the bread fully.

He had a sudden vision of Naomi in those early years. Her hair had been long in those far off days and surprisingly fair, her eyes wide and slanted slightly upwards at the edges. With a smile he recalled how her mother, a fierce woman, kept a strict eye on her precious daughter and never let her walk out on her own. She wasn't completely innocent though; where there was a will, there was a way.

There had been a hay barn at the back of their semi-rural house in the countryside just south of Toulouse. She had sneaked into the barn with him, telling her mother she was out collecting apples. Many were the furtive kisses and scrambling that had taken place there, Moshe recalled with a smile, but that was as far as it went. Moshe was but a year older than she and no more experienced than she was. Naomi wasn't really interested in him then, not in that sense anyway; she was just avid for attention and he certainly provided it. On many an occasion, as he was kissing her neck, his hands roaming freely over her body, her eyes would stare past him out into the fields and dream of the future.

It had been Naomi, he recalled, who reminded him all about the Passover festival. After all he'd endured from the Nazis, for a while he'd wanted nothing more to do with religion, ever. She told him that the evening which ushered in *Pesach* was known as the *Seder night*. It was always a joyous occasion, when the family would usually invite strangers to join with them in partaking of the special meal. That's what he liked to do now, in fond remembrance.

Anyway, Moshe with a distant glint in his eye, could still see his Naomi wiping her hands on her apron, dusty with *Pesachi* potato flour, whilst whispering sweet nothings in his ear when her mother wasn't looking.

Oh why am I always in such a fluster, she told him later, *whenever I meet someone nice? Whatever will Moshe think of me with this old apron on and covered in potato flour?*

He recalled how she had excused herself as politely as she could, before rushing into the scullery where she splashed cold water onto her burning cheeks. She had then fished out of a cupboard a hairbrush, and bent her head forward so that she could first brush out all the tangles, and then throw her hair back again before brushing it until it shone. She had then somehow pinned it back into a tidy and, she hoped, not too demure knot at the nape of her neck. She had then changed into her best dress and smoothed it down over her ample hips. Oh, how Moshe remembered those hips.

It was then that her brother Eli had rushed in. Moshe could still remember every bit of that magical evening, just as if it had happened yesterday.

"Oh, where have you been?" cried Naomi. "Mama's been looking everywhere for you. Do you know your *Ma nishtana* (child's prayer) for this evening?"

"'Course. I did it last year, didn't I?" he replied with little concern, as he munched on a green apple and shooed some chickens out into the back yard again.

"Oh, who's that I saw with Papa?" he asked his sister.

"Oh, it's just some boy Papa brought home for our *Seder* meal," she replied with an air of non-concern. It didn't fool Eli, though, who knew his sister better than anyone else.

"Oh ho, someone you like the look of, eh?" he smirked.

"Oh, be gone with you. Who'd have brothers!" she replied, throwing his apple core after him with evident irritation.

After the meal and the rest of the proceedings, Moshe had asked her father whether he could take a walk with Naomi. It was a fine evening, and Naomi had worked hard preparing for the festival all day, so her parents agreed – not, though, without some misgivings. Her mother was tearful: "Naomi's so grown up now; she's no longer my little girl. Soon she will be married and I will have lost her," she cried.

"Nonsense," he replied, "She knows how to look after herself," but inwardly remembering only too well when he himself was a boy, with all the mixed and turbulent emotions that adolescence brings.

That evening must have heralded a watershed in Naomi's life, thought Moshe all these years later. They had spoken long into the night, Moshe telling her of his difficult childhood and that terrible time in the camp.

After walking for quite a while, they found themselves in the hay barn at the back of the house where they rested a while. Soon, Moshe turned over on his side and pulled Naomi to him in an embrace. This was something she thought she knew all about. She responded joyfully, pulling his head down to hers and responding to his kisses. But when he pushed her back onto the sweet-smelling hay, she cried out. This was not something she was used to, but he was a man of the world and told her that this was as natural as the lambs in the field. She was frightened and tried to push him away, but he was too strong for her. Sweat was palpable on his brow and on his muscular forearms as he had his way with her. Slowly she became aware of the moon and the stars in the heavens above, and of the chill of the night air as it crept in all around them. Soon, he rolled off her and lay by her side, a piece of straw between his teeth.

Later that night, she went home, in a dream and feeling very different from the person who had left earlier that evening. She told him how she had felt she didn't want to see anyone, just to be left alone to reflect on the immense thing that had happened to her. On seeing her mother she said she was tired and managed to escape to her bed without too much difficulty. She had agreed to meet with Moshe again two weeks later when he would next be free, but by then she was already worried. Her courses, which usually were as regular as clockwork, had not arrived. After another two weeks, she told her mother who was hysterical.

"Whatever have you done?" she cried. "You have ruined your life!"

"No, mother. I have told Moshe and he has agreed to marry me as soon as it can be done. All is arranged."

Moshe grinned as he remembered his father-in-law's dry comment on hearing the news. "He's a Jew, isn't he? So," spreading his hands in a wide shrug, "what's the problem?"

But the birth of Simon had not been easy.

Moshe and Naomi were living in an old, converted barn, as they had very little money.

The following Spring proved unusually wet and windy. The winds blowing in from the sea attacked the olive trees, bending the spindly branches this way and that. The inclement weather rattled the door frames of their small dwelling and sent cascades of moisture coursing down to form stagnant puddles on the straw-strewn floor beneath. The dark sky gave a deep portent of foreboding to the occupants within, exacerbated when a sharp gust suddenly blew out the only source of light from a wax candle perched precariously above their heads.

The occupants of the bedroom seemed unaware of the raging elements without as they concentrated on the job in hand. With a chapped, work-worn hand the midwife wearily brushed away a straying tendril of mousey hair before standing up and slowly stretching her aching back muscles in a vain attempt to ease her tiredness and frustration. Today not even the usually successful trick of moving her neck round in a laborious circular movement seemed to make any difference. With a suppressed expletive she reached up her muscle-bound arm to the mantle and lit a new candle. She emitted a sigh of relief as the candle stub sprang back into life and cast a shadowy ring again around the tired, sleeping woman in the rumpled bed beneath.

The room showed signs of hasty removal of furniture to one side of the room, most of it stacked precariously in one corner. All that remained in the centre was the high creaky bed with its uncomfortable rail, flaking here and there with rust. At the far end of the room, orange embers from the small fireplace spluttered sporadically in their vain effort to warm the room, their bright glow casting ghoulish reflections on the room's inhabitants. On an old wooden table by the bed stood a large jug of hot water, various jars, a sharp knife and a length of grey cord. On a wire slung above the fireplace were hung some clean but worn white cloths, brought in by the midwife. The cloths were perfectly placed to ensure a gentle airing from the steadily rising warmth from the fire.

With a sudden scream Naomi was jerked awake by the

insistent pain. She shouted out for Moshe, her new husband, but the midwife said:

'Hush, my dear, this is no place for a man. Just push when I tell you. There›s nothing to fear.'

Reassured, Naomi quietened again until another spasm rent her weary body. It seemed to be working of its own accord, entirely separate from her free will. It forced her to push with all her might in a massive bearing down action, her head lifting involuntarily off the pillow as she grimaced with the supreme effort. The midwife placed her ear against Naomi's stomach, looking down at her pocket watch. With a frown, the midwife left the bed for a moment and crossed the room to whisper to a neighbour, who had stood by agonisingly to offer what assistance she could. The two whispered conspiratorially, out of earshot of the agonised Naomi.

"I'm worried about the baby. I can't hear a heartbeat. It's already been nigh on eighteen hours. If it doesn't come soon, I'm going to have to do something drastic or it'll be a dead thing I'll be bringing into the World, an' no mistake."

The woman nodded in agreement, as she cast a quick look at the poor woman in the bed. She remembered all too well bringing her own sons into the World all that time ago. All women feel a bond of empathy at such times, and the woman was no exception, having brought three into the World already. Although the whole family had been shocked that Naomi had had to get married so soon, she was not about to abandon her now in her time of need. The midwife now pushed her sleeves up in determination, ready for the ordeal ahead.

Outside, a streak of lightening momentarily illuminated their faces, as if agreeing with the unfairness of life, then was gone literally in a flash. They returned to Naomi's bedside again and resumed their positions either side of the bed, in preparation for the grand climax. With another agonising scream, Naomi shouted:

"Get it out of me, just get it out. I can't stand any more."

And with that, the midwife saw the dark fluff of the baby's head. Praise be! She eased its ears gently out of the birth canal, twisting the baby's shoulders slightly as the rest of its slimy body slithered and wriggled out into the yellow ring of candlelight that illuminated the room. The tiny baby, red and wrinkled, lay still at the foot of the bed as the midwife's hands worked feverishly over its body. She gently massaged its chest rhythmically and methodically whilst the other woman rushed to wipe away the mucus from its tiny nose and mouth. Suddenly a gasp, then a plaintive mewling cry rent the air, as the two women sighed simultaneously with relief. With luck and divine guidance, the baby would be none the worse for its ordeal. The midwife reached down for the sharp knife and cut the umbilical cord sharply and cleanly in a practised way, before cleaning the area carefully and efficiently. She carried the now crying baby over to the ready-prepared large bowl of water, which Ester had topped up with warm water in readiness.

'Praise Be to the Lord," she said, as she went to Naomi's side in a subconscious move of solidarity and reassurance. The midwife finished patting the baby dry before enfolding it in a warm towel. The baby yawned and began to sleep the exhausted sleep of the newborn. The midwife walked over to the bed and placed the baby in the crook of Naomi's arm.

"Congratulations, you now have a healthy son. He's a little

small and delicate due to the long labour you had, so he'll need looking after very carefully."

Tears of joy glistened momentarily on Naomi's cheeks, as she closed her eyes and succumbed to the warm drowsy feeling of complete exhaustion. She was so glad it was a boy. There would be time enough later to give Moshe more children.

Her mind floated back to when she had first realised she was pregnant. They had had such plans, she and Moshe

But then her morning sickness grew.

Another gust of wind outside the house brought Naomi back to the present, where she could only reflect on the circumstances with which she was faced. However, she was nevertheless awash with love for her new baby son.

The midwife carefully removed the infant and placed him down safely as if he were a china doll about to break. She re-adjusted the folds of the cloth in an attempt to keep the baby as snug as possible. She then went out to fetch Moshe to tell him about his new firstborn. She found him slumped in an old chair, the brown material cracked and strained as if in very sympathy with the cares of its occupant. She smiled to herself as she realised that he seemed just as exhausted as his wife by the protracted worry and tension of it all. She hadn't the heart to awaken him. After all, there would be time enough for the two of them to share in the joys of bringing up their first child together. The midwife yawned herself, suddenly realising it had been a very long night, as she carefully closed the front door silently behind her.

Finally, Moshe awakened and rushed in to his wife and new born son.

"I'd like to call him Simon,' said Moshe, "after my father *Shimon*.

Naomi agreed. "I rather like the name."

"Welcome to the world, Simon. But first, we need to organise the *Brit* ceremony."

The next day Naomi felt a little better, but was still not strong enough to leave her bed. She let her mind drift back to how her life had changed during her early life. As a child she had been brought up to respect all the ancient Jewish traditions. Even when there was not enough money for many candles, her mother had always lit a candle stub at dusk each Friday to welcome in the day of rest, and to commemorate the Festival of Lights at *Chanukah* time. But then had come Moshe.

Her father had always been a good and kind man and he recognised these qualities in others. She was sure this was why he had always remarked that there certainly existed a man called Jesus and that he was clearly a good man. "There is no greater good than healing the sick," he had always told her. But that was as far as it went. Her father said that every century there were men who are wise beyond the age in which they live, but to ordinary folk who are unable to understand such wisdom, such men appear to be cloaked in mystical or spiritual halos beyond comprehension. Her father, therefore, refused to believe that Jesus was the son of G-d, but continued to believe that there's always room in the world for a caring human being.

Naomi remembered particularly what her father used to tell her, over and over again. "It's unfair to accuse the Jews of any of the New Testament tragedies. I firmly believe that it was the Pharisees and the Romans who were the chief protagonists in all of those things. I do hope that in the future, long after I have gone (and I don't have long for this world, child), the Jews are not continually persecuted over this."

Now back in the present, Moshe could only shake his head at how much had happened since then. He had always admired his father-in-law. He was a wise man before his time. And Simon, their only son, had been born strong and healthy and had always been a good boy.

What more could a man need?

The day of the *Seder* arrived. Moshe was glad he'd been able to collect the lamb joint and bone they'd need from the kosher butcher around the corner. He was also grateful to Simon for thoughtfully bringing as many *Haggadah* prayers books as he could find. He had a feeling that Menes and his family might well be able to read the Hebrew texts, too, because so much of the two languages was widely understood in the area."

Right on time, at 20h prompt, Menes, his wife and four sons arrived. "Er, Sami couldn't come, I'm afraid. He's been coughing really bad for a few days now and so I told him to stay in bed at home. I didn't want him to bring any germs into your house, not with Simon's wife being nearly due."

Moshe thanked Menes for his thoughtfulness, accepting the lovely flowers which he'd brought from the market.

Simon acted as host, ushering the family into armchairs whilst Menes' wife joined Leah in the kitchen. The table was set with Moshe's special *Pesachi* tableware, and the traditional symbols were present. There were the hard-boiled eggs in salt water, their round, life-like shape depicting mourning. There were the traditional herbs: *maror (bitter herb)* representing the bitterness of slavery, and *haroseth* (sweet apple and honey) representing mortar used by the Hebrew slaves in Egypt. There was also a lamb shank-bone, depicting the sacrificial lamb. Moshe, despite his failing eyesight, read out loud the service, following the story of their people's exodus from the promised land. Menes was astounded how similar the Hebrew letters in the *Haggadah* prayer book were to the Arabic letters of his childhood. Both languages were read from right to left on the page.

Truth be told, Menes and his four sons were surprisingly fascinated by the similarities between the ancient Hebrew text and Arabic. The family dutifully followed the symbolic Pesach practices as Moshe read them. First, though, Moshe took the middle *matza* from the stack of three and broke it into two pieces. He then put one aside for the *Afikoman* that concludes the meal part of the *Seder*, the other piece he held up to the family.

It was amazing how much Moshe remembered of his religion, despite his early setbacks.

"*Ha lachma anya*…this is the bread of affliction," he reminded them all. "In good times, this *matza* stands for the affliction of Egypt. This is what we have, this is what we eat, because there wasn't time to bake the bread properly before we had to flee. But when times are really bad and we are being persecuted again….*ha lachma* anya..this is *our* bread of affliction," he told them solemnly.

Fingers were then dipped in the wine and drops put on the side of their plate, to symbolise the plagues that were endured. Then, Menes' youngest son was asked to read the traditional *Ma nishtona*, asking: "why is this night different from all other nights...?." Once the service was finished, Leah served the meal, and much wine was drunk.

Afterwards, Moshe gave a broad hint to Menes that he wouldn't mind being invited to his place for when they celebrate... ."what do you call it?....oh, I know *Eid*. Isn't that your celebratory festival following that month long fast you do?" Chuckling, momentarily, "I'm glad that on *Yom Kippur*, we only have to fast one day!"

They all laughed.

In truth, Menes was inwardly very worried about what Sami would think about this Jewish family visiting them for *Eid*. But often these days, Menes followed his instincts, thinking that the future often solved itself. In any case, the date in late May was still a long way off, so readily agreed and said how delighted they would be to welcome Moshe and his family to their humble home.

Time, though, would tell.

CHAPTER NINETEEN

Albi

2020

I N THE CORNER of the *Hotel de Police* stood an *agent* grunting non-committedly into a telephone. Ever since his conversation with the Jewish president of Paris, LeBrun had been thinking hard. At home, in relative peace and quiet, he'd replayed the tape of that conversation several times. At first, there had seemed to be nothing much of use to him until he had a thought and replayed the section near the end where there'd been mention of the Toulouse Jewish community living in poor areas, near to the city centre, and who walked to the synagogue on the sabbath and holy days.

Soon, this triggered an idea. The site of the explosion had been in the middle of a pedestrian area, so it wouldn't just be the Jewish people who weren't using their cars, it would be the general population too. Some would be walking but many used either the ubiquitous motor scooter or an ordinary push bike.

So, in mounting excitement, LeBrun set his aide the task of researching the fragments they'd found at the bomb site.

There was a timid knock on the glass door. LeBrun's aide walked in. "Sir, I think I've finally got a lead on the Toulouse bombing."

Instantly, LeBrun's head cleared.

"Well, lad, go on. Spill the beans, and it'd better be good."

It seemed that Forensics had come up trumps. A tiny fragment of metal found at the bomb site, with a five-figure number etched on it, had been analysed and found to originate from a bicycle repair shop in St. Antonin.

Now grabbing his jacket from the back of his chair, LeBrun slurped the last dregs of coffee out of the bottom of the Styrofoam cup whilst slinging his jacket over his shoulder. He dropped the cup into the waste bin by the door, then shouted to his colleagues that he was going to investigate further a new lead he had received on the Toulouse bombing.

Outside the blistering summertime heat scorched down unabated, the humidity rising in line with the frayed tempers of the passers-by. Détective LeBrun and Jean-Paul, his assistant, jumped into their squad car parked out the back, frantically searching for the cooling system that would alleviate their discomfort. After a few muttered curses, the engine finally fired allowing them to back up and speed out of the compound and onto avenue Francois Verdier heading for St. Antonin.

But, before they'd even gone a thousand metres, Jean-Paul complained he was hungry. He was something of a mother's boy and liked to eat at the same time every day, in true French fashion. So, grudgingly, Détective LeBrun agreed to stop for lunch at a little place he knew, in the central pedestrian area, left after the fountain. He screeched to a halt in a No Park zone outside. One of the perks of the job.

LeBrun knew that Jean-Paul, unusually for a French lad, was vegetarian, so headed for rue de *l'Ort de Salvy*. Carefully fixing their masks over their faces, LeBrun looked at the menu outside, his glasses as usual fogging up.

The restaurant was situated in a narrow lane, not far from the famous red brick Cathédrale. It was a good job he'd been there before, thought LeBrun, otherwise it was very easy to miss. But it was worth the inconvenience. The Middle Eastern menu was sumptuous, full of things like falafels and couscous so that even he, a meat eater, was satisfied. But he had to steer clear of the wine list. He was driving.

After wiping their plates with the crusty bread always provided free with every meal, making sure they didn't miss any of the tasty sauce, LeBrun paid the proprietor. As usual, he left no tip on the table.

Where did they think this was, America? thought LeBrun. This was the land of *le bien manger*, so good food was to be expected. As he said to young Jean- Paul afterwards "Can't understand the Americans or the English. What's the point of spending thousands on expensive things for the house or a new car, then pouring cheap *merde* into your body? To him it was stupidity. The body determines how long a person lives, so why would you use the cheapest, worse fuel imaginable to keep it running? "I bet they don't put two-stroke in their Rolls Royces," said LeBrun.

"*Bouff,*"said Jean-Paul.

Now racing back to the car at the top of the cobbled pedestrian street, hurriedly fixed that damned mask over his face as he ran, he only narrowly avoided upending a sudden horde of tourists emerging from the miniature train which regularly circuited the town. At last LeBrun and Jean-Paul were at last buckling up and on their way.

There was something about the after-effects of strong French coffee, with which they'd completed their meal, that gave them a real boost. They felt at last ready to cope with what lay immediately ahead. They sped off, LeBrun sounding off generally about the standard of driving of the other road users.

Reaching St. Antonin, LeBrun drove up *Avenue Paul Benet* looking for somewhere to park. *At least it isn't market day*, he thought. Eventually finding a space on the left, in front of the *notaire*'s office, LeBrun yanked the handbrake upwards, as usual ignoring the need to first press in the button on the end. It wasn't his car, so what did he care?

Slamming the driver's door shut, not bothering to lock it, LeBrun checked his notes. Turning to his young assistant "Where did you say that *velo* repair shop was?"

"Think you have to go down the hill and turn left past the bank."

Now skittering down the cobbled alleyway, avoiding the *merde* from the many loose dogs in the area, they peered at the buildings either side. No shop there. At the end of the alley, they came to a T junction. They looked around with difficulty. A thick mist was everywhere, obscuring their vision. Jean-Paul said "I think this is common round here. I remember my mother telling me. It's a combination of rising mist from the river over there, pointing behind him, and wood smoke from all the chimneys."

"But this is high summer," grumbled LeBrun. "Why would anyone light a fire in this heat?" shaking his head.

"Have you ever been inside these houses?" asked his assistant. "The chill is everywhere, even on a summer's day like this one."

"*Bouff*," replied LeBrun. "OK, clever clogs; find the *velo* shop then," shrugging his shoulders as he looked first left, then right.

But Jean-Paul was already ahead of him, darting around the corner before pointing up the slope leading to a square at the top of the lane. "There it is!" pointing his thin arm to a small shop with a chipped, faded blue sign with the owner's name next to it.

Panting with exertion as he rushed after Jean-Paul, LeBrun struggled again with his mask.

"You have to pinch the top wire over your nose and then pull your glasses on top of it," said Jean-Paul.

When will this damned pandemic be over? Life's difficult enough.

Their masks now in place, the two men pressed down on the heavy door knob before pushing open the splintered door. The two détectives were met with a loud chime, totally at odds with the size of the tiny shop.

The back of an elderly man, wearing a brown overall, could be seen. He seemed to be checking his stock of rubber inner tubes and puncture repair kits, all arranged haphazardly on wonky wooden shelves behind him.

Turning at the sound of the bell, the man peered from beneath wire spectacles perched on his nose. "Can I help you?"

LeBrun moved up to the counter and flashed his professional card in front of the man, who took it off him and studied it awhile before saying "Yes, Détective LeBrun, what can I do for you?"

LeBrun decided to come straight to the point. "We're investigating that bomb attack in Toulouse. I expect you've heard of that on the news?" eyebrows raised questioningly.

The shopkeeper looked a bit nonplussed. "Of course, Monsieur Détective. Who hasn't? A terrible business, terrible. But what could that possibly have to do with me? I'm just a small shopkeeper who repairs bicycles."

"Quite so," responded LeBrun, studying the man closer. Turning to Jean-Paul, he asked him to empty their evidence bag onto the counter. "But nevertheless, I want you to look very closely at what you see in front of you. Can you see the number on that scrap of metal? You see, the thing is *Monsieur*, our forensics' team have analysed that fragment which was found at the crime scene in Toulouse and they tell me that it came from a *velo* from this very shop."

To his credit, the shopkeeper looked shocked. Scrabbling for a handkerchief, he mopped his brow several times. "I can't believe that, *Monsieur. C'est incroyable!*"

LeBrun looked the man in the eye. "Perhaps you keep some records of *velo* transactions, something to show *les Impots* tax officials every Spring, eh?" tapping the side of his nose with his finger.

Considerably flustered, the shopkeeper disappeared into the back of the shop, eventually reappearing with a large hard-backed ledger.

Turning to Jean-Paul, LeBrun muttered "Clearly, the digital age has passed this man by."

"This may take a while, *Messieurs*. Perhaps you might like to take a seat whilst I check off my sales. When did you say the crime was committed?"

"*N'importe quoi*, it doesn't matter when the crime took place, as the perpetrator would have brought his bike in to be repaired before that date. So, I suggest you look through, say, the last twelve months."

"Might take me some time, *Monsieur*. Perhaps you might like to partake of some refreshment at the *Gazpacho* café on the main *Avenue Paul Benet,* while you wait?"

The two detectives returned to the shop an hour later. "If I have any more coffee, I'll burst," grumbled LeBrun before, his glasses again fogged up, stepping into something in the alleyway leading to the *velo* shop. "*Merde!*"he said.

"*Exactement,*" said his companion, grinning.

The loud doorbell again announced their return. The shopkeeper was at his counter, the open ledger in front of him. "Ah, *Messieurs*, I have found something," he replied. "See here," pointing with his finger at an entry some months before the date of the crime.

LeBrun put his spectacles on and squinted at the small, copperplate writing. The entry read "New inner tube fitted. Ali."

"Is that all you've got? Who is this 'Ali'?"

The shopkeeper frowned. "I seem to recall that he's a friend of my son's who lives in Toulouse. He sometimes comes up here to see Seth. They're friends from school."

"And your son, *Monsieur*…can we have a word with him while we're here?"

"Unfortunately not….. He's away."

"Well, do you have an address for this Ali in Toulouse?"

"Yes, I do actually," citing an apartment above the site of the bomb blast.

"*Voila*!" exclaimed LeBrun.

Thanking the shopkeeper, the two detectives made their way back to the main road, LeBrun careful to avoid any more *merde* on the cobbles, before sliding into the car again.

LeBrun was thinking furiously.

He knew he now had a valuable lead.

CHAPTER TWENTY

St. Antonin
2020

S AMI WAS FEELING delirious. He didn't know what was wrong
with him. His head was pounding and the bed was soaked.
Every time he moved his head from the pillow, he was consumed with coughing, which wouldn't stop.

He couldn't ask his mother for help, as the whole family
had gone down to Toulouse to visit that stupid old friend of his
father's. What the hell did his father think he was doing anyway,
acting all friendly with a Jewish family?

On a whim, he grabbed his cell phone and tried to call
Seth, so that they could laugh together about the stupid things
old people get up to. But, Sami was surprised to hear Seth's
mother's voice on the other end, explaining that No, Seth
couldn't answer because he wasn't at all well. She said she'd get
him to call Sami as soon as he felt better.

Flopping back on his pillow, Sami mulled over his life and
how everything seemed to be going wrong. An English tune was
buzzing through his head. *Why does it always rain on me?* It exactly
matched his thoughts. Maybe friend Ali in Toulouse could cheer

him up. He jabbed at his contact list, eventually reaching Seth's friend, the one who had helped them with their project. But the call sound eventually finished, no-one having picked up.

So, in disgust, Sami threw his phone onto the bed and with difficulty struggled to the bathroom. Tugging the large wash bag towards him, which contained the cheap, generic medicines that his mother picked up from the *pharmacie*, he scrabbled inside until he found some paracetamol. Swallowing down a few tablets in quick succession, in the vain hope that they would make him feel better, he washed them down with a glass of cola. He never drank water from the tap anyway and the cola was at least palatable.

Hours later, Sami woke up. His bed was even more drenched before. No-one there. *The family must still be in Toulouse*, his fevered brain surmised. What to do? His head was hot, he felt weak and his damned cough just wouldn't stop, making his chest hurt. No point calling his local *médecine traitant* doctor at that time of night, and in any case he never made house calls.

Eventually, there was no other option. He felt too ill to care, so he grabbed his cell phone and jabbed *121*. His head fell back on the pillow as he put the device onto speaker phone.

"Allo. You have reached SAMU. What is your emergency?"

With an immense effort, Sami turned his head towards the phone. "Uh, I'm ill and my family are all out. Can you help?"

After establishing the nature of his call, his full name, address, and *carte vitale* details, they agreed to send an ambulance. "Please make sure you're wearing a face covering," was the last thing he remembered before falling into another deep sleep.

Hammering on the door woke him. His head feeling even worse, Sami managed to stumble towards the front door. A blue light was flashing through the window. People wearing blue PPE overalls, head coverings, face masks and visors met his startled gaze. "What on earth…?"

"Can you walk, *Monsieur*?" asked the alien at the front of the group.

Later that night, when the family returned, Layla frantically called SAMU, but it wasn't until the following morning, during normal working hours, that the family learned the truth. Sami had been diagnosed with Covid 19 virus and was in a special Covid ward in Albi.

"Well, when can we visit him?" asked Layla, shocked.

"I'm afraid not, *Madame*. No visitors are allowed."

Menes grabbed the phone from her and spoke loud, as he always did, into the speaker. "Look, he is our son and we demand to see him."

A pause the other end. "I'm sorry, *Monsieur*, but this is a pandemic and we are governed by the French Health Service. Normally," in more placatory tone, "we'd suggest you call him on his cell phone, but I'm afraid he's now in the intensive care unit, so this isn't possible. I'm sorry but I suggest you call the main hospital switchboard later for an update."

Sami was feeling groggy. He'd just been wheeled into yet another unit, but this one seemed much worse than the last one. People dressed as aliens and machines everywhere.

Sami was drowsy and lacking the will to live but first asked whether he could talk to his father. The kindly nurse agreed, calling his home number for him before passing him his cell phone. She knew that shortly they'd have to put him on a ventilator so there'd be no chance for him to speak to his family later.

"Hello," shouted his father into the phone.

"Hello Papa. It's Sami. I'm sorry."

"Quick, quick," Menes shouted to the family. It's Sami," before pressing the speaker phone button.

"Look son. I know this isn't the time but I simply have to tell you something about when I was in Egypt. I should have told you sooner, but somehow the opportunity never arose. I was in the army and dying in Sinai when something remarkable happened. A Jewish soldier in the Israeli army saved my life. Without him I would be dead and you would never have been born."

There was a pause the other end, then sounds of muffled sobbing. This in itself was a surprise to Menes. Sami had never been known to show his emotions before. Clearly, the boy was suffering.

"I'm so sorry Papa but I've done something terrible. If only I'd known, I would never have done it. Now it's too late. Please forgive me…"

Menes was perplexed and leaned closer to the cell phone. "What, Sami, what did you do?"

"I'm sorry, *Monsieur*," came an official voice. "But your time is up. We're just about to anaesthetise your son in order to put him on a ventilator. He is very sick. Please call back later."

The following day, before Layla had a chance to call the hospital again, a blue flashing light could be seen through their kitchen window. Foolishly, Layla said to her husband "Is it the paramedics?"

But a heavy thump on the front door told its own story. There was only one branch of the emergency services who announced their presence like that.

Layla rushed to the front door, shocked to see two police cars on their driveway.

A burly man introduced himself, thrusting his id card under her nose. She couldn't read it without her glasses on. "Détective LeBrun, *Madame*, and this," indicating his colleague, "is Détective Brient,"

Menes rushed to the hallway, just as the two men lumbered along the hallway and into the salon. "What's all this about?" he asked the older of the two men.

"Can we speak to….," pausing to glance down at his notes, "a Sami Khaled?"

Menes replied. "Sami's our son, but I'm afraid he's not here. He's in the hospital and very sick. He's got the virus."

The two detectives politely said they were sorry to hear that. The sat down on the sofa, whilst Layla and Menes took chairs directly opposite from them. LeBrun did a cursory glance around the room, as he always did in unfamiliar surroundings, noting that the furnishings were poor. The parents were dressed in traditional African-style robes, Layla with her hair covered. In contrast, the four sons wore what all French teenagers wore these days: jeans with holes at the knees and hooded tops.

"Is this all the rest of your family, *Monsieur?*"

Menes nodded.

"We're here to investigate a crime," began LeBrun. "On

Saturday 11th July, an explosion occurred at a Toulouse synagogue in the Esquirol sector, and we have reason to believe that your son Sami may have been involved."

The two detectives peered closely at the family to see any evidence of guilt or pre-knowledge.

"What?" Menes exclaimed. "You can't be serious. You think our Sami could do something like that?" Menes was close to tears, Layla already sobbing into her handkerchief. The rest of the family stood mute in the doorway. All looked absolutely shocked.

LeBrun glanced at his colleague. They could both see that the whole family looked completely shell shocked. It didn't look as though as they had any idea of what took place.

At last, Menes turned to LeBrun. "What makes you think that our Sami was involved?"

LeBrun looked down at his notes. "Does Sami have friends called Seth and Ali?"

Layla responded. "Why yes, Détective. Sami has known Seth since they were at school together. I think Seth's father runs a *velo* shop in St. Antonin, a few kilometres down the road from here. It's not far from where we run our own market stall."

Jean-Paul was busy scribbling down notes in his notepad, whilst she spoke.

"And the other one, Ali?"

"That one I don't know at all, really. I just remember Sami mentioning him as a friend of Seth's. I believe he lives in Toulouse, but I've never actually met him."

"I see," replied LeBrun. "And your son, Sami? What kind of boy is he?"

Layla looked at her husband, not knowing what to say, without implicating him.

Eventually, Menes spoke up. "Sami is our eldest. I admit he's always had strong views on what he sees as the troubles in the world. But he's always been a loyal member of our family and helps me every Sunday at my market stall in St. Antonin. Look, Détective, like most teenagers today, he's sometimes a bit wilful, but he'd never be involved in something as terrible as you describe. Never. Not our Sami."

Layla continued to sob. The rest of the family looked on, mortified.

LeBrun closed his notepad. "Oh, just one more thing, *Monsieur*," turning to Menes. "Which hospital did you say that Sami's in?"

"Hello, Sami. Can you hear me?"

A big, burly man was leaning over his bed. Sami stared. There were two of them, wearing full PPE. The big man was speaking to him but his voice seemed to be coming from a long distance away. "We're police, Sami, and need to ask you some urgent questions. Is that OK?"

Instinctively Sami knew why they were there. His number was up, but somehow he no longer cared. He nodded.

The big man spoke slowly and clearly. "Sami, did you plant the bomb under the synagogue in Toulouse?"

Tears were forming in Sami's eyes, moisture running down his cheeks. "I didn't understand," he whispered. "I kept feeling so angry and didn't really know why. I've always hated everyone and everything. Ever since I was a child. So, yes I did it. It was the biggest thing I ever did."

"Who else was involved, Sami. Who else?" asked LeBrun urgently. He could see the patient was losing consciousness.

"Tell them I'm sorry. So sorry….," his voice fading away as his eyes closed. His chest was heaving, continuous coughing bubbling up from his sore lungs combined with the tears still oozing from his eyelids.

"I think that's all we're gonna get, Sir," said Jean-Paul, tugging on LeBrun's sleeve.

Frustrated, LeBrun agreed with him. "Well at least we got a confession," he said. "Did you get it all down?"

"Of course, Sir," said Jean-Paul, adjusting his visor.

The ICU team then approached. "I'm sorry but that's enough. The patient is unconscious. You'll have to leave."

LeBrun nodded to the medical team, as they quickly left the room and, after finally discarding the PPE kit, they walked out into the fresh air, ready to return to their desks and type up their report.

Once back in the car, LeBrun turned to his colleague. "Although Sami didn't give us the names of the two who abetted him in the crime, I think we now have enough evidence to convict the three of them, Sami, Ali and the velo man's son, Seth. Only a matter of time before we find them," he grunted, with some relief.

At least something was happening right at last.

Back in ICU, the kindly nurse was leaning over Sami's bed. "The monitors told us you weren't getting enough oxygen so that's why the decision was made to put you on a ventilator. It will help you, but first we need to anaesthetise you to set it up. Do not be afraid. You won't feel anything." She wasn't sure that Sami could hear her but felt obliged to explain anyway. Sometimes, although patients looked unconscious, they could still hear. It was always important to explain what was about to happen. It was something drummed into all nurses and doctors during training. These were real people, with lives, families and feelings, not numbers on a graph.

Chapter Twenty-One

Albi
2020

T HE CAR PARK in front of the Clinic, usually jam-packed with cars both day and night, was strangely empty. Since it had been requisitioned by the French health service as a major Covid centre, everything had changed. Barriers now barred visitors. Marquees had been positioned in front of the main entrance, and a line of ambulances and local medical taxis were parked alongside the marquees.

In the intensive care unit, large yellow banners had been pasted across all doors. No visitors allowed. This is a restricted area. Medical professionals only. Imperative that full PPE gear, masks and visors are worn at all times.

The ICU team were hovering over Sami's bed, trying not to convey their concern. This patient was very young to be so sick, but it was a phenomenon they'd seen before in patients whose families were of non-Caucasian origin.

Sami struggled to hear what they were saying. "First, we insert a tube through your mouth or nose directly into your trachea. This tube allows the machine to push air into your lungs and forces you to inhale. You can't swallow, speak or cough. You might be sedated, if you are lucky. But you won't be sedated the whole time. Do you understand?"

Sami nodded.

"It's a machine that breathes for you," the doctor continued. "Usual breathing uses negative pressure, meaning you open your mouth and air flows in. The machine uses positive pressure to force air into your lungs. Think of standing in front of a leaf blower. With the virus causing so much damage to your lungs, the ventilator allows you to rest and to heal while the machine does the work of your lungs." He told Sami that the machine would blow air in for one second, than pause for roughly three seconds to allow him to exhale, then repeats for as long as the machine is in use. And that could be a long time," he warned.

Before being made unconscious, Sami managed to say to the nurses "Please promise that I will see my father again. There's something I desperately need to say to him." There was a look of abject fear on his face as he struggled to say these words.

Sami couldn't fail to see what was happening to the people in beds near to his, even though they were shielded by curtains. Whilst trying to take in what had happened to him, every time he turned his head, he could see others who were struggling with masks and tubes over their faces. Every so often, a nurse wearing horrendous, alien, overalls, visor and helmet with tubes attached would arrive at a patient's bed alongside him and draw the curtains. He never saw that patient again.

The nurse tried to reassure him, but in truth she had to hide her inner feelings. She'd seen too many patients die on this ward.

Sami was frantic as he watched what the doctors and nurses were doing to others in the ward. They seemed to be repeatedly adjusting ventilator settings, checking X-rays and Sami could hear alarms chiming as oxygen levels fell. Patients were being flipped back and forth in a bid to improve their situation. But the worst thing of all was seeing some family members arrive and sit with their loved one.

Suddenly it became clear to Sami. The hospital wouldn't normally allow visitors. Therefore, when this happened, it must be the end for the patient. Sami's fear was palpable despite the nurse's reassurances. "Please promise me that I will recover so that I can see my family again. I must talk to my father and try to explain. I desperately need his forgiveness for what I've done." Tears streamed down his face. All that the nurse could do was hold his hand.

The nurse confided to her colleague, out of earshot of Sami's bed. "I hate the fact that I make promises to our patients when, I know that all too often, they're promises that I can't keep."

"I know. I feel the same, but what can we do? The people are so terrified, we just have to try to reassure them, despite there being only one probable end."

Just before the anaesthetist had put Sami under, the nurse saw only too well the look of abject fear on Sami's face. Ever since the pandemic started, it was one of the indelible memories on all the nurses' faces. Every patient they treated was the same.

As soon as they decided to intubate them, fear was evidenced in all of them. But in those patients who arrive already very ill, they tended to be sedated immediately. At least in those cases, the nurse thought, those poor people had no time to dwell on the possibility of not waking up.

"Is there anything else you'd like to say before we sedate you?" the nurse asked Sami.

Sami was in a panic, but suddenly he knew what he had to do. He indicated he needed a pen and paper. Although he couldn't contain his coughing and his chest hurt, he managed to sit up enough to scribble some words on the paper the nurse gave him. "Please," he whispered, "give this to my father," before collapsing back down on the bed.

The nurse put the paper in the desk in the nurses' station, after writing on the folded sheet in her gloved hand "Private. Sami Khaled. Give to his father."

Once Sami had been anaesthetised, one nurse began the difficult procedure of pressing his tongue down whilst inserting a tube down his throat. She knew that patients suffering from Covid are only put on ventilators as a last resort to help them breathe and ensure their bodies are getting enough oxygen while they fight the virus. But there were so many risks and so many had died whilst on the machines.

With Sami, they'd already tried positive pressure ventilation, inserting a tube into his windpipe. They'd also used continuous positive airway pressure, allowing oxygen to be delivered through a tightly-fitting face mask. But the hospital was still seeing an increase in the number of deaths. Just yesterday, another three ventilated patients had died in just one night.

In St. Antonin the phone was ringing. In trepidation, Layla answered. "Yes, yes, thank you," she said. "We'll leave right away."

The drive to the hospital in Albi was tortuous. Every traffic light was against them. Menes, a cigarette hanging from his lip, struggled to contain his feelings. Layla, in the passenger seat, nervously wrung her hands in her lap. In the back, crammed into the rear seats, sat the four boys. No-one said a word. No-one noticed the green fields along the route, the birds singing in the trees nor the general absence of other road users.

A police car drew up and indicated they should pull over.

"Votre attestation, Monsieur?" said the uniformed, masked gendarme, noting their dress and appearance.

In these foolish days of pandemic, the French had invented ever more bureaucratic means of ensuring their citizens obeyed the current rules whenever they ventured out.

Layla scrabbled in her bag before finding the statutory form she'd hurriedly completed before leaving the house. "Here you are, *Monsieur,*" she said, pushing the paper out through the passenger window. Thanks to *Allah*, she'd remembered to put the reasons they were making the long journey. Otherwise, there'd have been even more delay.

The gendarme took the form in his gloved hand, gave it a cursory glance, before handing it back.

Turning to Menes, "Your id, Monsieur, s'il vous plaît,"

Grumbling, Menes patted his pockets before finding his id card and his carte vitale. "Here you are, officer. Please be quick. We're in a great hurry. Our son is very ill with Covid and we must get to the hospital in Albi."

The gendarme understood, asked which hospital, then indicated they should follow him. They were only too pleased to oblige. It was about time that the French police gave them some help at last.

With blue lights flashing, the police car sped off, with Menes following. Suddenly it didn't matter about red traffic lights. They were on an urgent mission, aided and abetted by the authorities.

In no time at all, they pulled into the hospital car park and, with the aid of the now very helpful gendarme, were able to park near the entrance. But the gendarme wasn't finished yet. He could be seen radioing through to the hospital administration, before telling them to wait for someone to come out to them.

"Thank you, *Monsieur*," said Layla gratefully as they paused to catch their breath.

Soon, a hospital nurse arrived, ushering them inside a marquee outside the entrance. "You must wear these, please," she said through her visor.

Five minutes later, Menes, Layla and the four boys were dressed in full PPE gear and were being admitted through a side door and along to the ICU ward. In a daze, they shuffled along clinical corridors and through various Perspex swinging doors before, at last, being ushered into the ICU ward where Sami lay.

Not understanding why they had been admitted to the ward, they sat around his bed and stared. Curtains had been pulled shut after them. Sami was no longer on a ventilator and lay on a bed, his eyes closed. No tubes were evident and his mask had been removed. He looked very peaceful.

The nurse came in. "I'm sorry to tell you that Sami passed away. We did everything we could to save him, but there was nothing more we could do. I'm so very sorry."

Layla and the four boys cried.

Menes stared. "What? He's just a young boy. How can he be dead? What did you do?"

The nurse said "I'm so very sorry. It's happening here every day. People of all ages, but particularly those, like your son, with ethnic origins. The doctors don't yet know why."

Menes was shaking his head. "Not Sami. Not my eldest. NO!"

The nurse didn't know what she could say, but then remembered the note. "There's something I must give you. Before your son was sedated, he asked especially that I give you a note, *Monsieur*. He was most insistent. Give this to my father, he said, so I put it in my desk. I'll go now and find it for you. Please remain where you are until I return."

Pulling open the curtains, she went off to the nurses' station and found Sami's note. Slamming the drawer shut, she made her way back to the family. Layla was still crying. The boys and Menes were all staring at the floor, utterly dumfounded at what had happened.

"Why is this happening to us?" asked one of the boys.

Layla could only shake her head in despair.

The curtain was suddenly pulled back and the nurse thrust a folded sheet into Menes' hand. "Here you are, *Monsieur,*" she said. "I'll leave you for a moment, to give you chance to read it," closing the curtain behind her.

"Menes. What does it say?" asked Layla.

Menes searched for his glasses, unfolded the paper and read it aloud to his family.

Papa,

I'm so sorry. I didn't mean to get ill, but this is judgement on me. I did something very stupid, so it's all my fault. I don't know why I did it, but my head was exploding. I felt that the whole world was against me, but particularly the Jews who seem to control the world. But, afterwards, when you told me that your life was saved by a Jew, I felt really bad. If only I'd known about that before, I probably wouldn't have done it. If that Jew hadn't have saved your life, I wouldn't have even been born.

Mama. I'm so sorry I didn't turn out to be the son you wanted. Maybe my brothers can somehow make up for my lack.

And finally, to my brothers. Please don't follow what I did. Be good people and look after Mama and Papa.

Goodbye. Try not to remember me with hate. I just took the wrong path.

Sami.

Chapter Twenty-Two

Toulouse
2020

T HE PAINS STARTED at precisely 3 a.m. on the very date given to Leah by her doctor. She lay quietly counting the seconds between each before waking Simon. The pains started to quicken, and she knew that there could now be no doubt: their baby wanted to be born and fast. They still didn't know whether the baby would be a boy or girl. She had to insist that the obstetrician refrain from telling them. She just had a feeling it would be better to await the baby's birth, just as her ancestors had.

She turned over to prod Simon but found his pillow empty. Turning to switch on the bedside light, she was surprised to see hasty signs of his departure. The clothes he'd worn yesterday, which usually lay on the floor where he discarded them, were gone. Rolling over to his side of the bed, she stretched her fingers in search of his cell phone. Leah knew that he never went anywhere without it.

The phone was gone.

Now in a panic, her pains coming more frequently, she reached for her own phone and jabbed 112.

After a nerve wracking ten seconds' wait, a voice "*Quel service d'urgence Madame?*"

"*Uh SAMU, s'il vous plaît.Vite, c'est urgent.*"

"*Oui, Madame*, but first your name, address and type of emergency," infuriatingly calm.

Simon had earlier agreed that this would be better than driving there themselves. She'd heard so many stories of disasters happening *en route*. Far better that paramedics were on hand should anything untoward happen.

But where the hell was Simon? He knew she was due any day so why on earth would he disappear just when she needed him the most?

Between pains, Leah managed to change out of her nightdress into the maternity dress she wore yesterday. Well, she didn't want the neighbours or the paramedics for that matter to see her in her nightclothes.

Her small suitcase was waiting in the hall, just where she'd left it, so she sat on the stair waiting and worrying.

It was only then she saw the note, hastily scribbled on the back of an envelope.

"Something's happened to Dad. They've taken him to the general hospital so that's where I'm off to now. Will let you know asap. Sorry! Simon x"

Leah felt the baby turn in her womb. She wondered if she had time to relieve her bladder one more time before the ambulance arrived. But then she heard the crunch of wheels on the drive. She peered through the glass in their front door, but as it was still dark, all she could see was a flashing blue light. Apparently there was a law that forbade vehicle sirens at night unless in extreme emergency, so undoubtedly she wasn't an emergency. Since the beginning of time, women had been giving birth. It was the most natural thing in the world. Everyone told her that. *What was it her grandfather used to call it in Yiddish?* Ah yes, *ein gute Krank*! But what did men know anyway?

The paramedics were at the door.

"Do you need a wheelchair, Madame?"

Leah declined and walked steadily to the waiting van, the paramedic putting her suitcase right by her. Despite the absence of her husband, she felt curiously detached and quiet.

On the journey to the hospital, she noticed that one of the paramedics kept looking back from his seat to check she was all right.

By now the pains were bad, but Leah was in another world. At the hospital entrance, they helped her down the step and into the night-time lights of the entrance foyer, depositing her suitcase at the reception desk. The receptionist took her details and a nurse guided her down to the Labour Ward.

"I'll just get someone to examine you," she said efficiently, as she bade Leah undress and put on one of those awful robes that never fit or cover you at the rear. She'd read somewhere that someone had designed a new style of unisex hospital robe which fastened at the side. A much better idea, but clearly this hadn't yet found its way there yet.

A midwife arrived, did a cursory examination, and tutted: "I thought you were just at the beginning of labour. You're already three-quarters dilated. There won't be time to shave you or administer an enema. I'll have to fetch the doctor straight away." She bustled away, clearly indignant.

The pain was by now agonising.

"Breech," said the midwife. "Call the doctor."

Everything went black

Hours later, Leah woke up. Still no sign of Simon. A nurse told her that they'd had to do an emergency caesarean but that the baby was fine and in the nursery.

The doctor arrived. "How are you feeling, Madame?"

"Sore."

"Ah yes. That's entirely normal. Nothing to worry about."

"And the baby?" asked Leah, entirely exasperated.

"Didn't the nurse tell you? It's a boy, thankfully healthy. We were a bit worried but I'm happy to tell you that all is well." Now looking at his notes, "your son weighed 3.7 kilos, which is a good weight, but because of the trauma of his birth, we're keeping an eye on him for the moment. This will also give you time to rest after your ordeal. I very much fear, though, that you will be unable to have any more children. The damage inside was too great."

Leah thanked him and tried to get her head around the fact that they had a son. She'd been sure she was having a girl. She was worried about something, but the effects of the drip were making her woozy. Her eyes fluttered then closed.

A bright light woke her. Simon was sitting by her bed, holding her hand. He looked ridiculous, in full PPE kit. But it didn't matter. Nothing mattered but that a new life had been born and was healthy.

"What time is it?" she asked.

"Oh, about 15.00 I think."

He leaned over to kiss his wife and to congratulate her on their new son.

"Have you seen him yet?"

"Yes, but only through a window. He's got a thick fuzz of black hair and his nose looks a bit like Papa's."

Leah opened her eyes fully and looked across at Simon, whose eyes were red-rimmed and moist. "How's Moshe, Simon?"

There was a long pause, before Simon broke down in tears. "He passed away in the night, love. The doctors did what they could, but he was old and tired. In the end, his heart just stopped," wiping away a tear.

"Oh, I'm so sorry, love."

Leah hated to see her husband so distressed. She tried leaning over to put her arm around him but was prevented by the drip wire, attached to the machine alongside the bed. "I loved him, too, you know," she told Simon. "Moshe was like a father to me, after my own Dad passed away. He was a constant, somehow. Always there."

"I know. I can't believe he's no longer with us."

Simon suddenly realised that he'd need to contact the Rabbi for another reason. He'd already contacted him to arrange the *Chevra Kadisha* pre-burial rites for his father and the arrangements for the interment, which in Jewish law take place, wherever possible, within twenty-four hours. The nearest Jewish cemetery was at Portet-sur-Garonne, a short drive south of

Toulouse. The Rabbi assured him of the necessary *minyan* of ten men to allow the burial to take place.

"Moshe ben Yitzach was a good man," said the Rabbi, "and a regular attender at our *shul*. He was a brave survivor of the holocaust and a true person of worth. I and all my rabbinical colleagues wish you and your family Long Life. May you be spared further sorrow for many years to come."

As his apartment was too small, and because of Leah's condition, Simon had arranged with the Rabbi to hold the necessary seven days' *shiva* mourning time to be held at the central

Espace de Judaism building. This would be a time when the community could come and greet Simon, who would be sitting on a traditional, low wooden stool, and pay their respects.

A nurse suddenly appeared with a cot, which she placed by Leah's bed. "Here's your son, Leah. Isn't he beautiful?"

Leah had been dozing again but was suddenly awake. The nurse propped up the pillow behind Leah's head. Leah winced from the soreness in her stomach, but managed to sit upright. Carefully lifting the baby out of the cot, the nurse put him in Leah's arms.

"Oh Papa, where are you? Why can't you be here to see him?"

Soon, Leah was being wheeled up to the day ward with the baby in his cot beside her.

Now, as Simon looked down at his beautiful baby, he remembered his father's dying words "Don't forget me, Simon. Don't forget me."

This was a new beginning for the family. Here was a baby just starting out in the world.

Suddenly the baby opened his eyes and Simon saw Moshe looking up at him. This was the message he needed. He now had a son. He must not fail him. Here was a Jewish child and must be brought up to know and understand his heritage.

"So," said Leah, smiling. "What's his name going to be?"

But Simon was thinking. "What was it Papa always used to say to me when I was small? Oh yes, what's the point of living if no-one remembers you after you're gone. That was typical of Papa really. But he needn't have worried. There is now a new Moshe to perpetuate his memory."

Simon realised he'd need to contact the Rabbi again, but this time with better news. There was a surgical procedure to perform.

"I think we should call our son Moshe ben Shimon."

Chapter Twenty-Three

MENES STILL FELT grief stricken, not only for his son and what he'd done but also on the loss of his dear friend Moshe. For Menes it was a double whammy.

He'd made sure he kept in touch with Simon, though, and was looking forward to the first showing of his film. Now more than ever Menes desperately wanted to see an improvement in the world, but especially in the Middle East. Hadn't his long friendship with Moshe shown that people with different upbringings could not only live side by side but do so in brotherhood and even love?

But there was one thing that Menes still needed to resolve. He'd thought about it a lot recently. He wanted to find and thank that brave Israeli soldier who saved his life in the Sinai, but how was he to find him?

He thought he'd ask Simon. Menes still hadn't got to grips with the digital world, so was glad to know someone who could help.

He and Simon were sitting in the *Gazpacho* café, opposite his market stall in St. Antonin.

"Well," replied Simon, in his usual pragmatic style. "You'll need to do a search on the web."

Menes grumbled. "How am I supposed to do that? I can't fathom all this technology. Why can't we use the old methods, like we used to have in Cairo?"

"And what's that?" laughed Simon.

"Why, the best way ever. We send smoke signals to the next village!"

"Oh come on. You're not that old," said Simon. "Look," pulling out his cell phone. "Let's start at the beginning. I'll go to the general site for Israel," his fingers moving like lightening over the keys.

Menes leaned over. "What does it say?"

"It says that Israel's always been asked by visitors to find family members who moved to Israel at some point in the past or others whose families were separated by historical events. It seems that it's common for visitors on arrival in Israel to ask how they can find long-lost family members."

Menes looked excited. "So, what does it say I should do?"

Simon scrolled down the screen a bit.

"Well, it says the first stage would be to open a site called Bezeq, which is the main telephone company in Israel. Then, you have to click on 'People' and type in the person's first and last name and the name of the city where the person lives, if known."

"Oh dear," replied Menes. "I don't know where he lived, just his name, Dov Cohen. Thanks to *Allah,* I at least remembered that. So, Simon, what do you have to do after that?"

"Well," after scrolling down some more, "you then click 'Search'. If the person has a Bezeq phone number, his contact information will appear."

"And," said Menes, "what next?"

"There doesn't appear to be anything more. The next bit is about finding holocaust survivors and that isn't relevant for you."

The *Gazpacho* bar man brought over their usual strong black coffee as Simon and Menes thought over the issue.

"You know what we should do?" said Simon, after a moment. Menes shook his head.

"But I'm not at all sure you'd want to do it," said Simon prevaricating.

"What?"

"I think we should go in person to Israel and make our own enquiries."

Two months later, and Menes was stepping off the plane at Ben Gurion airport. He couldn't believe it. Here he was, a man from Cairo, and he was actually visiting Israel.

"Thank the Lord, we no longer have to bother with face masks or temperature tests," said Simon as they ventured through immigration control and out to the line of taxi cabs on the airport forecourt.

"Yes," said Menes, very relieved. "I remember back in the old days in Cairo, when there was one plague after another, but especially polio, diphtheria and meningitis. So many people became disabled, even my own father, and so many children died."

"Well, now that the worst of this modern plague called Covid is finally over, and most people have been vaccinated," said Simon, "at least it gives me a chance to show you what the Jewish people are really like."

It had felt right that the two of them, who'd each suffered so much, should make this pilgrimage to the old world. After Simon's suggestion in the *Gazpacho*, Menes had felt a sudden surge of boldness, deciding that yes they would go. His remaining sons could now be trusted to look after the business while he was gone. So, flights had been booked from *Blagnac* airport in Toulouse, strangely routed via Rome through to Tel Aviv. To Simon, it was like a scene from his film. Even the plane was following the ancient route of his people's old adversaries.

After an uneventful flight, Simon and Menes checked into adjoining rooms in a Tel Aviv hotel on *Josef Trumpledor* Street, just up the road from the famous beach area. The following day, the two men – one the son of a Jewish holocaust survivor from Poland, the other an Egyptian survivor from the Six Day War – took the opportunity to walk along the shore towards the ancient port of Yafo. Some said it was the oldest port in history. To many an onlooker, the men might have looked like strange bedfellows, but in fact they felt a special empathy for each other.

Menes was still grieving for his eldest son. *If only I'd talked to him sooner*, he kept repeating, *he'd still be alive today and those poor people in the Toulouse synagogue would not still be suffering*.

Simon put an arm around his father's old friend. "Ah, Menes. It was a terrible thing that Sami did, but his mind must have been disturbed. I'm just so relieved that, in the end, no-one died directly from his actions. I wish you and your family Long Life. That's what we always say to the family after someone has died. We always look to the living. Life is everything. At least, my father had lived a full, if somewhat eventful life, before he passed away. But Sami was so young. My life seems to be full of could've, would've, should'ves! What's done is done, I suppose, and we can never change the past. But the future, ah all our tomorrows, is still full of possibilities."

"But I feel so bad," said Menes. "What my son did was wicked and it's all my fault. I must have been a bad father not to have spotted his feelings sooner. I knew he was unhappy, yet did nothing to help him. That's what grieves me so much."

"My friend, despite what Sami did, I feel deeply for your loss." Seeing the sorrow in Menes' eyes, Simon changed the subject. "Did Dad ever tell you about what happened to him in Poland when he was no more than a baby? You remember that lady he told you about called Hanna?"

Menes nodded.

"Well, she did such a wonderful thing for him when she was but a teenager herself. She could easily have concentrated on her own survival in the midst of all that terror. What I'm trying to say is this. We never know what's going on in other people's minds. Let other people do what they may, even our own children. All we can do is make sure we, ourselves, do the right thing."

They stopped for a moment to catch their breath and looked out to sea, squinting their eyes to the far horizon. Every so often, a water skier would zoom past, leaving a wake of white surf behind him. In front of them, sitting on a blanket spread over the fine sand, sat an Arabic family enjoying their home-prepared lunch. It didn't matter that the women had their heads covered, for walking past were many an orthodox Jewish woman, her hair too covered with a headscarf. What was important was that everyone there was free to live, to follow their religion exactly how they chose, to work even in government or the army and for all of them to be equal Israeli citizens.

"I never realised how many Arabs live in Israel," said Menes in surprise.

"Did you know that all the Arabs you see here are actually all Israeli citizens," said Simon, pushing his toes into the ancient sand dunes beneath his feet, cooled intermittently by the in-rushing shallows. "In fact, I read that a recent survey reported that some Arabs actually prefer the term Israeli Arab to describe themselves. In point of fact, whilst many call themselves Israeli Palestinians, the irony is that all Israelis could identify themselves as such. Similarly, the citizens of Jordan often call themselves Jordanian Palestinians, all of them recognising correctly that the term Palestine refers not to one country but to the whole historic region.

As they continued their amble along the warm sand towards the ancient port, Menes cast his eyes to the right, amazed at all the high-rise hotels that lined the promenade.

"You know, Menes," said Simon, seeing in which direction his friend was looking, "in December there's even a giant Xmas tree, adorned with lights. That's how cosmopolitan and free this land is today. And, in Hebron, the three monotheistic faiths all pray to Abraham at the same site. Yes, it's probably the only thing they all agree on: that Hebron is the place where *their* patriarch is buried."

But Menes was thinking about France, the country where he, Moshe and Hanna had decided to live all those years ago, but for very different reasons. "I couldn't believe it when you told me about what had happened since you spoke to your film colleagues."

"I know," replied Simon. "Who would have thought that one chance comment could have led to such amazing possibilities? They tell me there'll be a French election soon, but the papers are all talking about the possibility of a new, radical, President taking charge. I don't like 'radical'. Neither did my father. To him, it signalled danger. I agree. When will the world ever learn?"

Menes nodded. "Yes. Between you and me, I've always been a bit worried about the French and their real intentions. What they say in public isn't always who they vote for in practice. They've always been a bit *fermé,* closed, you know, the French. Moshe used to tell me stories of how, after the Nazis marched into their part of France and took the Jews away, their erstwhile French neighbours apparently rushed in and took all their valuables."

"Terrible. Just terrible. But many countries are probably the same. Sometimes war brings out the worst in people. We each should be worried about the future. But, who knows, maybe my film will make a difference."

"Let's hope so," said Menes. "But maybe I'm being a little unkind to the French. After all, they did take me in when I had nothing."

"They're already talking about the next G7 summit, you know," said Simon. "Apparently, there's a chance they'll establish a satellite symposium to discuss the whole Middle East conundrum, and it may even be held in Jerusalem!"

"Yes, I heard that too," responded Menes, as they resumed

their slow, bare-foot walk along the sand dunes, "I do so hope all the Arab nations will agree to attend. It would mean so much."

"Yes. If only the G7 nations could build on what was achieved single-handedly in the Abraham accords: to get many more Arab nations to sign a peace/economic, normalisation accord with Israel. Just think. Already," listing them on his fingers, "there are the UAE, Egypt, Jordan, Sudan, Bahrain that I can think of off the top of my head."

"Well, as you say, if this new symposium idea takes off, I can die happy," sighed Menes. "We'll just have to see, I suppose. Miracles have happened before," thinking of that long ago day when his life was saved by a Jewish soldier in the hot sands of the Sinai.

Before heading back to the hotel, the two men stopped at a fish restaurant overlooking the old Yaffa harbour and ate fish and chips, served to them in a newspaper-lined basket.

A thought came to the old man. "Why are there still Jewish people living all over the world when now they have their own land?"

Simon smiled, still licking his fingers after eating the wonderful fresh fish caught in the very waters they overlooked. "Well, for me the answer is simple. If some future madman (and I don't use the term lightly: only madmen would target an ancient, peaceful people whose only aim is to live in peace) decided to bomb the whole of Israel, then there would still be Jews left living in the diaspora."

"So, you mean," said Menes thoughtfully, "that it's simply a question of guaranteeing your survival."

"Yes, my friend. But, as I've said many times before, I have never met a fellow Jew who harboured hatred in his heart. Never."

"Well, for me, I'm just grateful to have had you and, of course, your dear father as a friend and that we can discuss such issues between us without coming to blows," sparring playfully together.

"Hah."

Back at the hotel, whilst Menes was resting, Simon worked hard to trace the man called Dov Cohen. Eventually, with some excitement, he traced the old soldier to an apartment in Tel Aviv, not far from where they were staying.

Quickly Simon jabbed at the phone numbers, hoping that his *Ivrit* modern language Hebrew would be sufficient to understand.

A woman's voice answered. "Yes?" in the often seemingly abrasive style Israeli-born people used.

"Er, I am a visitor here and would like to speak to a Dov Cohen. Is he there?"

There was a long pause.

"Who did you say you were?" said the women suspiciously.

"I'm sorry, I should explain. I'm a Jewish visitor from France and I'm enquiring on behalf of a friend who this Dov Cohen saved in the Sinai back in 1967. My friend's name is Menes and, before he dies, he's desperate to trace this Dov to thank him from the bottom of his heart."

The woman could hear the sincerity in Simon's voice, so took a risk, giving him her address and telling him to come over with his friend the following day at 10 a.m.

Menes was feeling nervous. What would he say to the man he'd thought about for so many years? How could he possibly put into words all his inner feelings?

He walked into the *en-suite* shower room and looked around in amazement. How his dear wife would have gloried in such luxury. The hotel had even thoughtfully provided complimentary soap and shampoo for their guests, even though these days Menes had little use for the shampoo, he thought wryly.

Now enjoying the full blast raining down from the shower head, he let his mind flow back to that time in the Sinai. They were the worst days of his life and he thought he was done for, his life over. His Egyptian leader, whom they all thought was their hero was, in effect, simply a killing machine, sending wave after wave of men into ultimate slaughter. And what chance did he, Menes, have under such conditions? He'd always been weak, physically, having no muscle strength to speak of and morally he'd never believed in what they were even fighting for. So why had he gone to war, a young, naïve boy?

Now stepping carefully out of the shower cubicle and towelling himself dry with the lovely, fluffy towels the hotel provided, he knew the answer.

Where we're born and the genes we inherit from our parents, are simply elements of fate, he realised. *But also, and most importantly, the age we're born into, the culture and the mindset of that country at that time — ah, that's what we all have to deal with. And in my case? It very nearly killed me!*

He'd arranged to meet Simon in the lobby at 08.30 to give them time to have some breakfast in the hotel's restaurant before making their way to their so important destination.

Eventually, having taken some time worrying over what to wear, Menes settled on a short-sleeved shirt and simple cotton trousers. He'd noticed how everyone in Israel seemed to wear very casual clothes, so decided against a jacket. Besides, looking out of the window, the day was already hot. Not a cloud in the sky. He hoped that was a good portent.

Simon was already at a breakfast table, as usual jabbing away at his cell phone. *What on earth do these young people find to look at for so long?* he thought.

Simon stood up. "Ah, there you are," giving his friend a quick hug. Menes couldn't quite get used to this modern style, but accepted it gracefully enough. These days Simon was like a son to him.

Together they crossed to the self-service breakfast bar where just about everything was on hand. For those more European types, there was a selection of croissants, fruit and yoghurt, and an array of local salad ingredients. For those more used to a hot breakfast, there was a hot counter providing baked beans, mushrooms, eggs and tomatoes.

So much food. Menes would never get used to all this abundance. Growing up in Cairo he'd always been starving.

Feeling slightly queasy at the thought of their day's mission, Menes picked up a tray and filled it with a pastry, some fruit and yoghurt. Simon, being younger, chose something rather more substantial. Even though Simon had been brought up French, he seemed to have inherited his father's Eastern European culinary tastes. When facing a hard day, fill up with *schmaltz*!

At least they didn't have to worry about coffee, as a waiter came and filled up their cups automatically.

By 09.30, after they'd digested their breakfast, they were ready to slide into a waiting taxi cab.

Leaning over to the driver, Simon gave him the address.

Soon, in typical Israeli fashion, the driver was zooming off on a hair-raising journey, beeping frequently at the other drivers and snaking in and out of the city lanes until they emerged into a much quieter, more residential, area.

At 09.55, the taxi squealed to a halt. Simon argued with the driver over the requested fare, until at last an agreement was made and the correct shekels were handed over. Shaking his head, they emerged from the vehicle, and brushed themselves down.

In front of them was a large, modern apartment building, the type that was increasingly popular amongst young Israelis. Glancing again at the slip of paper with the address written on it, Simon led the way up to the outer door and jabbed at the apatment number.

After some crackling, "Allo?"

"It's Simon here. I made an appointment with you yesterday over the phone."

More crackling before "Come on up. I'm on the second floor."

The outer door sprang open. They walked into a wonderfully cool lobby after the heat of the outdoors. Simon moved over to the stainless steel doors of the lift, but Menes tugged on his sleeve. "No, no. I never like lifts. They break down when you least expect it."

With a sigh, Simon demurred and looked around for the stairs.

At last they arrived on the second floor, after having to pause every few minutes for Menes to catch his breath.

An old woman was at an open door. "Come in, come in," she said slowly in *Ivrit*, ushering them through to a modern interior full of glass and chrome. "Welcome. My name is Sabra Cohen," extending a hand in greeting.

After introducing themselves, the two men sat on the sofa facing Sabra. After a pause, the woman spoke in heavily-accented French. "I didn't want to say over the phone, but I'm afraid I have some bad news for you. My husband, Dov, died ten years ago from cancer. He was already seventy years old and had been diagnosed with lung cancer. He knew that it would take him but remained cheerful to the end. He always said that all that smoking during the war would be the end of him and so it proved. At least," looking carefully at Menes, "he wasn't taken by enemy gunfire."

Menes was crying. He tried desperately to stem the tide, but couldn't help it. For over fifty years he'd been searching and now it was too late.

"I'm not sure if your husband, sorry late husband, ever told you but I am eternally grateful to him for what he did back in 1967," Menes at last managed to say, wiping his eyes. "You see, I was a soldier in Nasser's Egyptian Army and was dying at the side of the road, when he picked me up and cared for me. Without him, my life would have been over all those years ago. Remember. I was the enemy, so what Dov did was absolutely extraordinary. He was truly a great man and now I'm too late to thank him. I'm completely devastated."

In sympathy, Sabra stood up and brought over some photos of her late husband. One of them, in particular, struck Menes hard. There was the man he remembered walking into that tent in the Sinai, when he was recovering. There was no doubt. It was the same smile, the lift of the eyebrows, everything.

Simon didn't know what to say, so was grateful when Sabra brought them a strong drink.

Suddenly he had a thought, but with not much hope of finding an answer. "Excuse me, Mrs. Cohen, but may I ask you something that may sound rather strange?"

Sabra laughed. "With the life I've lived, with the constant rocket sirens, nothing would surprise me, nothing, so please go ahead."

So Simon told her about his film and how a *meleke* stone came to be passed down via Jewish women for thousands of years.

Sabra leaned forward, suddenly interested, telling him to continue.

"Well, a friend of my father's, a Polish lady called Hanna, inherited the stone from her mother who was murdered by the Nazis before she could tell her daughter how she had obtained it. So now I'm struggling to find an answer."

"What was this Polish lady's name, I mean the mother?"

"Adela Siskowski."

Sabra looked shocked. "Are you sure? Adela Siskowski?"

Simon nodded.

"Well, you're not going to believe this but I was born on a kibbutz, in the north. Like so many others, it was run in a so-cial, collaborative way. All the children grew up together, away from their parents. Anyway, my best friend who was also born in the kibbutz was a girl called Ruth. But she never knew her mother. It was said that her mother had worked picking grapes for a while but became pregnant with Ruth. No-one knew if the mother had a husband back home, as she never spoke about her home. Soon after the birth, Ruth's mother returned to her own country, Poland. But, and here's the interesting bit, Ruth showed me a special stone that had been left for her by her mother."

Simon sat bolt upright. "And, Sabra, what was this Ruth's surname?"

"Siskowski."

Menes, who'd been listening attentively to the whole story butted in "But, if this is the same family, how did the stone get back to Hanna?"

Simon too was puzzled. "Any ideas?" turning to Sabra.

"Yes. I think I can help you there. You see – and the ways of *HaShem* are indeed strange – my friend Ruth Siskowski went into the Israeli army. We all did. It's mandatory, even now. But Ruth joined the same regiment as my Dov. I remember him telling me about her. But, Ruth was killed by enemy gunfire during the six day war. So, as Ruth wasn't married, I believe the Israeli army would have tried to trace her mother to return Ruth's effects, including the stone. But, thinking about it, maybe that's how this Hanna (Ruth's half-sister) obtained the stone. Perhaps, Adela left a note for her. I know so many East Europeans who did things like that when they realised the Nazis were approaching. They buried their most precious possessions in secret locations in their homes or gardens."

"Yes, that makes some kind of sense," said Simon. "Hanna told my father long ago how her mother and all the rest of the family were murdered at Auschwitz. I still can't believe, even now, that Hanna and my father escaped when everyone else perished. So, maybe Adela addressed a note to 'Daughter'. Only she knew she had two daughters, and in those times of grief, crisis and fears for the future, how could she know who would live and who would die? All I can think is that Adela's note was found after she died and passed to the authorities.

They were all lost for words, thinking about those terrible times.

Just then a door slammed and into the room rushed a young boy, looking surprised to see two strangers there. It was rare for there to be visitors in their home.

"Come over here, love," said Sabra. "I want you to meet these gentlemen, who've come a long way to see us," beckoning the boy over.

Turning to Menes, in particular, she introduced the boy who bore an uncanny resemblance to his saviour.

"This is Dov," our grandson.

CHAPTER TWENTY-FOUR

Jerusalem
2022

T HE NEXT DAY, Simon planned to show Menes a bit of Jerusalem.

Ah Jerusalem. That city of the bible, glorious in its antiquity, but pitted by centuries of struggle and strife.

'I've always wanted to go there," said Menes enthusiastically. "Everyone agrees it's one of the oldest cities in the world. I can't wait to see it with my own eyes.".

"Yes, me too," agreed Simon. "What many don't realise is that in ancient times the area west of the Jordan was called Judea, and it's that place, set amongst the Judean mountains, which gave its name to the people who lived there and yet..... still its ownership is disputed. But the important thing to me, as it was to my father, is its holiness."

"I agree," replied Menes. "Jerusalem is a holy shrine to us, too, as well as the Christians.

Simon closed his eyes for a moment. *Why, oh why, can't the three Abrahamic faiths – Judaism, Christianity and Islam – grab hold of that uniting fact? We're all descended from one man, Abraham. So, we're not just friends; we're actually family!*

Yesterday, Simon had been poring over an old map of the whole Palestinian area at the time of the historic Balfour declaration. He saw that a large area to the east of the Jordan river used to be part of Palestine before it was handed, free of charge, to the Saudis as thanks for assistance given during world war one. *Of course*, he thought, *it was initially called Trans-Jordan, but this subsequently became Jordan.* Simon scratched his head in frustration. If only that huge swathe of land had still been part of the Palestinian area, the land of Israel wouldn't have been such a narrow strip of land west of the Jordan. There would have been so much more land then to accommodate all those who sought to live there.

As Simon now planned the next few days, he knew that already he'd learned a valuable lesson. Sometimes he could be too trusting. After being diddled by the Israeli cab driver taking them from Tel Aviv airport to their hotel, he discovered to his cost that you can't trust everyone. That first Israeli lesson was repeated in the *Ha Carmel* market in Tel Aviv where a trader boxed up not the gift Simon had chosen, but a broken one from beneath his counter. Up until now, he had treated other Jewish people as his family, but this was a country. As with all nations, there were clearly good and bad citizens everywhere.

Now looking out at the old city, Jerusalem was bathed in an ethereal light, reflecting age-old yearnings. The Mount of Olives rose majestically behind the Temple Mount, a reminder of the passage of time, the individual yearnings of its people, their messages buried deep under its surface, and of the mortality of man. Further south lay the Dead Sea, the lowest point on Earth, its waters thick with the salty tears of Jewish people, past and present.

Everywhere were signs of Jewish hospitality, particularly in the old, walled city, with its various quarters. Vibrant colours abounded making a rich tapestry of both ancient and modern dress, some casual, others orthodox. Tourists, with their cameras and cell phones, looked incongruous against the ancient backdrop.

As Simon and Menes wandered through the narrow lanes, every so often a gap in the buildings let a strong beam of sunlight flood down, coating the ancient brickwork in a pink glow.

"Just like in Toulouse," said Menes.

"Yes," agreed Simon, looking at the kaleidoscope of colours refracted at every corner. "It's a film set mosaic. But these aren't actors, the clothes belong to them, and the buildings are not constructed for effect. This is the real deal."

The scent of cooking and spices gave Menes a nostalgic pang for Egypt. In a flash, he forgot all his early anguish. "Oh, how Layla would love all of this. She'd be packing her suitcase full of all the spices she could cram in." Menes made a mental note to take Layla to the *Mahane Yehuda Shuk* market, where she'd have a field day. But would she want to come? He wasn't sure. She'd probably prefer to go back to Egypt, where she was born.

But Simon's head was far away. He could hear the Jewish prayers coming from the Western Wall, and he was accosted many times by Rabbis on street corners wanting to teach him the correct way to put on *tephillim* (phylacteries) so that he could say the correct prayer. This place was said to have been continuously inhabited for thousands of years. It was as if time had no meaning.

But once out of the old city, everything changed again. Simon could now forget Sodom and Gomorrah and the Maccabees, as he was instantly transported to today's world of high rise apartments, restaurants, businesses and coffee shops.

Menes was in a sense bewildered. This was Israel, the country of the Jewish people which they'd built from the barren deserts, yet he could hear the Arabic language all around him, mingled with the local *Ivrit* Hebrew and English, which he could speak well from a combination of his school days and the many American films he'd seen.

Simon too was puzzled. In their hotel, the sign next to the lift was written in Hebrew characters but when he managed to pronounce the letters, they came out as e-l-e-v-a-t-o-r! As he said to Menes "Shouldn't it sound out the Hebrew word rather than the English?"

Israel was surely an enigma. He just couldn't get his head around it.

Yet another corner and they were assaulted by the hot, dry desert *khamsin* wind, said to arrive on fifty days of the year.

Jerusalem was absolutely extraordinary. Simon found it surreal to see actual place names and features from the Old Testament standing right in front of him. At the Western Wall, both men knew that it was customary for visitors to leave a personal message on a scrap of paper in one of the many chinks in the ancient bricks. For Menes, with tears in his eyes, his personal message was to the man who saved his life. And for Simon, it was a chance to remember his father.

Simon wondered how there were still spaces left after so many visitors, but this was soon answered for him. He was told that one of the duties of the appointed Wall Rabbi was to regularly remove all the messages and then to reverentially inter them under the ancient Mount of Olives nearby. Such messages forever lie in the land of Israel long after the message giver has gone. He recalled also reading that Princess Alice, the mother of the late husband of Queen Elizabeth, was buried at the foot of the Mount of Olives. It had apparently been her dying wish to be buried there, as a deeply religious woman and a heroine who had saved a Jewish family during the Nazi era.

Afterwards, the two men visited the poignant *Yad Vashem* museum. Simon wondered what Moshe's feelings would have been, but suspected that he wouldn't have wanted to go. The memories would have been too painful.

He explained to Menes that the museum was Israel's official memorial to Jewish victims of the holocaust like Moshe. Their tour driver that morning had taken them, first, one thousand metres above sea level to the western slope of Mount Herzl on the Mount of Remembrance in Jerusalem. But even that trip wasn't without incident. Because of several security alerts *en route*, they were seriously delayed in getting to the Museum. This meant that by the time they actually set foot inside, a female security guard repeatedly urged them to hurry along because they were to close in half an hour. Eventually Simon said to the guard "Look, *Madame*, I am the son of a survivor myself.

It's taken me years and much heartache to get to this very spot, so please stop pushing me to leave!"

"You know Menes," said Simon, "do you remember my mentioning the mother of the Duke of Edinburgh being buried under the Mount of Olives?"

Menes nodded.

"Well," Simon continued, "in this museum, there is a history of people being awarded a special honour when they've helped the Jewish people by individual acts of bravery. It seems that Princess Alice had, during world war two, sheltered a Jewish family called Cohen in her own home in Athens. At that time, if you remember, the Nazis were hunting down all the Jewish people they could find to systematically murder them. Well, after the war, the *Yad Vashem* museum anointed Princess Alice as one of the 'righteous amongst nations' for her actions."

Menes sighed, thinking of the Nazis. "Why is there always so much hate in the world? Why can't we all see the good in one another and recognise, not our differences, but the things we have in common?"

The two men commented in like vein as they walked around the museum. To her credit, the museum guard looked abashed and didn't bother them again. Another highlight for both men was the International School for Holocaust Studies which honours non-Jews who saved Jews during the Holocaust at personal risk to themselves, as the Righteous Among the Nations.

As Menes said to Simon "It's only at times of war, struggle and strife that you discover who your real friends are – and they aren't always the ones you think."

Menes was thoughtful. "I like this idea of having a national depository for the names of Jewish victims who have no one to carry their name after death. Also, at the Western Wall, it's fitting that, even if the family line dies out, as so many did after the holocaust, family lives can still live on in perpetuity on that tiny scrap of paper buried under the Mount of Olives."

But there was one more important thing that Simon needed to do. When his wife had given birth to their wonderful son, the doctor had told her that they wouldn't be able to have any more children. So, once the family were back home, Leah had asked him "What should I do with this *meleke* stone that Hanna gave me before she died? She said that I must give it to another female in the family but there isn't anyone else."

Simon knew only too well, particularly after making his film, of the stone's significance to the Jewish people. So, when he had decided on the trip to Israel with Menes, he made sure to pack the important stone in his luggage.

He thought back to his scenes about Sodom and Gomorrah as far back as 1900 BCE, followed by the Maccabees in 167 BCE, and still struggled to comprehend the long history of the place. And later, when King Herod instructed the priests to begin the reconstruction of Solomon's first temple, even that was around the year 25 BCE. Absolutely extraordinary. But, in Simon's mind, there was no doubt that *meleke* stone would have been used in the construction of both temples. Such a stone would have been around in the time of Sodom and Gomorrah and still in abundance during Herod's time. After all, the gigantic proportions of Herod's temple at fourteen hectares, doubling its previous size, would have required the use of masses of the local *meleke* stone.

"What do you think, Menes? Shall we go to the Old City and look at the Temple Mount today?" he said to his friend as they were enjoying their buffet breakfast in the hotel.

"Why not?" said Menes. "I know how much it means to you. Whilst you're doing that, I'd like to look at the *Al-Aqsa Mosque*. It would mean a lot to me if I could go there."

"It's a deal," said Simon, giving his friend a high five. Menes smiled. Maybe at last he was getting to grips with today's world after all.

They decided that, because they each had different sites they wanted to visit, they wouldn't take a professional tour but use a local taxi, Simon making sure he paid the driver what he knew to be the correct fare!

"Do you think I'm dressed correctly?" asked Simon, as he knew there were certain dress requirements when visiting the holy site.

"Yes, you're right. I can't believe how many tourists think it acceptable to arrive in shorts and skimpy tops."

"I read that, although women don't have to wear headscarves, their shoulders must be covered and they need to wear long trousers, and definitely not shorts!"

"Yes, that holds true for men also," replied Menes, not that I ever wear shorts. I wouldn't feel comfortable and would feel immodest. It's not how I was brought up."

On arrival, after agreeing with the taxi driver a time to pick them up for the return journey back to their Tel Aviv hotel, the two men entered the complex through the *Mughrabi Gate* near the Western Wall. Fortunately, they'd arrived early so didn't have to wait long. There was no admission charge, but they were checked by guards to see that they were not carrying any weapons.

"Can't believe I'm not allowed to bring in a Jewish prayer book or a *tallit shawl*," whispered Simon to Menes. And I'm not even allowed to recite any Jewish prayers. Is this Israel or isn't it?"

"It's because of the holy *Dome of the Rock,*" replied Menes. "There, they don't allow anyone of other religions to enter at all."

Simon was looking around wide-eyed. Although he, of course, knew about Israel's history, actually being there brought a whole new dimension to it all. Within the *Temple Mount* area, there were a hundred different structures to see, spanning so many time periods that his eyes glazed. He felt the weight of thousands of years bearing down on him. But suddenly, from nowhere, he could hear his father Moshe's voice in his ear. Foolishly, he looked behind him, so clear was the voice. But, of course, his own innate logicality stepped in. Moshe was gone. So what was it? The insistent tingle came again, reverberating deep within his brain. *Simon, Simon,* the voice said, *remember what I told you. You must tell the world!*

Simon felt himself inwardly responding *But I did, Papa, I did. I made that film.*

It isn't enough. That was just a few instances. It's now necessary to tell the world of ALL the attacks, all the tribes who have murdered us for over three thousand years…… .

The voice faded away as Simon slowly became aware again of the world around him. He felt shivers up and down his spine.

"Are you OK, Simon?" asked Menes, concerned. "You seemed to be in a world of your own for a moment."

Simon blinked several times, before reassuring his friend. "I just had a crazy dream all of a sudden, but it's gone now. Let's carry on," steering Menes towards the centre of an open area not far from the Western Wall.

Ahead of them they could see a large crowd, so they edged closer to see what was going on. A rabbi of indeterminate age had turned his pale, lined face towards the blue heavens above. His hooded eyes, almost hidden behind wire-rimmed spectacles, were closed and in his clenched, arthritic hand was a twisted, wooden rod. He looked for all the world like a biblical prophet just returned from Mount Sinai.

Was he then about to give them the latest Commandment?

The rabbi was helped up onto an orange box by onlookers eager to hear what he had to say.

A younger man, also very pale, the fringes of his *tsitsis* prayer vest peeping out from his white shirt, was distributing a leaflet. As Simon felt the paper being shoved into his hand, he glanced down and at first could only make out thick, black Hebrew letters, but on the reverse, the text had been translated into English. Luckily, Simon's good English was enough to comprehend its meaning, as his Hebrew knowledge was not up to the task.

Menes leaned in. "What does it say? I haven't got my reading glasses with me."

"Looks like a chronology of events over time," replied

Simon. "Seems to be a list of dates from ancient times, leading up to the present day." Peering closer, he concentrated on understanding the English words underneath each of the dates. "Yes, see here," he indicated to Menes, "if you run your finger down the page, there are some interesting facts here."

But as the crowd waited for the old rabbi to start speaking, Menes spoke very quietly, in their native French so that no-one else might hear. "I may not have understood all of this, but one thing's clear. This isn't a normal list of events."

Simon was intrigued. "Well, what is it then?"

Leaning in closer to his friend, Menes said "Look. It starts right at the beginning, when Israel was first documented, but then chronicles every time an enemy has ever attacked, killed or ousted the Jewish people from their original homeland."

Simon was quiet for a moment, as he re-studied the leaflet. "Yes, I see what you mean. It doesn't seem to list the Jewish prophets, kings or temples or any of the success stories. It simply shows the many instances when the people have had to suffer."

Pushing his sunglasses further up his nose, whilst they waited for the rabbi to speak, Simon read the leaflet more attentively.

Dates of persecution / murdering of Jews and the number of times they have been ousted from their homeland

1500 BCE. First documented reference to Israel. The Meneptah Stele. An inscribed stone slab.

928 BCE. Judah, an area of Israel, formed. Our people called themselves Jews, from the people of Judah.

721 BCE. *Northern kingdom of Israel destroyed by Assyrians.*

604 BCE. *The centuries-old aggression against the Jews by the tribe of Philistines in the land of Israel ended. (Modern confirmation: in 2016, a large Philistine cemetery was discovered in Ashkelon).*

587 BCE. *Israel's capital Jerusalem, including Soloman's temple, destroyed by the Babylonian tribe.*

165 BCE. *Jewish people living in the Israeli area of Judea terrorised by the Hasmonean tribe.*

134 BCE. *The Israeli capital Jerusalem destroyed by the Roman, Antiochus.*

63 BCE. *Jerusalem again attacked by the Romans.*

66 – 138 CE. *Jews continually persecuted in their own land by the Romans.*

570 CE. *Birth of Muhammed. Spread of new religion called Islam.*

711 CE. *Muslims invade large areas of Spain, forcing Jews to flee.*

1066 CE. *Muslims massacre Jewish community in Grenada.*

1096 CE. *Massacre of Jewish community in Rhineland.*

1099 CE. *Massacre of Jews in their own capital of Jerusalem by the Christian Crusaders.*

1190 CE. *Massacre of Jews in York, England.*

1278 CE. *Hangings if Jews in London.*

1290 CE. *Edward I expels all Jews from England.*

1306 – 1394 CE. *All Jews expelled from France.*

1492 CE. *All Jews expelled from Spain.*

1497 CE. *All Jews expelled from Portugal.*

1516 CE. *Italian Jews forced to live in a ghetto in Venice.*

1550 CE. *Jews expelled from Genoa, Italy.*

1655 CE. *Massacre of 65,000 Jews in Poland.*

1674 CE. *Jews of Yemen expelled.*

1720 CE. *All Ashkenazi Jews expelled from Jerusalem by an Arab mob.*

1775 CE. *Mob Arab violence against Jews in Hebron.*

1791 CE. *Russia establishes Pale of Settlement ghetto for all Jews.*

1799 CE. *Arab mob attack Jews in Safed.*

1834 CE. *Muslims attack Jews in Safed, Hebron and Jerusalem.*

1881 – 1920 CE. *Pogroms massacre thousands of Jews in Russia and Ukraine.*

1903 CE. *A giant hoax is published in St. Petersburg called 'The Protocols of the Elders of Zion." Many believe the appalling libel that the Jews practise cannibalism, even though this is forbidden in Jewish law and goes against the very tenets of Judaism. Unfortunately, the libel is still believed today.*

1919 CE. *2000 Jews decapitated in pogrom.*

1929 CE. *Muslims attack Jews over access to the Western Wall in Jerusalem.*

1933 – 45 CE. *Rise and progression of Nazism in Germany. Methodical extermination of 6 million Jews in Europe.*

1941 CE. *Pogrom against Jews carried out by Muslims in Baghdad, Iraq.*

1948 CE. *Hours after formal re-establishment of a Jewish state, Israel is invaded by Syria, Iraq, TransJordan, Lebanon and Egypt Muslims.*
   One million Jews expelled from all Arab and Muslim nations. No condemnation of this by the rest of the world.

1956 CE. *Egypt calls for total destruction of Israel. No condemnation by the rest of the world.*

1967 CE. *6 day war between Egypt and Israel. Thousands of Muslims* chant "No recognition of Israel. No negotiation with Israel. No peace with Israel. Death to all Jews." No condemnation of this by the rest of the world.

1972 CE. *Massacre of Israeli athletes in Munich, Germany by Black September terrorists.*

1973 CE. *Syria attacks Israel during holy day of Yom Kippur.*

1980 CE. *Israel under attack by PLO in Lebanon. The very term Palestine Liberation means the extermination of the Jewish people from their own land.*

1987 CE. *Intifada against Israel.*

1991 CE. *Israel hit by Scud missiles from Iraq.*

2000 CE. *Israel agrees to withdraw its vital defence forces from S. Lebanon.*

2005 CE. *Israel agrees to withdraw its vital defence forces from Gaza strip in exchange for peace.*

2006 CE. *Terrorist group Hezbollah cross border into Israel. 159 Israelis killed.*

2008 CE – present. *Continuous rocket attacks from Gaza into Israel by ruling Hamas regime. The world condemns Israel for 'disproportionate' defence of its own people and its own land.*

Simon and Menes had just finished their first full perusal of the leaflet when there was a sudden hush in the crowd. The old rabbi was speaking.

"My friends. I have been consulting with my rabbinical colleagues and they all agreed that it should be I who speaks to you today. It's significant that we are gathered here in this most holy place as what I have to say will reverberate all over the world very soon."

A few onlookers in the crowd shuffled nervously, not knowing what to expect.

"Do not be afraid, my friends. I speak only the truth. Now, listed on the leaflet that you hold in your hands are some significant dates. Of these, the most important is the first one. Look closely at it and understand its import. Yes, it's 1500 BCE when this land of Israel was first officially documented. That's over a thousand years *before* the Christian religion began, and over two thousand years *before* the birth of Mohammed and the rise of the Muslim religion. Think about that for a moment. Now put it into the context of our various enemies over the years calling us such things as 'usurpers' and 'occupiers'.

"I want you all to take home the leaflet and study it very carefully. You will see how many enemy tribes have ousted us from our original land, how many times we've returned, then only to be ousted once again by yet another tribe. It's evident when you look at the various enemy tribes that they all disappear after a time. But, my friends, the Jewish people are still here and will always be here. On our many enforced wanderings, we needed no idols or graven images as do some other religions. We kept the laws of the *torah* in our heads and close to our hearts, somewhere where no-one could ever encroach. In that way, our faith and our laws could be passed on. Our grand-parents ensured that they always taught us the tenets of our faith, so that, in turn, we could do the same with our children and grandchildren. It has ever been so."

The old man paused to catch his breath, as his eyes roamed over the crowd. His eyes flicked over Simon and Menes and the corners of his mouth creased.

"Yes. The old must always pass on their knowledge to the young. That's how we as a people have survived. But, my friends, as we think of today's world of mass communication via every digital means, we must do more. If we do not, biased views can quickly become mainstream. Don't forget, there are many, many Muslim nations but only one Jewish one. That means that the votes of international committees are likely to be biased automatically against little Israel, as a minority of one. So, what can we do to stop this? Well, whenever you hear the words 'usurper' or 'occupier' when referring to our democratic coun-try, show them this leaflet and say "How can we be a usurper or an occupier in this land, when there is archaeological and scientifically-proven evidence to support the fact that we were here long, long before any others? Think of the names Samaria and Judea, commonly called the West Bank by the media. The very name Judea is where the name Jew came from!"

Simon whispered to Menes "See, I told you so."

"In fact," continued the Rabbi, "back in 1948, it was Balfour's original intention to give the Jewish people the whole of Palestine, but he was persuaded to give a large tract of land east of the Jordan river to Saudi Arabia for favours given. This piece of land was then named Transjordan, which soon morphed into the current large country called Jordan. Let me ask you, my friends, does anyone call the Jordanians usurpers?"

The crowd murmured No.

"Just look on the map," said the Rabbi, "and see how minuscule our tiny piece of Israel is compared to Jordan."

The old man mopped his brow in the increasing heat as he came to his conclusion. "A friend of mine recently returned from a trip to Jordan. He purchased a bottle of whisky in the duty free shop at Amman airport, and glancing at the receipt, saw the word Palestine printed at the foot of the piece of paper. Clearly, even Jordan understands that the word Palestine refers to the whole region, of which Jordan is but a part. My friends, we are all Palestine and, as neighbours, we should love each other. I hold no hate against others. We are all HaShem's children. Whether Jew or Muslim, we all stem from Abraham and as such could be termed cousins. Yes, we're all one family."

Glancing down to the front of the crowd, he spotted two small children, a boy and a girl. He smiled and threw them a boiled sweet each.

Simon smiled, remembering his Papa doing just that in their synagogue in Toulouse.

"That, my friends, is our future," said the Rabbi, smiling "The children. Always do the right thing by them and teach them all you know and to respect everyone. Above all, never teach them to hate and kill others, as do many from neighbouring countries. And never, never, dance in the streets to celebrate when another soul has died. That is something the Jewish people never do. Despite everything that has been thrown at the

Jewish people and all those who have murdered and subjected us to appalling torture, forcefully removing us again and again from our homeland over the past three thousand, five hundred years, I say this. The Jewish people do not harbour hate in their hearts and will always survive, no matter what."

Now lifting the leaflet up in front of the crowd, the Rabbi's eyes roved over the sea of faces in front of him. "I am now an old man and my physical strength begins to fail me. So, I need you, especially the young who understand today's digital world, to transmit far and wide the proven facts listed on this leaflet. Maybe then, and only then, will the world come to its senses and understand how it has let our people down. Remember," looking down at the leaflet, "think of that terrible aggressor Hitler – the one listed against the dates 1930s and 1940s in Europe – there's no point in trying to appease a terrorist. Often today I see in the media that major broadcasters attempt to show both sides in a misguided attempt at fairness. You can't compare a terrorist organisation, sworn to eradicate another nation, with a democratic, established, modern state like Israel. Just as Churchill correctly understood, there is only one way to treat a terrorist organisation that advertises its wish to exterminate a whole people.

"Thank you, my friends."

Slowly, and humbly, the crowd began to disperse, murmuring amongst themselves. Simon thought he saw his father's face amongst the crowd, smiling. Both he and Menes were unusually quiet as they carefully deposited their leaflets in a safe pocket and turned away from the mass of people.

As Simon walked across the flat plaza area, enclosed by ancient retaining walls, he looked up at the three dominant structures rising up into the blue heavens above his head. Menes naturally wanted to visit the *al-Aqsa* mosque, but there was also the Dome of the Rock and the Dome of the Chain.

So much to see, so much to think about as history was literally laid out as a tableau before their eyes. There were minarets, alongside Herodian walls and as many as eleven gates. Simon knew that many Jewish people will not walk on the Mount itself because, by so doing, they might unintentionally find themselves face to face with the *Holy of Holies* site. A Rabbi once told him that there remained at the site elements of the divine presence himself.

For Menes, his thoughts centred on his own faith. Since the passing of Sami, his eldest son, his emotions were very vulnerable and simply being in that place was an emotional experience for him. For him, the Mount was one of the three sacred mosques, which were the holies sites in Islam. But, as he told Simon "You may not know but the location of our holy prophet's journey to this place and his ascension to heaven is associated with the Jewish biblical prophets, who are also venerated in Islam."

"Wow," said Simon. "That's yet another reason to bring us all together."

"If only," said Menes, shaking his head. "If only…."

"I know what you mean," replied Simon. "Jerusalem must be the most fought over religious site in the world, yet it's our capital."

Later, after Menes had joined a group touring the sites he wanted to see, Simon had a very important mission in mind.

He hadn't told Menes as this had been something personal to his father and to his friend, Hanna Siskowski. Simon had already written private messages in their memory when visiting the Western Wall and had been pleased to know that their names would be forever remembered when his pieces of paper were interred in perpetuity under the Mount of Olives.

As Simon walked around the three sides of the Temple Mount, he saw that parts of the original supporting walls still stood. During all those terrible centuries when Jews were excluded from the Temple Mount, its Western Wall became Jewry's holiest shrine. But since 1967 the wall had been further exposed, and a large plaza had been cleared in front of it.

He began to get excited. He knew what he had to do.

His thoughts kept returning to his film scenes of the Six Day War, after which Israeli archaeologists had begun some excavations very near where he was standing at the southern wall. They had apparently discovered many finds from Herod's second temple, including a number of tunnels.

Now, peering closely, Simon noticed a kind of bulge in the retaining wall just ahead of him. He was wondering whether the earthquake which probably occasioned the events in his Sodom and Gomorrah scenes a thousand years before might have caused such a thing. He didn't know. But a thought was buzzing through his head.

Pausing to reflect for a while whilst a tour guide passed him, leading another group of excited visitors, he waited. Eventually, he found himself alone. He knew, of course, that it was important not to take away any of the historically significant archaeological material on the site.

But no-one said you couldn't leave something there.

Acting quickly, before the next tour group came along, Simon pulled from his pocket a small, smooth stone. Bringing it to his lips, he kissed it reverentially and said a prayer for all the females who had preserved it over the centuries and passed it down the line, generation to generation. Of those who were known to him, he whispered the names of Ruth, Adela and Hanna.

But it was clear, this particular *meleke* stone had succeeded in its long journey and had fulfilled its mission with aplomb. Now it had completed its circle of deliverance, there was only one thing to do.

Very carefully, Simon pushed the small *meleke* stone into a tiny fissure near the ancient bulge in the wall standing in front of him.

Welcome back home, he whispered, before walking back to where he'd agreed to meet his friend.

"You know, Simon. I wish I had a magic wand to stop so many Muslim countries teaching their children to hate. It's something I've not seen in Israel."

"No," replied Simon. "Israeli children are taught to love and help others."

"Maybe next time, that's something I could put on my message inserted in the Western Wall," said Menes. "Don't know what else I can do but trust in Allah."

Together, Simon and Menes embraced each other.

Just then Simon's phone pinged. The first review results on his film had come in. Everywhere, viewers were applauding it, and major companies all over the world were clamouring to show it.

What d'you think of that, Papa? Looks like your lifelong dream is actually happening.

Jewish and Egyptian, arm in arm, Simon and Menes made their way homewards again, reciting a poem that Simon had especially commissioned for the finale of his film:

"At early morn' I had a dream
that man would cease his futile scheme
Blazing battles, suicide missions
Murder, hatred, crazed seditions

Plumb the depths, re-appraise
Be none so blind, none so fazed
Halt the fight, tribe v tribe
Suffused with hate and diatribe
But see with eyes afresh from birth
We're all one tribe – that of Earth"

The world still had a lot to learn, but for the two of them – one Jewish, one Muslim – their mission had been accomplished.

"Come, cousin," said Simon smilingly, remembering the Rabbi's wise words.

Arms around each other's shoulders, friends for ever, they returned to their hotel in Tel Aviv, ready for their journey back to Toulouse.

Author's Note

Someone once said to me that truth often takes a back seat for those with subliminal, obsessional, lifelong-held racist views. It seemed to me, therefore, that in these days of free access to social media, which unfortunately gives a voice to many ill-educated, unsubstantiated, racist viewpoints, it was time to put the record straight.

So, the foregoing story is the culmination of a project I have been working towards all my life. I wanted to write an enthralling, engrossing narrative but with a serious moral behind it. By bringing together two fictitious characters from different ethnicities, one Jewish, the other an Egyptian Muslim – conflating their alternative personal histories and previous mindsets about each other – the story leads them to a lifelong friendship.

I built on the knowledge I learned at first hand when living in Toulouse, France, over a twelve year period. In so doing I was able to give my characters a shared, common background in being expelled from their original homelands and struggling to establish a new life in a different country.

By researching the true, peer-reviewed, archaeological evidence which substantiates the rights of the Jewish people to return to the land of Israel – from whence they've been ousted countless times by wave after wave of different tribes over four thousand years – I've attempted to alleviate much heartache in the world and draw on man's similarities rather than perceived differences.

I hope I've succeeded, not for any personal reasons, but on behalf of all the Jewish people in the world who are crying out for justice and to put a stop to all the passed-down inaccuracies and hurtful personal parodies that continue to this day. All the Jewish people have ever wanted is to live in peace in their own, tiny piece of land.

Let us hope that, whatever colour, faith or creed people espouse, we can all learn to live in peace and brotherhood with each other.

Olga Swan
2021

Acknowledgements

I'm grateful to Jerusalem author Miriam Drori, who kindly read through my early manuscript and helped with the factual details about Jerusalem and the biblical citations.

BIBLIOGRAPHY

Danon, D. 2012. Israel. The Will to Prevail. Palgrave Macmillan.

Julius, A. 2010. Trials of the Diaspora. A History of Anti-Semitism in England. Oxford University Press.

Montefiore, S. S. 2011. Jerusalem. The Biography. Weidenfeld and Nicholson.

Schama, S. 2013. The Story of the Jews. The Bodley Head.

Printed in Great Britain
by Amazon